In The Shade of the Shamiana

By

James Sinclair

©2015 James Sinclair

All Rights Reserved

This ebook is licensed for your personal use only. This ebook may not be re-sold or given away to other people. If you would like to share this ebook with another person, please purchase an additional copy for each recipient. If you're reading this book and did not purchase it, or it was not purchased for your use only, then please return to the website where this book is being retailed and purchase your own copy. Thank you for respecting the hard work of this author.

This book or any portion thereof may not be reproduced or used in any manner whatsoever without the express written permission of the publisher except for the use of brief quotations in a book review.

The purchaser of this book is subject to the condition that he/she shall in no way resell it, nor any part of it, nor make copies of it to distribute freely.

Dedication

In loving memory of my mother and

Grandparents

Contents

Introduction

Chapter 1

Chapter 2

Chapter 3

Chapter 4

Chapter 5

Chapter 6

Chapter 7

Chapter 8

Chapter 9

Chapter 10

Chapter 11

Chapter 12

Chapter 13

Chapter 14

Chapter 15

Chapter 16

Chapter 17

Chapter 18

Chapter 19

Chapter 20

Chapter 21

Chapter 22

Chapter 23

Chapter 24

Chapter 25

Chapter 26

Chapter 27

Chapter 28

Chapter 29

Chapter 30

Chapter 31

Epilogue

Glossary

INTRODUCTION

The Vestiges of Empire

India—that exotic land of jewels, silks, perfumes, and spices, drew many a young adventurer to that distant and alluring land. Like a moth to a candle, it was often a fatal attraction as some found not fortune awaiting them, but only dust, flies, disease, and death. They readily succumbed to the ravages of the hot blazing sun or cholera, malaria, and the dreaded smallpox, so the only evidence of their flirtation with India were their bones still resting in half-remembered graves. However, the fortunate did succeed and amassed vast riches.

Since Elizabethan times, the British had been wooing India for the establishment of a trading company to compete with the Portuguese, Dutch, and later, the French. This took the form of the Honourable John Company, better known as the East India Company, whose directors sat in London but whose trading posts were in Bombay, Madras, and Calcutta. The "golden age" of Mogul rule was now on the wane, and the European powers rushed in to fill the vacuum. At the time, the sub-continent was fragmented into kingdoms, some ruled by fierce warlords, and was at odds with itself as battles raged between these independent kingdoms. The British and French formed their allegiances with local rulers, and many a battle was fought as each aspired for dominance of the land. In the centuries that followed, it was mainly the British who gained their foothold in India, stealthily acquiring territory after territory.

Since there were few, if any, English women in India, many a senior Indian Civil Service administrator sought comfort by taking an Indian wife, or maintaining a harem of several mistresses they accommodated in *Bibi Ghurs*. Others entered into marriages with the daughters of Indian princes, and this gave rise to a generation of mixed-race children. The ordinary British soldier too sought comfort by taking a native Indian wife, and this was actively encouraged by giving the soldier a special allowance and even married quarters to house his wife and family.

As a consequence, the woman would immediately be disowned by her Indian family and cast out, as by marrying a Christian, she lost her Hindu caste. This native wife was probably kept in the background within the family, as she would have been socially unacceptable to her husband's friends. So, she took the role of an unpaid servant in the household, and kept very much behind the scenes.

Any children born from this union would have been brought up to follow British traditions and to attend Anglo-Indian schools where they would speak only English. Their white father would have actively discouraged Indian habits and mannerisms, and their mother would play a minor role in their lives where she would not be acknowledged or introduced to their friends. So she just cooked the food, looked after the house and children, and provided sex for her husband whenever he felt so inclined.

When they grew up, these mixed-race children would find employment in the Indian Railways, Telegraphs, or other government jobs. They were hardly accepted into the Indian Army except, perhaps, as drummer boys. Hitherto, this mixed-race community became known as Eurasians, but later they wished to be called 'Anglo-Indians' which was a term reserved for the country-born British of pure ancestry, such as Rudyard Kipling. This label had a certain ambiguity about it, as it did not admit to having Indian heritage.

For two hundred years, the British, Eurasians, and Indians lived peacefully together. But in 1857 the first rumblings of discontent began to brew in the ranks of Britain's native soldiers, the *sepoys* and *sowars*. Not only because of the high-handed attitude their masters adopted, but significantly at the introduction of a new cartridge for the Enfield rifle, which, it was rumoured, was coated with a mixture of pig and cow fat—repugnant to both the Hindus and Muslim soldiers who served in the Company's army. As the ends of these cartridges had to be bitten-off before loading into the rifle, it was *haram* to the Muslims and broke the caste of the Hindus.

Insurrection was in the air, and the native soldiers mutinied. The horrors of what became known in history books as the Indian Mutiny of 1857 ensued. It was a "Devil's Wind" that breathed over the land, engulfing, sometimes, entire towns like Cawnpore, and wiping out all the European and Eurasian residents in a massacre—man, woman and child alike. Vultures, jackals, and pi-dogs grew fat on the glut of bodies that were strewn over town, village, and paddy-field.

The British retribution was swift and terrible, and the corpses of any native Indian suspected of being a participant or collaborator of the rebels, hung from the branches of many a banyan tree. When at last the bloodbath was over, the East India Company was disbanded and India was incorporated into the British Empire in a period of what is popularly known as the "British Raj," and India became the jewel in the crown of Empire.

Relative peace reigned in the land in the years that followed, with administrators attached to the Indian Civil Service coming out from England to rule native and countryman alike. As the British built bridges, roads, and canals, commerce grew as more and more merchants and traders set up businesses. Transport and communications were greatly improved, and railways linked most important towns. Fortunes were made in the trade of Indigo, raw cotton, jute, and the opium poppy—the latter being exported in ships to China.

The population of the cities grew as, now, Englishwomen began to arrive in the country—many of them unmarried—arriving in shoals, which became known as "the fishing fleet"—in search of a husband.

Hitherto, under British Rule, Hindus and Muslims lived peaceably together. The mixed-race community, the Eurasians or Anglo-Indians, also enjoyed the privileges and protection offered to them by the British—who represented an awning of shelter—a "Shamiana." It is here our story begins …

CHAPTER 1

Going Home Day had arrived. Jamie Donaldson, squeezed in on one of the benches in the Assembly Hall, tried to ignore the other boys who talked excitedly to each other. He felt some apprehension, as there were rumours abroad that in fact his school, Fern Hill, was being closed down permanently at the commencement of the three month winter holidays, never again to reopen. The prospect saddened him, as he loved the school and its friendly walls and had been happy during his four-year term there. The hubbub subsided when the Headmaster took his place on the podium and addressed the assembled boys.

"My boys," the Headmaster said, "I know how excited you are to be going home today for your three month vacation, but there is something I have to say to you, which I am sure will sadden you all. Fern Hill is to be closed down permanently, so you will not be returning here next year."

A hushed silence met these words, as the boys looked at each other. So the rumours were true. Fern Hill, their beloved school, was closing down forever! This put a real damper on the excitement of the school holidays.

"I know this news is upsetting," the Headmaster continued, "because I know how fond you have become of the old school, as much as I am fond of all of you. But the situation is a financial one and cannot be avoided. I would dearly love the circumstances to be otherwise, but unhappily it is the sad truth." He continued to drone on, and Jamie only half-heard what he was saying, through the gloom that descended upon him, like one of the mists rising suddenly from the valley. *Oh no*, he thought, *not Fern Hill*. Now it would mean having to be admitted to another school, and making new friends all over again. Even in Sing La the only other schools were the snobby St. Paul's or the RC St. Joseph's, neither of which he felt his father could afford. He only came out of his meditation when the Headmaster announced that they were to sing one of the old school songs. All the children rose to their feet, and the music teacher played the tune on the piano. It began:

> *Old walls are friendly walls*
> *Friendly walls, farewell!*
> *Old walls hold memories*
> *That breathe a kindly spell.*
> *Breathe then your benison*
> *On me as I depart,*
> *I'll always keep your memory*
> *Warm in my heart.*

Jamie could not help but wipe a tear away with the sleeve of his blazer as the song came to an end.

Anyway, they were going home today. Going home after nine months hard slog of maths, history, and French. The prospect of three idle months lay deliciously ahead of him. The thought cheered him up, although he loved Sing La, nestling high in the Himalayas in India, with its range of high, snow-covered mountains fringing the northern horizon—in fact the highest mountains in the world.

The British had established Sing La as a health resort for weary soldiers and for tired government officials who wished to escape the heat, dust, and flies of the unhealthy plains of India during the summer months. The British soon discovered that the climate was ideal for the growing of tea, so tea bushes—originally imported from China—flourished, and soon a lucrative tea-growing industry began. The cool and healthy climate attracted people from Calcutta and the *Mofussil*, and a small community of residents built up in the town—mainly retired folk who set up small businesses or ran boarding houses. The town boasted of cinemas, clubs, a museum, and even a racecourse, all tucked away in this remote region of the Himalayas. It was also a place of worship, with the spires of churches, minarets of mosques, pagodas of Buddhist monasteries, and *sikharas* of Hindu temples, all seeming to point to one universal God.

The journey from the high Himalayas to the plains of India began with a ride on the "toy train": a narrow-gauge railway that connected Sing La to Kholagari Junction, where meter-gauge rail tracks connected it to the vast Indian Railways network. To eleven-year-old Jamie, this first leg was the highlight of the journey back home, as the tiny train looped, twisted, and zigzagged on its track through the hills, until it reached the plains of the Ganges. Here, his mother was to meet him and he would leave the rest of the school party and return with her to Panchpani.

"It's bad luck we won't be at school together again next year," the small boy with glasses said, as he squeezed into the seat next to Jamie in the crowded railway compartment.

"Yes," Jamie agreed. He was apprehensive now about what school he would be sent to next term. "What school are your parents going to send you to then?" he asked of the boy.

"Don't know. Probably La Mart, in Cal. It'll be easier for my dad and mum, and I'll be able to go back home for the summer hols. Where are you going?"

Jamie shrugged, as he tried to put the thought behind him. At the moment, he just wanted to revel in the excitement of seeing his family and pets again. It was November of 1945 now, and these were the holidays. He looked at the other boys crowding into the tiny railway carriage, pushing and jostling and fighting over seats, their voices high with anticipation and excitement.

Jamie's class teacher, who among other schoolteachers was accompanying the boys on the journey, entered the compartment, his bald head gleaming with sweat. "All right you boys," he hollered. "Quieten down now. You, Smith, get back into your seat. Long, put that suitcase on the luggage rack. Yes, that's a good chap. We'll soon be off."

The boys settled down and the hubbub subsided a little, though there was still some squabbling over the window seats.

After what seemed an eternity, there came a shrill blast from the guard's whistle, followed by two acknowledging toots from the little saddle-tank engine. A hiss of steam, and the wheels spun as they slipped on the track, then the train lurched forward. The boys raised a cheer and broke into one of the familiar school-break-up songs.

"Going home day has come at last,
Doo dah, doo dah,
Going home day has come at last,
Doo dah doo dah day.
We travel all the night,
We travel all the day,
We spent our money on the HMR,
Doo dah doo dah day."

The Himalayan Mountain Railway pulled out of the station, gaining speed and billowing volumes of smoke, soot, and steam. It followed the Tonga Road, as it would for most of the journey, criss-crossing it again and again whenever the bends were too sharp for the little train to negotiate, and under full steam made its way determinedly towards Soong.

As it rounded the Loop, the great wall of the Snowy Ridge and Sing La town disappeared from view, and Jamie felt a twinge of sadness. He loved those snowy mountains standing so high and serene in the sky. On many a clear morning as, teeth chattering, he had climbed out of bed, he could see the mountain range, framed in the dormitory window, glowing a fiery copper colour from the first rays of the rising sun. Now he wondered if he would ever witness this beautiful sight again. The thought made him pensive.

The train reached Soong station, which was shrouded in mist. He remembered his father telling him about the old Soong Witch who used to live here many, many years ago. She was a terrifying old hag, and Jamie remembered seeing a portrait of her hanging up in a corridor of the Himalayan Hotel when he was little. The witch would beg at the station, and it was believed she would place curses on you if you didn't give her any money.

The train moved off again and the engine made less noise now because it was downward all the way from Soong and it didn't need full power. It twisted and turned as it snaked along the track, sometimes hugging the embankment, at others riding precariously on the edge of *khuds*, with sheer drops to the valley far below. Jamie could often catch glimpses of the other two carriages at the frequent bends, and jubilant schoolboys leaning out of windows, sometimes squirting a water pistol, or hurling a paper bomb, at an unsuspecting bystander at the side of the track.

They reached Kumsong Station after three hours. The boys were let out of the cramped carriages and, under the keen eye of the teachers, allowed to stretch their legs along the platform. The station restaurant served refreshments, and there were the inevitable queues for the toilet. Then it was back to the carriages again, hoping that someone else hadn't bagged your seat.

As the little train reached lower and lower elevations, the scenery changed from alpine to deciduous forest, and now and again Jamie caught glimpses of the vast Indo-Gangetic plain, with rivers meandering lazily like silver ribbons over it. The track ran round loops and through zigzags, losing elevation in the process. Finally, and just before dark, they reached the plains, and the little train made its way through thick forests, where sal trees stood tall in their shrouds of vines. Then, coming out of the gloom, it followed a straighter track and picked up speed for the last few miles to Kholagari Junction. Here, it entered the dimly lit platform under the eaves, where it jerked to an abrupt halt, sweating in the steam of its own exhaustion.

A flood of activity ensued as the boys collected their belongings, with more pushing and shoving, until they all tumbled out of the railway carriage and stood on the platform in an untidy group—blazers off, shirt-tails hanging out, and ties awry. The teachers tried to be everywhere at once, shouting at boys and coolies alike, and at the same time trying to take a head-count of all the children.

It was amidst this chaos that Jamie spied his mother, dressed in her familiar flower-pattern dress, and a scarf tied round her hair, looking in this direction and that, in an attempt to find her son. Beside her stood Abdul, their driver.

CHAPTER 2

Lydia Donaldson didn't notice her son until he was standing right in front of her. She hardly recognised him for a moment as he had grown during his year at school. "Darling," she cried, hugging him and showering him with kisses despite his protests. Then, dampening her dainty handkerchief with a little spit, she rubbed the lipstick off his cheeks.

One of Jamie's teachers came towards her with a smile. "Ah, Mrs Donaldson, I see you've found your boy. Now all we need to find is his luggage!" He looked around the accumulation of tin trunks and bed-rolls that had been unloaded from the luggage van. "Yes, I think this is it." He beckoned to a coolie. Another helped the tin trunk on to the coolie's head, and Jamie's bed-roll was also handed to the coolie, who carried it in his free hand, using the other to help steady the trunk.

"Thank you for bringing him down safely," Lydia said. "I hope he's been a good boy."

Jamie groaned in embarrassment. "Oh, Mum ..."

"Oh yes, very good. No trouble at all. Wish I could say the same for some of the other lads though." He looked grimly in their direction.

Lydia addressed her son. "Better say good-bye to your friends now, darling."

She watched him as he sauntered off in the direction of the group and exchanged handshakes awkwardly. The rest of the school party would be boarding the big train, waiting on the opposite platform, for their onward destination to Calcutta, which they would reach the next morning.

Jamie re-joined her, and together with Abdul—who carried his suitcase—and the coolie, balancing his battered tin trunk and walking with an unsteady gait, they set off along the platform, up the steep steps and over the gangway that crossed the rows of railway lines, and out of the station to where the dusty old Ford estate car waited for them. The cook's son, Jubra, had been left behind to look after it. He grinned at Jamie, his two big front teeth showing prominently, and raised his hand to his head in a salaam. Jamie placed his hand on Jubra's shoulder in a gesture of friendship.

"We're staying at the *dak* bungalow tonight," Lydia said as they settled themselves into the car, and Abdul and Jubra loaded the boot with the luggage. "It's too late to travel now, and besides, you must be tired."

"Not really, Mum," Jamie said. Truthfully, he looked quite exhausted.

Abdul got into the car and Jubra sat alongside. He started the engine, put the car into gear and drove out of the station yard and into the crowded bazaar streets, mostly driving on the horn and swerving to avoid cycle-rickshaws, pedestrians, and stray cows alike. From the brightly lit shops that bordered the streets, came the blaring sound of Indian music, punctuated by the delicious aroma of Indian cooking that wafted into the car from the multitude of snack-shops. Jamie's stomach growled. "I suppose you're hungry, darling," Lydia said. "Did you have anything on the way?"

"Only at Kumsong, Mum."

"I expect you must be starving then, poor darling. Never mind. The *khansama* at the *dak* bungalow will have some *khanna* for us when we arrive." She used the Indian term for food.

As she lit a cigarette, Lydia filled her son in with all the family news; how his father was so busy managing all the Estate affairs; how his elder sister, Frances, was held up in school waiting for her examinations to finish; how his younger sister, Cissy, had spent her fifth birthday. All this her son absorbed without much comment, or questions. He only listened more attentively when she told him that Blackie, their Labrador, had got a porcupine quill stuck in his paw and how his father had taken it out with a penknife.

"How's Gingernut, Mum?" Jamie enquired. His father had bought him this hill-pony the previous year for Christmas.

"Very well," Lydia said. "And getting fatter than ever. Kaila has been overfeeding him, and of course, he hasn't had much exercise."

They had left the boundary of Kholagari town, and now drove along a quieter road with peepal trees bordering both sides. Soon, Abdul made a turn and they were on a rough track that led to the *dak* bungalow. It appeared gloomily as the car's headlights swept across it, and he brought the vehicle to a stop.

The *khansama*'s moustached face appeared at the window, and he opened the rear door with a stately salaam. They all got out, and Abdul and Jubra went to the boot to deal with the luggage, which included Lydia's bed-roll and overnight bag. The *khansama* led Jamie and Lydia onto the long veranda that fronted the *dak* bungalow, and ushered them into a large room.

It was gloomy inside, being lit only by a single electric light-bulb that dangled from the ceiling. Two beds lay alongside each other, with their mosquito nets pulled up into a canopy on top. Under the light, stood a square dining table and two chairs. A small vase of faded marigolds sat in the middle as a centrepiece.

"Will I bring in the food now, memsahib?" the *khansama* asked in Hindustani.

"Yes, very well," Lydia replied.

He disappeared, only to reappear some minutes later with a large tray. He laid the dishes on the table. The meal was simple but tasty. They had dhal soup with croutons, a large dish of potato chops, another dish of salad, and a caramel custard pudding. Jamie tucked into all this with relish; not even minding his mother's mild admonishment that he should eat more slowly and chew his food.

"Gulping your food fills you full of wind, darling," she said.

After the meal was over, Jamie yawned and rubbed his eyes with both fingers.

"I think you ought to go to bed now," Lydia said. "We have to be up early in the morning."

As she spoke, the *khansama* appeared at the doorway to clear away the empty dishes. He asked what time he should bring in their *chota hazri*. She said seven o'clock and added that they would breakfast an hour later.

"Very good, memsahib. Should I inform the driver of this?"

She nodded. Abdul and Jubra were being accommodated in the servants' quarters for the night, and probably would be eating their meal now.

Jamie got up. "I'd better get undressed then." He unpacked his night suit, sponge bag, and rubber slippers from his suitcase, then disappeared into the bathroom, and returned a few minutes later.

Jamie tested the beds. "Which one, Mum?"

"The softer of the two."

"They're both the same."

She joked, "The one *without* bugs then."

Jamie lifted his bed-roll onto the bare coir mattress and undid the straps. He opened it out and arranged his pillows and bedding, then hopped onto the bed. He pulled down the mosquito netting and set about tucking it under the mattress. Lydia came across and helped him with the final tucking in. "Goodnight, darling," she said, and kissed him.

"Goodnight, Mum," he mumbled.

She tucked in the last of the mosquito net. "I think I'll go out on the veranda for a quiet smoke," she said.

"Okay, Mum," he said sleepily.

Lydia went out into the cool night air on the veranda. She sat down on one of the green-painted wicker chairs that lined it. The night was alive with sound—the chirping of crickets and the croaking of frogs. In the distance she could see the haze of Kholagari's lights, from whence came the muted sound of Indian music mingled with the yap-yapping of pi-dogs. A bright moon cast a silvery light, and stars sparkled in the night sky. She struck a match and it exploded into flame, almost blinding her for a moment. Then she held it to the tip of the cigarette, and inhaled deeply. Alone with her thoughts.

How happy she was to have Jamie back, and Frances expected shortly too. It had been dull without them, and her husband's job as manager of the Panchpani Estate often left her alone, with only the *ayah* and little Cissy for company. She was glad that Jamie was turning into such a handsome lad, with fair skin, large grey eyes with long dark lashes, a dimpled chin, and thick, wavy brown hair. His fair complexion could be quite an advantage in his later years.

One could hardly progress if you had a swarthy skin or looked the least bit Indian. Then it was only the Railways, Customs, or Post and Telegraphs that was open to you, or perhaps a mediocre job in a mercantile company. She had suffered from such discrimination in her teaching career before she met and married her Domiciled European husband, Howard. At least that had given her some sort of status, and she was more accepted among the better circles. Of course, Howard's parents, particularly his stepmother, had never approved of her. "What! Marry an Anglo-Indian?" Horror of horrors! She smiled to herself, feeling the irony. It wasn't as if she had a very dark skin—more olive than brown, really. But it wasn't just the skin colour; her features were slightly oriental, which was further evidence of her mixed heritage. Francis had taken more after her—the boy after his father. She wasn't so worried about Frances. It wasn't so bad for a girl, and she might make a good catch. But for boys, she felt, it was more important. They needed to get on in life and not be bound down by racial prejudice. And what if the British left India? She stubbed out her cigarette in anger. She didn't even want to think of that eventuality.

CHAPTER 3

The next morning dawned fresh and clean, with only a thin haze that veiled the peepal trees. Their *chota hazri* was brought to them by the *khansama* exactly on time as promised—a hot cup of tea and a thin, green Singapore banana. Breakfast was served in the morning sunshine of the veranda; Quaker Oats followed by fried eggs for Lydia and rumble-tumble (scrambled eggs) for Jamie. Four thick slices of toast waited in the toast-rack and there was a dish of fresh butter. Two mugs of hot coffee completed the meal.

Abdul, accompanied by Jubra who still wore a broad grin on his face, appeared from somewhere. They took the luggage out and loaded it in the car. The *khansama* came up to Lydia with the bill on a tray. She opened her bag and counted out the required money.

"I hope memsahib and baba have been very happy and comfortable here," the *khansama* said.

The *dak* bungalow's facilities were a bit primitive, but nevertheless Lydia gave him some coins as *baksheesh,* and after he examined them in the palm of his hand, he salaamed with exaggerated graciousness.

They all climbed into the car and started off on the sixty-mile journey to Panchpani, following a southerly direction from Kholagari, past the tidy tea gardens of the Dooars and then the bamboo thickets and paddy fields of Bihar. The road was un-tarred in some sections, and Abdul often had to swerve to avoid the many potholes. At one point, they reached a narrow river, and the car had to be ferried across on a small country boat specially designed for the purpose. Finally, they reached Panchpani, and drove through the town along the main road, passing the railway station, post office, and government buildings. They crossed the bridge on the far edge of the town, and finally pulled up outside the large wrought-iron north gate of Lal Kothi.

The house was a large rectangular building made of red brick that sat in the middle of extensive grounds, surrounded by a high wall and fringed by tall eucalyptus and other trees. It had been built for the manager of the Estate, as the Nawab—who was the landed proprietor of the Estate—no longer resided permanently on the property, and the original palace, where previous generations of the Nawab had lived, had long since fallen into decay and been completely taken over by the jungle.

Abdul sounded the horn and a khaki-clad *durwan* came running up to the gate. He fiddled momentarily with the latch then swung the heavy gate open. They went down the gravel drive, skirting past the fan-shaped traveller's trees, round the large circular rose garden, and finally stopped at the front of the building. Howard Donaldson, a tall, gaunt, and slightly balding figure, stood on the marble steps that led onto the covered veranda, holding little Cissy by the hand. A small semi-circle of the house servants stood to one side. The car door opened, and Jamie climbed out. Blackie immediately jumped up on him, barking and wagging his tail in excitement.

"How are you my son?" Mr Donaldson asked as he embraced Jamie and kissed him on the forehead. "Glad to be home and all that, eh?" He helped his wife out of the car, gave her a small peck on the cheek—being aware that displays of affection between sahibs and memsahibs could embarrass the servants—then held her by the elbow and escorted her up the stairs to the veranda, where tea was already being served on the round marble table.

Jamie hugged little Cissy then greeted the semi-circle of servants—each one in turn, and they all smiled and salaamed him. It felt good to see all the old familiar faces again, and some new ones. He then followed Abdul and Jubra, who were carrying the luggage, upstairs.

The Donaldson family occupied the upper-storey of the house, which consisted of a large airy bedroom with slatted doors on each side leading onto the terrace, and off the large room were two smaller rooms at the back—one for Jamie and the other for Frances and Cissy. The children's bedrooms shared one bathroom, which did not have sanitary fittings, but the one attached to the main bedroom had a WC, washbasin, and shower. All the rooms were light and airy with high ceilings, while a wide veranda all round offered good views of the gardens. The bedrooms downstairs were empty and usually reserved for the *Nawab* when he visited with family or friends.

Abdul and Jubra dumped Jamie's luggage on the floor of his bedroom, then Abdul took his leave to attend to the car—his primary duty—as it needed a good wash before being put back in the garage. He seemed a little disgruntled at having to do most of the humping of luggage when there were now plenty of other servants about to do it.

Jubra hung on, still smiling while Jamie slooshed his sweaty face with cold water in the bathroom. The bathroom was three-cement-steps-down from the main room. It was large, dank, and gloomy. A portion of the floor had been separated off for the bathing area, and a large water-drum stood on a stand with a brass tap fitted at the bottom. A small zinc tub stood up on end, leaning against the wall. In the other portion of the floor, a washbasin and jug stood on another stand. The washroom also housed two commodes, one encased in a box, which looked more comfortable, and another alongside, standing in a metal frame and supported by three legs. Jamie thought he'd better do his business and get it out of the way. He hadn't been in the morning, what with all the rush of leaving school. He lifted the lid, pulled down his shorts and underpants, and sat down. He strained, and there was a dull clunk as his droppings hit the bottom of the pan. It sounded odd, as he half-expected the usual plop-splash of a modern WC. He chatted away to Jubra as he completed his business, then looked round for the toilet paper. "Oh God," he groaned as he noticed there was none on the roll. He thought of asking Jubra to fetch some but decided instead to wash himself as the natives did. He filled the battered aluminium mug with water from the tap, and Jubra poured the water while Jamie washed his backside with his left hand.

Back in the bedroom, Jamie took off his shoes and stockings and changed into his cotton khaki shirt and knee-length baggy shorts, freshly *dhobi*-washed and laid out for him on his bed by Cissy's *ayah*, Tulassa. His discarded flannel pants and crushed shirt and school tie lay in a heap on the floor, and he was surprised how quickly he was becoming accustomed to having servants to pick up after him again.

"Oh damn!" he exclaimed as he realised that he was missing a belt. He picked up his discarded pants again, and slid out his striped school belt with its buckle in the form of an S-shaped snake. This he threaded into the loops of the khaki pants he had just put on. Like a reptile discarding its skin, he was glad to be out of his uncomfortable hill clothing and into something cool and fresh, also not to be restricted by tight underpants. He slipped on his leather sandals while he chatted to Jubra, trying hard to remember some of his half-forgotten Hindustani. Jubra replied to his many questions with "*hah's*" and "*gee's*" and smiles and nods.

They clattered down the stairs.

"Just going to see Gingernut," he yelled to his parents.

"Your tea's getting cold," his father said.

Jamie rushed to the table and gulped down his lukewarm tea.

"Now, don't forget your sola topee," his mother said. "You know how burnt you get in the sun."

Jamie turned to Jubra. "Go fetch my topee. It is hanging on a peg in my room."

Jubra dashed eagerly upstairs to collect the khaki pith helmet, then down again to the waiting Jamie.

"Don't be too long. Tiffin's going to be ready soon," his father called after them as they ran towards the stables with Blackie in pursuit, barking furiously.

The stables were situated at the far end of the large back compound, next to the garages that housed the Estate's cars. Each of the children had their own pony, even little Cissy, whose tiny piebald, though fully-grown, was only a few hands high. Howard Donaldson rode one of the Nawab's thoroughbreds, which he kept on the Estate for riding and pig-sticking.

Kaila, the *syce*, a short, stumpy middle-aged man, groomed a reddish-brown pony standing in a bamboo-fenced pen as the boys arrived, panting.

"Gosh, he has got fat!" Jamie said as he stroked his pony affectionately. Gingernut responded by nudging him with his muzzle.

"Yes, Jamie baba. All this time he has been waiting for you to come back from school and ride him. Then he will become thin again," Kaila said, grinning through teeth stained with betel juice. "You go now and have your food, and in the meantime I will put on his saddle so that you can take him for a ride."

When he returned to the house, tiffin was just being served on the front veranda by Tulassa's husband Dawa, their Nepalese house-boy, suitably attired in his starched white uniform and silk pill-box hat with a pom-pom on top.

He sat down to a delicious meal of mulligatawny soup, chicken curry and pilau rice, with an assortment of pickles and chutneys as accompaniments, and there was fresh papaya for dessert.

"Can I go for a ride, Dad?" he asked, and spooned down the last mouthful of papaya.

As he spoke, Kaila arrived in the front courtyard with a smart and freshly-saddled Gingernut.

"I see you've arranged that already." His father lit his pipe. "All right, but don't go too far, and take someone with you."

Jubra arrived magically, wheeling a ramshackle old bicycle.

"Yes, Dad."

"Can I go too?" Cissy asked.

"Not today, pet," her father said. "We can all go for a ride tomorrow."

"Oh." Cissy pouted. "I want to go now."

Her father tousled her hair. "Tomorrow. I promise."

"Yes, I'll take you tomorrow," Jamie said.

"Be careful now," his mother said, "and don't go galloping about, and remember to keep your topee on."

"Yes, Mum." Jamie felt weary with all the fussing and bother.

"And be back in an hour," she called as Jamie mounted his pony with the help of the *syce*. He trotted off down the pathway to the west gate, Jubra going ahead on his cycle to open it for him, while the *syce* held back a barking Blackie.

They made their way over the level-crossing of the meter gauge line that connected Panchpani to other stations in the region, and onto a narrow cart track that led to the mango groves of Ahm Bagh, a mile away. Gingernut trotted briskly and Jubra rattled behind on his cycle. The track ran beside the riverbank for a while then it turned and skirted around the orchards. They passed the burial grounds where the bones of the old nawabs lay under ancient gravestones; then the jungle began—tall trees and thick bamboo clumps. The ruins of the old palace lay in this vicinity. When they rode past the crumbling walls and turrets, Jamie could hardly distinguish it from the surrounding jungle, so well was it camouflaged by the vines and trees that had rooted deep into the brick.

Jamie called his pony to a halt while Jubra alighted from his bicycle. He dismounted and led Gingernut into the gloom.

"Jamie baba, do not go in there," Jubra called after him. "It is a bad place full of snakes."

"Come on, have you no courage?" Jamie said over his shoulder. "There is nothing here to be afraid of."

"Sahib and memsahib will be angry."

"They will not know if you do not tell them. "I am only going as far as the well."

Jubra hesitated, and then laid the bicycle down on the ground while Jamie tethered Gingernut to a low branch of a tree. They went through a ruined archway and into a clearing where a well stood, its eroded wall half-concealed in undergrowth. They peered into the dim interior through the tangle of vines and tree roots.

"They say there is treasure buried here," Jamie said, remembering the legend that one of the old *nawabs* had hidden his treasure in the well when, in the distant past, a neighbouring warlord had besieged the palace.

"The *djinns* would surely have claimed it by now," Jubra said.

Jamie had heard about these supernatural spirits before — how they could assume human or animal form, and could dwell in all sorts of things, like stones and trees. Anything odd, mysterious, or unusual was put down to the work of *djinns*, especially among the Muslim servants.

"I will give them something to drink then," he said wickedly. He lifted the leg of his pants and peed into the mouth of the well, watching the stream disappear into the depths.

Jubra, anxious to support his friend and yet not wishing offend the evil spirits, squatted down and urinated against the well's surrounds.

Jamie retrieved Gingernut, who was busy munching on a grassy patch, and led him out of the gloom and back into the sunlight. Jubra picked up his bicycle, and they both mounted their respective steeds and made their way back to Lal Kothi.

CHAPTER 4

The family sat in their garden chairs on the front lawn, sipping their drinks as the evening light faded and the air filled with the faint scent of jasmine and wood-smoke. Howard entertained the children with extraordinary stories about his experiences.

Cissy pleaded, "Tell Jamie about the python, Daddy."

"Yes, go on, Dad," Jamie said.

Howard knocked the ash from his pipe. "Well," he said, "as I was returning from Surjapur in the Jeep a few weeks ago, I came across the body of this python lying on the side of the road. It hadn't been run over by a truck or anything because the body was quite intact, but what was so unusual about this snake was that it had horns." He paused deliberately to fill his pipe.

"Ooooh," Cissy said in a mixture of awe and disgust.

"What, horns on its head?" Jamie asked.

"No, protruding from its mouth."

"Gosh, how weird."

"Yes, I thought it strange too," his father said. "But when I took a closer look, I could see what it was. Apparently, this python had tried to swallow a bullock, after crushing its body to a pulp, but when it came to its head, it couldn't get past the horns, so it obviously choked to death."

"Don't believe your father," their mother said. "He's telling a load of yarns."

"No, honestly." Howard pulled at his moustache.

"Come on, Dad, a python can't swallow a bullock, surely," Jamie said.

"Well, this one apparently tried. Took on more than it could chew, I expect." He laughed at his own joke. "Anyway, we'd better get up on the veranda now. You know — snakes and all that."

They got up from their chairs, Jamie and Cissy looking cautiously about, and made their way to the veranda, where Dawa was already placing a paraffin lamp on the round marble table. Electricity hadn't been brought to Panchpani yet, and except for the Indian cinema house in the town, which boasted of its own generator, one had to rely only on paraffin lamps. At night the atmosphere of Lal Kothi could become quite sinister, the oil lamps hardly illuminating the dark corners of cavernous rooms. Gaunt shadows swept over the walls as people moved about, and the figures themselves became shadowy and indistinguishable.

Dinner was served at eight in the large dining room at the back of the house, close to the kitchen which was across a small court-yard and where Jubra's father, Ishmael the cook, presided.

"When are you up going up to Kumsong to get Frances, Dad?" Jamie asked as he helped himself to some cutlets from the dish Dawa held.

"In a couple of weeks."

"Are you taking the estate car?"

"Good gracious, no. That old thing will never make it up the hill to the school. No, I'm taking the Jeep and the trailer."

"Are you going up to Sing La, then?"

"Yes, your father has to get the stores and things first, darling," Lydia said.

"Are you going to bring a tree and crackers and things for Christmas, Daddy?" Cissy asked.

"Yes, my pet, and if there's anything special you want me to get you, tell your mother and she'll put it on the list."

"And don't forget the letter to Father Christmas," her mother said. "Daddy can post it from Sing La." She winked at Jamie.

"Can I come?" Jamie said.

"Not this time, son," his father said. "Why, you've only just come down. I thought you would have had enough of the hills by now."

"Yes, but there're no pictures here or anything. Can you get me some comics then?"

"Yes, put it down on the list."

"I want some comics too," Cissy said, not to be outdone.

"All right, pet."

Jamie changed the topic. "What school am I going to next year?"

"Your father and I haven't decided yet," Lydia said. "But when Daddy's in Kumsong he's going to see the headmaster of Turnbull's to see if he can admit you there."

"Oh no," Jamie groaned. "Turnbull's!"

"There's nothing wrong with Turnbull's," his mother said. "Your father went there when he was a boy."

"Only for a short while, Liddy," her husband said. "It was St. Paul's for most of the time."

"That snob school," Jamie said.

"Yes, I didn't like it much either. Turnbull's was better. Anyway, we'll see. We haven't decided finally yet. It just depends on whether they can take you or not."

"Daddy's going to ask if they'll take you as a day scholar first," Lydia said. "I want to go up and stay in Kumsong for a while with old Mrs Sheehan at Eagles' Crag. It'll give you the chance to get used to the school and make new friends before you go in as a boarder."

"How long for?" Jamie asked.

"You mean as a day scholar? Oh, just about a month or so."

Jamie helped himself to some jelly and custard. He warmed a bit to the idea of going to Turnbull's, especially if he started as a day scholar first. Perhaps it wouldn't be so bad, although Kumsong was such a dump.

After dinner, the family retired to the front veranda for a while, not talking much but watching the fireflies and listening to the medley of night sounds. Howard puffed contentedly on his pipe. The general tranquillity was broken from time to time as Jamie slapped at mosquitoes, which had become quite active.

The ghostly figure of Tulassa, in her white sari, appeared carrying a hurricane lantern.

"You children better get off to bed now," Howard said.

Cissy was already half asleep when Tulassa picked her up from Lydia's lap.

Jamie yawned. "Goodnight, Mum," he said, getting up and kissing her. "And goodnight, Dad," he called, as he made his way off.

"Come back and give your father a kiss," Lydia said in sharp tones.

Jamie hesitated momentarily, then went up to his father and gave him a peck on the cheek.

"Goodnight, son," his father said. "Becoming too big for a goodnight kiss and all that, eh?"

After they had gone, following Tulassa and the lantern, Howard said, "The boy's growing up."

Dawa brought in a tray of drinks—a whisky soda for Howard, and a gin and lime juice cordial for Lydia—and set it on the table.

"Yes," Lydia said, picking up her glass. "I wish he were a bit more affectionate though."

"Oh, come on, Liddy," Howard said. "Being shut away in boarding school naturally makes a boy a bit reserved. They don't get much affection there."

"Yes, I wish he didn't have to be away from home all the time."

"Can't be helped."

"I hope he won't pick up any bad habits at Turnbull's," Lydia said, "or a *chee-chee* accent. He talks so nicely now."

"Well, we can't afford St. Paul's."

"If only we could get him into school in England," Lydia said and sighed.

"We haven't the money, dear, and besides, that would only mean a bigger separation."

"No, I mean couldn't we all go?"

"What on earth for? There's nothing there for us, and what sort of job do you think I could do?"

"Oh, I expect you could find something."

"Looking after the property of some old duke or other, I imagine." The sarcasm deepened his voice. "Anyway," he continued, "things are still very hard over there, you know — rationing and all that."

"But what do you think is going to happen, what with all this talk of Indian independence?" Lydia asked.

"I don't think anything much will happen, dear," Howard said. "Although, with Atlee in charge of things, one never can tell."

"Yes." Lydia nodded. "Churchill would never have dreamed of such a thing. What did he call Gandhi?"

"A half-naked *fakir*."

"Did he really use that word?" Lydia said, her eyes wide with incredulity.

"Um ... it's not the word you think it is, dear—it means a sort of Indian holy man." He took a swig of his whisky and made a face. "Dawa's given me the Indian whisky again. Don't we have any Scotch left?"

"It's probably all gone now. You'll have to get some more in Sing La when you go up." She called out to Dawa who appeared out of the gloom and asked him if all the *Sadha Ghora* (White Horse) was finished.

"It is all finished," Dawa said, grinning.

"Oh well, I suppose it'll have to do," Howard said. He drank down what remained in his glass. "As I was saying," he went on, "I don't think much is going to happen in spite of all the talk. The British can never leave India. Why, they've been here for three hundred years. The Indians will never be able to rule themselves, what with all the religious and cultural differences. I don't think you need to worry too much."

"But what if it *did* happen? What would become of people like us?"

"What, you mean the Anglo-Indians? It'll be no different for you than it will be for us. We're all Indian born after all, and in the same boat, so to speak. There's no place for us in

England. We'd be complete misfits. Why, already the ones that come over here look down on us 'country born' and call us box-wallahs."

"It *would* be different for us." Lydia frowned and put her glass down. "The Indians have never liked us because we've always sided with the British, and they consider us their lackeys. It would mean there would be no jobs for the likes of us, and they'd expect us to adapt to their culture and become like Indians."

"It won't happen," Howard said, "and if it ever did I don't suppose it would make very much difference. They'd still need us to run things for them." He looked at his watch. "Well, I suppose we'd better get off to bed." He called out to the *durwan* who appeared from somewhere and told him to lock up for the night.

"*Gee huzur,*" the durwan said, and pulled the heavy steel trellis gates together. These sealed the veranda off, and ensured that no wild animal could enter the building during the night.

Dawa appeared with a hurricane lantern and escorted the couple upstairs.

CHAPTER 5

Howard drove the Jeep down the narrow and hazardous track that zigzagged down to the tea plantation, and the trailer bumped behind dangerously. It had been a long, dusty drive from Panchpani to Kholagari, where he stopped for a short break. Then it was up to the hills on the winding Tonga Road for the remaining forty miles or so. His parents' tea plantation, Stone Valley, was situated below the Pokhari Road that branched off at Soong and led to the more remote regions of the Singalila Ridge. Howard had left Abdul, the driver, back at Panchpani because he had no experience of driving in the hills, and had brought only Dawa with him. But he had dropped him off at Soong so that his house-boy could spend a couple of days leave with his family in Sing La.

He reached the bottom of the rough track, and the road levelled out onto a large open plateau that had been carved out of the mountainside. Here the bungalow stood, surrounded by a neat garden ablaze with poinsettias and various flowering shrubs. A long veranda fronted the house, and geraniums and other flowers in pots stood on tiered wooden benches that ran along its length. Corrugated iron sheeting, that had been painted green, made up the roof. However, Howard noted, some of the paint had weathered away, and rusty patches showed through here and there.

He brought the vehicle to a halt under the bougainvillaea-covered porch, and the *khitmagar*, suitably liveried in a starched white uniform and turban, came up and greeted him with a salaam. "Burra-sahib and memsahib are waiting for you on the back veranda," he said in Hindustani. He escorted Howard through the large, familiar drawing room with its framed pictures and bric-a-brac, through the dining room and on to the glazed back veranda that had been made into a sort of conservatory, and where an elderly couple sat in deep wicker chairs.

Stanley Donaldson rose unsteadily to his feet. "Hello, my boy," he wheezed. "We've been expecting you since tiffin."

"Hello, Pater. I'm sorry I'm a bit late. Got held up in Kholagari." He hoped the lie wouldn't be detected in his voice. "And hello, Mattie," he said, going over to his stepmother and kissing her on the cheek, which she presented to him with a little tilt of her head. She smelled strongly of peppermints and lavender water.

"Yes, we waited tiffin for you hoping you'd arrive earlier," she said. "But then it became too late. You'll have some tea, naturally." She reached for a little bell that stood on the small square cane table, covered with a damask tablecloth.

"Well, actually, I'd prefer something a bit stronger," Howard said.

"A whisky soda then?"

"Yes, fine."

She rang the little bell, and the *khitmagar* appeared. "A *burra* peg of whisky for the sahib."

"I think I'll have one too," Stanley said.

"So early in the day?" She gave him a stern look.

"Well, I thought I would join Howard," Stanley said, abashed.

"Oh very well then." She turned to the *khitmagar*. "Two pegs," she said. "One *burra* and one *chota*, and some soda-water."

"Does memsahib require anything?" the *khitmagar* asked.

She hesitated. "A dry sherry." She turned to Howard. "The children well?"

"Oh fine," Howard said. "Jamie's just back from school and I'm picking Frances up on the way back."

"And the little one. What's her name?

"Cicely. Yes, she's fine too." He waited for her to ask after Lydia, but she changed the subject.

"We thought it would be much nicer here instead of the drawing room. The view is so splendid, don't you think?"

Howard looked out beyond the end of the terraced garden at the panorama of the Snowy Ridge, broken up into squares by the panes of window glass. Sing La town spread out in the shape of a horseshoe over the adjacent mountain ridge, the clutter of tiny buildings tumbling down the mountainside.

"Yes, I've always loved this view," he said.

"Not enough to want to live here though." Her voice sounded reproachful.

"Oh, come on, Mattie. You know I have my job."

"Yes, working for someone else in that awful backwater. I sometimes wonder how you can tolerate it, what with all the dust and flies and heat of those unhealthy plains."

"You can get used to anything if you have to," Howard said in as light a voice as he could manage.

"Yes, but you *don't* have to. That's just the point." She tapped the wooden floor irritably with her walking stick to emphasise the words. "You know that you can always stay here and help your father. Goodness knows, he finds it hard enough to manage."

"That's enough, Matilda dear," Stanley said in a soft voice. "Howard has his own life and his own responsibilities. We've been over all this before."

"Yes, silly boy. Ah — here's *khit* with the drinks."

They talked on, Matilda filling Howard in with snippets of the latest town gossip. Quite a large European community resided in Sing La, comprising mainly of elderly boarding-house keepers or retired people. These were mostly widows and spinsters or the odd Indian Army colonel. There were not many young families, as the town offered little means of employment. Of course, there was the tea planting community, but they didn't mix very well with the town residents, as they were usually snobby British sahibs covenanted out from England, unlike the Donaldsons who had been planting tea in India for generations. Howard listened inattentively, sipping his whisky. His father hardly entered the conversation. The late afternoon sunlight slanted over the garden and cast long shadows. Tea was served, and Matilda filled the delicate china cups with the pale amber liquid from a silver teapot, and then passed around a plate of hot buttered scones.

"There's nothing like Sing La tea," Matilda said, then she sipped from her cup. "Stanley, you must give Howard a few packets to take back."

"Um ... thanks, but just a packet will do," Howard said. "We don't drink much Sing La. Liddy prefers something a bit stronger, like Assam or Ceylon."

Matilda clicked her tongue in disapproval. "And you, a Sing La tea planter's son! Whatever next."

Stanley, who had remained silent for most of the while, cleared his throat and eventually spoke. "Did I tell you I've had most of the tea garden machinery replaced?"

"No, Pater."

"Yes, it had to be done. Of course, this meant taking out a heavy mortgage on the garden, and the interest is simply crippling. I've hardly made any profit this year, despite the second flush being so good."

This meant the growth of the tender new shoots, or pekoe, which was the "two leaves and a bud" that the tea-pickers plucked so deftly from the tops of the tea bushes, and which produced the best quality teas.

"Let's not bore Howard with our troubles, Stanley dear," Matilda said. "I'm sure he has enough of his own. Let's go into the garden, shall we, before the light fades completely."

Howard helped her out of her chair. She got to her feet, leaning heavily on her stick. They all went out into the garden and down the crazy-paving stones. Matilda pointed out a plant or other to Howard, who tried to show some interest. They went down the steps to the lower terraced garden, where a sun-dial stood, and to the wrought-iron railings at the end. The hill dropped down steeply from here, and tea bushes stretched right down into the valley.

They stood against the railings in silence and watched the sun set on the Snows. At first, the mountains and the streaky clouds above were a delicate rose-petal pink, but this soon deepened into fiery crimson. Eastwards, the last rays touched Sing La town, reflecting off the countless window-panes of the houses, which lit up into a thousand flashes of light. Then, as darkness descended all at once, the town's street lights came on, covering the hillside with a glitter of sparkling gems.

Matilda pulled her shawl more tightly about her shoulders. "We'd better get inside now," she said. "The chill air isn't good for Stanley's chest, and I expect you'll want to freshen up before dinner. We've put you in your old room and I hope you're going to spend a few days with us."

"Um ... well, actually, it'll only be for tonight," Howard said. "I've booked in at the Himalayan Hotel for tomorrow and I have to collect Frances the day after."

"Such a short trip," Matilda said. "And that awfully expensive hotel."

"It's only for one night, Mattie, and I have to be in town to do the shopping and all that. I also promised to meet some friends at the Gymkhana Club in the evening." His last statement was a lie and he hoped his stepmother would not question him too closely.

"Well if you must, you must." Matilda sighed. "We see so little of you these days."

They went into the house, and Howard went upstairs to the bedroom. He noted that the *khitmagar* had taken his suitcase out of the Jeep and placed it in his room. He had a quick wash and, before dressing for dinner, sat on the edge of his bed and pulled out a crushed brown and slightly sweat-dampened envelope from his jacket pocket. Inside, was a letter on lavender-coloured note-paper. He sniffed it, and through the smell of his own perspiration, he could still make out the scent of some exotic and mysterious perfume, then he read it for the umpteenth time.

> *My precious love,*
> *How I've missed you all these long and lonely months. Anyway, we'll soon be together again at last. I have booked in*

at the Himalayan Hotel for a week, so if you can manage to get in there for the 20th, at least we'll have one night together. I wish it could be longer, but I'll make it one to remember, I promise, my darling. I managed to persuade Alex that I needed a break, and he agreed. He, poor dear, doesn't suspect a thing – too absorbed with all his stocks and shares and racehorses! I can't tell you how excited I am at the thought of seeing you. It makes the waiting all the more worthwhile.

I must close now, my darling. Alex is due back from his race meeting any minute, and I must give this to the bearer to post.

Always, your loving,
Veronica

Like Alex, Howard was glad that Lydia too suspected nothing. All the *dak* came directly to his office, which was a small bungalow beyond the west gate and outside the compound of Lal Kothi, where all the Estate business was carried out. Howard had three *babus* who formed the clerical staff, and had pointed out to them that no letters, personally addressed to him, should be opened by anyone else. He put the envelope back in his jacket pocket, and changed for dinner.

When he went downstairs again, the *pani-wallah* was lighting a fire in the grate of the drawing room. Matilda and his father sat in easy chairs, listening to the BBC news on the big HMV radio set, Matilda's fingers busy with crocheting a dainty doily or something, which rested on her lap. She looked up at him over her pince-nez as he entered the room.

"Ah, that looks much better," she said, indicating his dinner jacket. "You must get terribly dusty in that awful American contraption—what do they call it?"

"A Jeep, Mattie."

"Yes, completely unsuitable for this climate."

"I don't know how we'd manage without one in Panchpani," Howard said. "Most of the roads are no more than cart tracks, and it's only a vehicle like this that can manage them. An ordinary car would probably break its axle. Do you still have the little Morris?"

"Yes." She sighed. "But your father's driving has become worse these last few years."

"Oh, I don't know, Matilda," her husband said, "I seem to manage all right."

"It's the terrible hill to Stone Valley that terrifies me," she continued. "The last time we went into Sing La, I almost thought we would roll down backwards off the *khud*."

"It's the hill gear that's playing up," Stanley said. "I'll have to get it seen to when I go into town again."

"Yes." Matilda frowned. "That's another thing that has to be fixed."

Howard changed the topic. "Do you still play?" He nodded in the direction of the upright piano that stood against the wall.

"Now and again," Matilda said. "But my fingers are a bit stiff now."

"Play something for us," Howard said.

"Not now, dear. Perhaps after dinner."

"You don't mind if I do?"

"Not a bit."

Howard went over to the piano, lifted the lid, and played a few notes.

"It's a bit out of tune," Matilda told him.

He sat down on the piano stool and played, hesitantly at first, then he broke into the syncopated rhythm of a popular boogie-woogie tune.

"You're not going to play that dreadful American jazz, surely," Matilda said. "Goodness knows we had enough of it when their servicemen were here, with their vulgar jitterbugging. Don't you remember any of the nice pieces you used to play when you were a boy?"

Howard broke off. He changed the tune to a light classical piece, his fingers moving awkwardly to half-remembered notes.

Matilda clapped her hands in appreciation. "Bravo!"

"Very good, my boy," Stanley said. "I'm glad you haven't forgotten your music."

Howard got up, and gave a little bow. Then he turned his attention to the framed pictures on top of the piano. One of him as a boy, dressed in his Sunday suit complete with Eton collar and boater hat, looked back at him. Beside it, stood another rather faded picture of his elder sister Isabel, with her long golden hair. A picture of his mother, who had died when he was twelve, was noticeably absent.

"I'm glad to see you've still got these," Howard said.

"Yes, you were fifteen in that one, I think." Matilda nodded. "And Isabel, nineteen. They were taken about a year after your father and I were first married."

"Yes, I remember," Howard said.

Like the photograph, the memory of his elder sister had faded somewhat, but he knew about the awful row that had taken place between her and his stepmother, when Isabel refused to return to her recently married husband. She had gone upstairs and locked herself in her bedroom, where she was found the next morning, an empty bottle of laudanum beside her. He had been in school at the time, so had been spared some of the trauma this tragic event had caused in the family. His father would carry it to his grave, but as far as Matilda was concerned, he felt that she was more affected by the disgrace this had caused, particularly as his sister had to be buried outside the cemetery in un-consecrated ground.

The gong sounded for dinner, and they all went over to the dining room. The meal was typically European—clear soup, roast pork and crackling with accompaniments, and an apple Charlotte to follow, all cooked on a primitive mud *chula* by the *bawarchi*, whose virtues Matilda frequently exalted throughout the course of the meal. Matilda disliked Indian cooking, derogatorily referring to it as coolie food. But his father relished a good curry, which he would eat on the sly at every opportunity when out of the home environment.

After dinner, they sat for a while beside the fire in the drawing room, sipping small cups of strong coffee, then, as promised, Matilda seated herself at the piano and played a few light classics, her fingers fumbling over the keys. She often struck a wrong note, and would click her tongue in irritation. Then she played a few of her favourites—songs like *Let Me Call You Sweetheart* and *After the Ball is Over*, singing in accompaniment in her high, cracked voice.

The next morning dawned bright and clear, and Stanley took Howard down to the tea factory. They followed a narrow path, and as they rounded a bend, the long building—constructed of brick and corrugated iron sheeting—came into view. In the dim interior, they passed through areas where the withering, rolling, fermenting, and drying processes were carried out, and Stanley pointed out the new bits of equipment he had invested in, shouting to be heard above the clatter of machinery.

When they came out into the quiet and sunlight again, Howard paused to light his pipe.

"Pater," he said, "I didn't mean to sound callous last evening when Mattie was saying that you needed more help with the garden. I know what you must be going through, and you're not getting any younger. It's just that Lydia and Mattie would never hit it off living under the same roof."

"I understand perfectly, my son," Stanley said. "Matilda knows that too. She's just trying to make you feel bad."

"I wish I could help in some way though," Howard said.

"What can you do? And I really wouldn't be able to afford to pay you the sort of salary you're getting now. That's why I haven't been able to employ a manager or anything. I'll just have to press on as long as I can." He sighed. "I do worry about Matilda though. It's harder for her."

CHAPTER 6

Howard left his parents and Stone Valley later that day, after tiffin. He felt a twinge of guilt as they stood on the porch steps, two frail and lonely figures that waved to him as he drove away. But with pipe clenched in teeth, he set off with determination up the steep ascent to the road above. He reached Soong, and then re-joined the Tonga Road, which led to Sing La. But before he reached the town, he branched off and climbed the hill towards the chateau-like Himalayan Hotel with its twin dunce-cap turrets at either end. Veronica had chosen the Himalayan because it was secluded and had a certain anonymity about it. The visitors were generally the more affluent holiday-makers and unlikely to know any of the Sing La residents, so if he and Veronica were seen together, it wouldn't get back to the town and cause gossip.

He parked the Jeep near the rickshaw stand on the road below the hotel and carried his suitcase up the steps to the entrance, where one of the porters took it from him. Once in the lobby, he checked in at reception, and when he filled in the register, he noticed Veronica's name—Mrs V. Hamilton-Smyth—in her large, round handwriting. Next to it was her room number. He was grateful there were three other entries after hers, as he filled in his own name on the next blank line.

"What room would you like, sir?" the clerk said. "The hotel is almost empty so you can have whatever one you wish."

"Ummm … what about Room 28? Is it available?"

"Yes, sir. Almost certainly, sir. Let me check for you." The clerk checked the rows of hotel keys and took one off the hook. "Yes, it is available," he said. "There is also one letter for you, I think." He took a small envelope from a pigeon-hole in the rack and handed it over to Howard, who put it in his pocket.

He followed the porter with his suitcase through the enormous, empty hotel lounge, with its low ceiling and deep leather armchairs, up the central staircase that branched into the two wings of the hotel, and down the long corridor, until he finally reached his room. He gave the porter some *baksheesh* and, when he had left, Howard took the envelope out of his pocket and tore it open.

Darling,
Have just had to go out to meet some ghastly friends at Peliti's. Will go on from there to Beech Hill and wait for you on the bench near the summer house. Meet me there at about 3 o'clock, darling. I'll be watching out for you.
Your Veronica.

PS – I'm in Room 26.

He glanced at his watch. It was just going on to two o'clock, so he had plenty of time. He took out the shopping lists Lydia had made out. Her handwriting was neatly written and well set out, and titled "O. N. Mookerjee's – Chemists," "The Johra

Rasta Stores," and "The Oxford Book Shop." There was also Jamie's list—a page torn out from one of his exercise books and written in his schoolboy handwriting, with several smudges, inkblots, and corrections. Cissy's letter to Father Christmas was in an envelope addressed in huge scrawly capitals, which Lydia had apparently helped her with. He could picture Cissy, her face deep in concentration, the tip of her little pink tongue sticking out from the corner of her mouth as she pressed hard on her pencil. She had even drawn the postage stamp in the top right-hand corner in crayons. Against the many items on Jamie's list and Cissy's letter were some of Lydia's annotations—*Don't worry about this. Have already ordered from Whiteaway's.* He was glad he didn't have to do much of the Christmas shopping. Lydia had ordered all the presents and other Christmas fare from a large department store in Calcutta, who would crate it up and despatch it to Panchpani by rail freight. It was mainly the stores and toiletries he had to get from Sing La, which were not available in the bazaar shops of Panchpani.

For the moment, he thought the best plan would be to leave Lydia's lists with the shops concerned, who would pack the stuff in tea chests ready for collection the next day. Then, instead of walking to Beech Hill along the top road, he would drive, via the Tonga Road below, to the bottom of Beech Hill and walk up to meet Veronica there. This way he could bring her back with him to the hotel in the Jeep and avoid the risk of being seen walking with her through the town.

After leaving the hotel, Howard went to where he had parked the Jeep and struggled a bit to unhitch the trailer. A grinning Bhutia rickshaw-man came up to him and offered his help in the hope of some *baksheesh*, but Howard politely and firmly declined. He got into the Jeep and drove further down the Auckland Road and into the town. Since the upper part of Sing La was sealed off to motor traffic, he parked the Jeep at the motor stand and walked along Commercial Row, where most of the Sing La shops were located. First, he popped into the chemists, then next to the Johra Rasta Stores. The shop was well-stocked—not only with wines, beers, and spirits, but also a glut of provisions the Americans had left in the wake of their departure. The Oxford Book Shop was only a few doors away from the Johra Rasta Stores, and he went in to get Jamie's comics—*Superman*, *Batman*, and the latest editions of the *Beano*, *Dandy*, *Wizard*, and *Hotspur*, and then some children's books from Lydia's list—Beatrix Potter's *The Tale of Peter Rabbit* for Cissy, *The Girls' Own Annual* for Frances, and *The Coral Island* for Jamie. Lydia also wanted a couple of issues of *Woman* and *Woman's Own*. All these he had parcelled up for collection the next day.

While he drove down Tendup La Road, past the Plaza Cinema, he noticed *Leave Her to Heaven* was being shown. He made a sharp right turn at the bottom of the hill and joined the

Tonga Road. Then it was through the Sing La bazaar and onwards towards Singamari. He managed to find a wide bit of road to park the Jeep just below the Old Cemetery. The climb up past the ancient graves was steep, cut into terraces on the hillside, and he was quite out of breath when he eventually reached the Beech Hill West Road above. It levelled out from here until he branched up the road that led to Beech Hill Park itself and to the summer house where Veronica waited.

She stood with her back towards him beside a magnolia tree, gazing out towards the snows, her hand resting lightly on the trunk. A slight breeze ruffled her auburn hair and fluttered the red gauze scarf round her throat. She turned as she heard his footfall.

"Darling," she cried. "I didn't see you."

"Too busy looking at those wretched mountains of yours instead of watching out for me," Howard said, with mock jealousy. He took her in his arms and crushed his lips to hers. She returned his kiss hungrily.

"I've been waiting for this so long, my darling," she said breathlessly. "A proper kiss from a proper man at last. I can't tell you how much I've missed this since that time in Calcutta such ages and ages ago."

"Has it really been that long?" Howard said.

"Uh-huh. Almost two years now. I bet you haven't missed me as much as I've missed you," she said sulkily.

"Of course I have. Been thinking of you every minute."

"Liar."

"Anyway, it's wonderful to see you again. You haven't changed a bit. Still as lovely as ever."

Her green eyes glinted with amusement. "Do you think so? Not even a teensy-weensy little wrinkle?" She tilted her face so that he could examine it more closely.

"Not even that," he said. He wondered at her flawless complexion—white and translucent as some rare marble. "You haven't aged by even a wrinkle. There now. Happy?"

She smiled and looked smug. "But you have, with all those lines of worry and care and responsibility, and that little bald patch on your head." When his face fell she added hastily, "Only teasing, my darling."

He ran his hand over his head. "Ummm ... I am getting a bit thin on top."

"That just means more virile. I hope you are anyway, darling. I don't want to be disappointed tonight after waiting for so long."

They walked over to the bench in the summer house, holding hands, and sat down.

"It was a good idea of yours to meet here." Howard took his pipe and tobacco pouch out of his pocket. "With just you and nobody else."

"I try to think of everything, darling." She opened her handbag and took out her gold cigarette case. She pressed the clasp and it snapped open. "Would you prefer one of these?"

"No, my dearest." He filled his pipe. Veronica leaned over towards him for a light as he struck a match.

She inhaled deeply and blew the smoke up into the air. "So, did Lydia let you off the leash without any trouble?"

"She's no problem that way," Howard said, feeling a little defensive of his wife. "She knows that I have to come up to Sing La now and again for the stores and all that. She's pretty much used to being on her own anyway, as my work takes me around a bit."

"Not like Alex," she said. "Sometimes I feel like a poor little bird trapped in a cage."

"A gilded cage."

She ignored his remark. "Whenever I get back from anywhere," she went on, "he wants to know all the ins and outs of where I've been and what I've done. He's not suspicious or jealous or anything, mind," she added. "It's just that he's curious and wants to know every itsy-bitsy tiny little detail of everything that I do. It's like having a faithful old dog watching and guarding you every minute of the day and not letting you out of its sight. It was hard enough to persuade him about this visit to Sing La. He wanted to know all the whys and wherefores and even asked me to wait a few weeks so that he could come up with me. You're so lucky with Lydia." She sighed.

Howard teased, "So, it's you who's on the leash."

"Yes, like a bitch on heat. Oh, doesn't that sound awful, darling?"

"Well, I hope I'm not just one of the pi-dogs in the queue."

"Oh, you're such a beast!" Veronica exclaimed. "Take that dreadful pipe out of your mouth and give me another kiss."

They walked down the hill, hand-in-hand, out of the park and through the cemetery, only releasing each other when they spied one of the *chokidars*. Once out of sight, Veronica stepped on a grave and posed, frivolously, like one of the statuettes.

"Look, darling," she said, "I'm an angel."

He joked, "I know you are, but don't do that, dearest. There may be one of my ancestors lying under all that."

"Are they all buried here?"

"Most of them are. Don't forget, we've been here for a hundred years or so — the Donaldsons."

"I hope they're not going to haunt me," Veronica said, "for leading one of their family astray."

"They might, if you don't get off their grave," Howard warned, with humour in his tone.

She laughed, put her hands round him and, standing on her toes, kissed him lightly on the lips, "You're such an old fuddy-duddy," she said.

They got back to the Jeep and climbed in, and Veronica tucked in her skirt so it wouldn't blow about in the wind.

Howard drove to Singamari, where he turned the Jeep around, then headed back along the road, peeping the horn frequently as they passed through the bazaar with its pedestrians and pi-dogs. The thought that few of the elderly residents ever ventured into this vicinity comforted Howard. They seemed to confine themselves to between the location of the two churches in the town above—St. Matthews along the Mall and the Methodist Church situated below the Himalayan Hotel. To be on the safe side though, he continued along the Tonga Road, past the railway station, until he reached Wernicke Road, then turned a sharp left up the hill and to the hotel.

As Veronica climbed out of the Jeep, Howard said, "Sorry, darling, but I have to go back into town again to meet some friends of Pater's at the Club." He hoped the lie would work, as it had with Matilda. The truth was that he wanted to avoid the dinner situation at the hotel. He couldn't very well sit at the same table as her, and it would be awkward to have to sit at a separate table, with her eyeing him seductively all the time.

"Oh darling." She pouted. "You're not going to leave me all alone in this ghastly hotel for the rest of the evening? I can't even have a drink at the bar, because ladies can't go in there unaccompanied."

"Can't be helped, dearest. I promised Pater that I would see these tea planter friends and get some information for him about the tea market situation. The garden's in a bad way and he needs all the help and advice he can get."

"What time are you going to be back?"

"Ummm ... well, I have to have dinner with them at the Club, so I'll probably be back at about nine."

"Oh, go to your friends then." She frowned. "Don't worry about poor little me locked up like a caged animal in my room. We've had such little time together as it is." She flicked her head to one side and stalked off in a huff, like a sulky little girl.

Back in town, he parked the car at the motor stand again. He didn't go up to the Club for a drink as he wasn't a member. Instead, he walked up to Peliti's and ordered a *burra* peg of whisky. He needed it. He felt very uneasy about the situation. He couldn't deny that he was terribly attracted to Veronica. At the same time he felt very guilty about Lydia. The moral dilemma confronted him. What he was doing wasn't right. However, it was too late to back out of the situation now. If only he had ignored Veronica's letter and delayed his trip by a day or two, the situation could have been avoided. But then the temptation was too great to resist. He drank his whisky and ordered another *burra* peg, and by the time he had finished this, he felt more relaxed and not so much at odds with himself. Since he had a few hours free, he decided to go to the Plaza and see *Leave Her to Heaven*. He had liked Gene Tierney ever since *Laura*, and she reminded him so much of Veronica in many ways, with the same teardrop eyes and high cheekbones. She played the part of Ellen, a terribly possessive bride who went to the lengths of letting her husband's young son drown in front of her, just because she didn't want to share his love with anyone else. After the film, he had a Chinese meal at the Peeking Restaurant.

When he returned to the hotel later, he had a quick wash in his room, then tapped lightly on the door of number 26.

"Oh darling," Veronica said when she opened it. "I'm sorry I was so horrible and beastly to you. I know you're always so busy. Not like poor little me who has nothing to do all day but wile away the hours just waiting and longing for you."

She wore a bathrobe, and was obviously naked underneath. "I'm going to unpack my present now." She began to undress him, leisurely at first but more hastily as she attacked the buttons of his trousers. Finally, he stood naked in front of her, and she threw off her robe in complete abandon. Then she flung her arms around him, kissing him hungrily, and dragged him down onto the bed.

They made love, urgently and ferociously, with something of the animal in their passion. She took him into hidden and unexplored places; between her warm red lips and in the valley of her voluptuous breasts, then into the soft, wet cleft between her thighs. Her cries, groans, and squeals of delight were noisy and unashamed, and Howard was glad that most of the neighbouring rooms were unoccupied. Finally, exhausted and sweating, they rested back on the pillows.

"Oh darling." She sighed. "You were wonderful." She leaned over and kissed him gently, then reached across him to the bedside table for her cigarette case. She snapped it open. "Would you like one?"

"Ummm ... all right," Howard said.

She extracted two cigarettes from the case and placed them between her lips, then found her lighter and flicked it a few times until it ignited. She lit the cigarettes and handed one over to Howard.

"Lydia is so lucky," she said. "I'm frightfully jealous of her, you know. She has you to herself every night, and here's poor little me going without you for ages and ages." She tapped the ash off her cigarette. "How is it—making love to her?" Her green eyes slanted at him through a curl of cigarette smoke.

"Not the same as it is with you," Howard said. It truly wasn't the same, he reflected, as he dragged on his cigarette, which tasted like straw. With Lydia it was always in the dark and under covers. Why, he had hardly seen his wife's naked body at all these last few years. And then when he did by chance—like entering the bedroom one day when she was still half-naked, she had been put-out and annoyed. With Lydia, sex was something that had to be regulated and controlled. You weren't allowed to show your feelings or emotions, or talk about it, and their lovemaking was carried out in silence. He felt that to her it was just a necessary duty a wife had to put up with, and this always left him with a sense of guilt—as though he were being selfish and thinking only of his own pleasure.

"Yes, it's not the same with Alex, either," Veronica said. "The poor dear can hardly manage it at all these days. But then," she added, "he always buys me a terribly expensive present to make up for it."

"I'm too poor for presents," Howard said.

"Oh darling. You don't need to buy me presents. You have the most gorgeous present for me right here." She reached under the covers and grabbed hold of him. "I think you're ready again."

Howard laughed and pulled her hand away. "Not quite ready yet, dearest. I want my batteries fully charged for you."

"All right then, darling. I can wait a few minutes. I'm used to waiting for Alex. The poor darling has practically no charge at all." She blew a perfect smoke-ring and Howard watched it drift towards the ceiling and finally break up.

"Veronica .... ah, do you ever feel guilty?" he said at length.

"Guilty, what on earth for?"

"You know, our meeting like this and getting together for a good screw every so often."

"Howard darling, you know as well as I that Sing La is famous for it!"

59

"I know, but I can't help thinking about Lydia—you know. I feel awfully guilty about being unfaithful to her. Don't you feel the same way about Alex?"

"Yes, he's a dear, really, and so filthy rich." She turned towards him. "But I don't want to be lectured right now, my darling; I just want to be fucked."

CHAPTER 7

Howard left the hotel and a tearful Veronica the next morning with promises that he would write. But this would be rare, as they didn't often correspond. It was more a physical thing between them. He was almost sure she had a string of other lovers on the go and he was just one among them. Both he and Veronica had their own lives, and there was no question that either one of them considered their brief encounters as anything more than just a diversion.

On the Johra Rasta, a smiling Dawa met him, carrying a young cryptomeria tree that he had chopped down with his *kukri* earlier that morning. This would be their Christmas tree. Howard employed three stalwart Bhutia rickshaw-men to carry the packing cases he'd collected from the stores. These they carried on their backs, with the help of a wide band of woven hessian supporting the case at the bottom, and the other end looped around their foreheads. They walked down the road in a small procession and, once they reached the motor-stand, they loaded everything into the Jeep's trailer which Howard and Dawa then covered with a tarpaulin. They both climbed into the Jeep and made their way down the road, past the railway station and onwards to Kumsong, a distance of about 20 miles. Once there, Howard branched off the Tonga Road and up the steep hill that led to the schools. He had to put the vehicle into four-wheel-drive as the road twisted and turned for about two miles. He went first to Turnbull's, passing Frances' school, Queen's Hill, on the way, and stopped the Jeep outside the main gate, just above the school chapel. He left Dawa in the vehicle and walked to the headmaster's cottage up a windy pathway, carrying a large brown envelope containing all Jamie's school papers that Lydia had given him.

Mrs Stalkey, the headmaster's wife — a plump little woman, wearing an apron, and carrying a feather-duster in her hand — met him at the door.

"It's Mr Donaldson, is it?" she said. "My husband's been expecting you. Would you like to come through into the study? Please do excuse me, I'm just dusting off some of my husband's cups. He doesn't trust the servants."

She ushered him through the parlour to a little room at the end, then tapped on the door before opening it. "It's Mr Donaldson, dear."

"Come in, come in." Her husband rose out of his chair and extended his hand, which Howard shook. "Please, do sit down. It's about your boy's admission, is it?"

Mr Stalkey was a lean, wiry Anglo-Indian gentleman, with thinning hair and thick glasses, which made his beady black eyes seem enormous. With a large hooknose, he reminded Howard a bit of Mr Punch.

"Yes, my son Jamie … er … James."

"Ah, yes. Your wife wrote to me about it. How old is he?"

"Ummm … Eleven, I think."

"And he was at Fern Hill?"

"That's right, for the last four years or so."

"A great shame they've closed down. Most unusual these days. We're having some other applications from Fern Hill you know, so your son will feel more at home if he's admitted here. You have his transfer certificate and last school report?"

"Yes, they're all here." Howard took the papers out of the envelope, and passed these over to Mr Stalkey who sifted through them and scrutinised each document carefully.

"Well, everything seems to be in order," he said finally, looking up at Howard, the light reflecting off his thick lenses. "I expect you'd like to have a tour round the school now, before we complete formalities."

"Ummm ... there's only one thing," Howard said, "and I don't know whether my wife mentioned this in her letter, but she would like Jamie to be admitted for the first month as a day scholar. The reason is my wife is coming up to Kumsong for short spell, and she thought it would give him a chance of getting used to the school before becoming a boarder."

"Ah, I see. No, she didn't mention this. It is a bit unusual. We don't have any day boys at Turnbull's." He drummed his fingers thoughtfully on the desk. "I just wonder if it will be good for the boy. He might feel a bit of a misfit at first, and then unsettled when he's admitted as a boarder. I feel it's much better to throw them into the deep end right from the beginning. But there's no problem otherwise, administratively speaking or as a matter of policy, that is."

"It'll just be for a month," Howard said.

Mr Stalkey deliberated for a moment. "Oh, very well. I'll show you round the school now, if I may."

"Well, I know what it's like. As a matter of fact, I was here as a boy."

"Oh, were you? But we've made a lot of changes since your day and I'm sure you'll welcome the improvements. Of course," he added, "all the boys have left now after the Cambridge examinations, so the school will be quite empty."

"Yes, I know," Howard said. "I have to collect my daughter from Queen's Hill on my way back. She was held back for the Junior Cambridge exams too."

"Ah, you have a daughter there," Mr Stalkey said as he collected a bunch of keys hanging from a peg on the wall. "As you know, Turnbull Boys' School and Queen's Hill have always been closely associated, being situated so near to each other. We like to think of Queen's Hill as our sister school."

"Do they still have their socials? I remember they used to be quite a lot of fun."

"Yes indeed. The two schools like to get together at least once a year to have an evening of games, music, and dancing. It's good for the boys and girls to meet each other now and again, and quite a few of the boys have their sisters there. Of course, it's all closely supervised, and the teachers enjoy taking part too."

They walked out of the study and back into the parlour, where Mrs Stalkey was dusting a clutter of silver cups and trophies, laid out on a table. She gave them a tight little smile.

Howard glanced at the array. "I see you're quite a sportsman."

"Yes, most of them from my schooldays. Does James like sports?"

"He's keen on cricket and hockey," Howard said. "Not so much on football."

"And boxing?"

"No, I don't think they had that at Fern Hill."

"We have a good boxing team here," Mr Stalkey said proudly. "In fact, I think it's one of the best in the district. We've even won against St. Paul's recently."

They walked down the pathway from the house, passing the junior boys' school building on their right. Howard had only been at the senior boys' school, which started from Standard IV. Dawa smiled at them as they came by the Jeep and salaamed Mr Stalkey.

"Do you mind if my house-boy comes along with us?" Howard said. "I'd like him to see the school."

"I don't mind at all," Mr Stalkey said.

Howard beckoned to Dawa to follow them. "Come with us and see the school that I came to when I was a small boy, and where Jamie *baba* is going to come as well."

Dawa's grin increased, but he enquired whether the Jeep and *saman* would be all right if left unattended.

"Your vehicle and luggage will be perfectly safe here," Mr Stalkey said. "There's nobody about—especially curious little boys."

Once through the large gates, they stepped onto the deserted junior school playing field—the sprightly Mr Stalkey walking with an energetic step. At its end, the main school building stood. It was just as Howard remembered it—a large, rambling structure with an extensive corrugated-iron roof interspersed with steep gables, and a long covered veranda that bordered it all round the front, following the contours of the building. Mr Stalkey unlocked the door and showed Howard his dark and dingy former classroom, which smelt of chalk-dust, pencil shavings, and school-books, and still redolent with the faint smell of scruffy schoolboys. The dining room had its rows of long tables, which they walked past to get to the flight of wooden stairs, worn smooth by the feet of countless generations of schoolboys, where the dormitories were.

"I expect this brings back some memories," Mr Stalkey said as Howard looked at the rows of empty beds.

"Yes, I think my bed was that one, right there, near the window." He remembered how homesick he had been the first night in school, unable to sleep and hearing the murmuring, and the tossing and turning of the other boys as they slumbered.

Mr Stalkey took Howard to the rear of the school, which backed onto the hillside, and up the cement steps to a covered walkway that led to the newly constructed gym. The lavatories beside still reeked of urine and Phenyle.

Back at the main school building, Mr Stalkey opened his office with one of the keys on the bunch. It was still very much as Howard remembered it, the heavy oak desk near the window, the shelves of books, and the upright leather chairs. In a display cabinet were the school trophies, together with some more of Mr Stalkey's. A small cabinet with diamond-shaped panes held an array of canes — some of which he had tasted during his term at Turnbull's.

"I'll give you our application form," Mr Stalkey said, "and a list of things your boy will require. The school outfit is supplied by Hall & Anderson's in Calcutta, and they can provide the school tie, blazer, and cap badges etc., etc. There's no need to fill in the form just now. You can send it on by post, together with James's transfer certificate and your cheque for the term. I trust that will be all right?"

"Perfectly." Howard took the form and list, and put them with the other papers he carried.

"I'll just show you the Assembly Hall, and then we're more or less finished. You'll see that it has been completely refurbished."

They entered the large room with its rows of chairs, and stage at the far end with the curtains drawn back. The school emblem and motto hung above the stage.

"We usually have a film here, about once a week," Mr Stalkey said. "Before we broke up for the holidays we had *David Copperfield* and *Captains Courageous* with Freddie Bartholomew. The boys enjoyed them immensely. As you know," Mr Stalkey went on, "there's little or no opportunity for the boys to walk down to Kumsong, and there's little there to amuse them anyway. So we're a bit isolated here, high up on the hill. This makes the films a very welcome treat indeed."

Dawa followed behind them as they walked back through the playground. The main playing field was on a plateau about sixty feet below. The bank of the hill sloped down sharply to it, but terraces had been cut into the bank to accommodate the cricket pavilion and the seats that would be required on occasions like Sports Day.

Howard and Dawa climbed into the Jeep and Howard shook Mr Stalkey's hand. "It was nice meeting you," Howard said. "Please give my best wishes to your wife. By the way, I expect you'll both be going down to the plains shortly, so will it be all right to send the forms, etc., here by, say, next week?"

"That will be perfectly all right," Mr Stalkey said. "We're not expecting to leave here until just before Christmas."

Howard turned the Jeep and trailer round and drove on towards Queen's Hill. He stopped outside the main gate, which was padlocked, and walked through the side entrance onto the playing field. He saw a group of girls in the distance. One of them broke away and came running towards him. It was Frances.

"Daddee, Daddee," she screamed. When she reached him she threw her arms joyfully around his neck, showering him with kisses.

"Whoa, whoa, steady on," Howard said.

"Oh Daddy, I've been waiting so long for you. All morning in fact." She beckoned to the other girls who were staring in their direction. "Come over here and meet my Daddy," she yelled. They came over slowly and shyly, and Frances introduced the group to her father.

"This is Maureen," she said, "and this is Katie and Peggy. And this is Milly."

They stood gawping at him, as he said hello to each of them in turn. He thought what a plain bunch they were, except for Maureen, who was quite a pretty little thing.

"We'd better go over and see your headmistress now," he said. "Where is she likely to be?"

"Oh, Miss Neale? In her office, I think. I left my luggage just outside. It's all ready and everything."

"Is there any way of getting that blasted gate open so we can bring the Jeep inside?"

As if in answer to his question, a *durwan* came running up and opened the padlock on the gate.

Howard waved and shouted to Dawa. "Take the *gari* to the school building." He pointed in the relevant direction.

"*Hah sahib,*" Dawa called, grinning with pleasure at the chance of being allowed to drive. He started the Jeep, which jerked forward as he let in the clutch, and progressed, kangaroo-fashion, towards the school building where he stopped beside the steps.

Howard put his arm around Frances's shoulders as they walked towards the school, followed by the gawky schoolgirls. "Everything all right, eh?" he said.

"Yes, I think so, Daddy. The JC exams were very hard though. But I think I may have passed."

Before they reached the building, the headmistress appeared on the steps. She greeted Howard with a smile. "Here at last," she said. "Poor Frances has been anxiously waiting for you since breakfast."

"Yes, I'm sorry. Got delayed with the headmaster at Turnbull's. Stayed on there rather longer than I expected to, I think."

"Frances's younger brother's going there, is he? Frances did mention it," Miss Neale said.

"Yes, it's more or less fixed up now." He turned his attention to the trailer and unfastened the tarpaulin. Meanwhile, Dawa, with the help of one of the school's servants, was struggling with Frances's tin trunk, bedroll, and suitcase. They loaded these into the trailer, having to shift a few of the packing cases about, until everything fitted in snugly. The tarpaulin was replaced, and Howard went over to Miss Neale who was talking to Frances. "Well, good-bye," he said. "Thanks for looking after Frances for us. I expect you're glad now the exams are over and you can get back to the plains. When are you leaving?"

"Tomorrow," Miss Neale said. "Anyway, it won't be too bad travelling with just the girls from the Junior and Senior Cambridge. Not like it is with the 'Going Home Day' crowd." She shuddered.

Frances said her goodbyes to Miss. Neale and her friends, with many PS's about staying in touch with each other during the holidays.

"Better sit on the back seat, love," Howard said. "At least until we get down to the plains. It's cold and draughty in the front. You don't mind, do you, if we drive straight through to Panchpani, except for just a cup of tea and something to eat at Kholagari? It'll take us about six hours, and we should reach there by about nine."

"I don't mind, Daddy," Frances said, and she climbed obediently into the seat at the back, moving Howard's suitcase out of the way to accommodate her feet. Dawa climbed in beside Howard, and with waves and goodbyes to the headmistress and the small group of girls, Howard drove across the playground, through the school gates, and back to Panchpani.

CHAPTER 8

Had it not been for Lydia's planning and organisation, Christmas Day would have been something of a non-event. The general ambience of Panchpani didn't lend itself well to the spirit of Christmas. There was no church to go to, no European or Christian community to share it with, and no carols heard, because the only radio set at Lal Kothi was battery-operated, and the battery had run out of power. However, the children received their complement of presents—a Diana air rifle and Mecanno set for Jamie, and a smart suede writing case and Eversharp fountain pen for Frances, together with an autograph album and a pretty party frock. For Cissy, there was a giant teddy-bear, a water-colour paint set, and story-books. Howard and Lydia didn't exchange presents, and only gave gifts to each other on their respective birthdays. Similarly, the children didn't give presents to each other or to their parents, as there were no shops to buy them from and the children had no money to buy them with. For Cissy's benefit, all the gifts they received were supposedly from Father Christmas.

The family bundled into the Jeep for a picnic to the Mahanada River, about twelve miles away, which could be reached by a cart track. They took with them Dawa and Tulassa and their eight-year-old twin boys, whom Howard had nicknamed *Humni* and *Thumni* (meaning me and you) and, of course, Jubra—who all travelled in the Jeep's trailer, along with the *degchis* containing all the food, Primus stove, crockery, and other paraphernalia.

After a bumpy ride, they reached the river and found a spot for their picnic on the wide, sandy bank, while crocodiles, with mouths agape, sunned themselves on a sandbank opposite. Dawa and Howard erected a *shamiana* to provide them with some shade, and spread coconut matting and *dhurris* beneath. It was almost like being at the seaside again. Cissy was already sitting on the sand, making sand-castles with her bucket and spade; Lydia played *Don't Fence Me In* on her portable HMV wind-up gramophone, while Frances sat beside, selecting records; Howard, seated on a camp-stool a little way away, attempted to fish, while Blackie — barking wildly — frolicked in the water. Jamie and the servants' children, Jubra and *Humni* and *Thumni*, took turns shooting at targets with the new air-gun, and Dawa and Tulassa occupied themselves with getting the food ready — hot *chapattis* with *dhal* and egg curry.

They returned home just after sundown, singing songs and carols. On their way, they encountered a leopard. It stopped directly in front of them, its eyes glowed in the Jeep's headlights, and then it slunk into the forest. At Lal Kothi, their Christmas dinner waited: roast goose, killed that morning by Ishmael from the stock of poultry, and a Christmas pudding from Whiteaway's, embedded with little silver charms and, of course, the Christmas crackers. On the veranda, Lydia had festooned the cryptomeria tree with Christmas decorations, and after dinner, Howard handed out presents to the servants. A *sari* for Tulassa, a pair of leather *chapals* for Dawa, and clothing for their two twins. Jubra received a *durzee*-made shirt and a pair of pyjamas, and there were a couple of *lungis* for his father. Gifts of clothing were very much appreciated by both adults and children alike, more so than trivial presents and toys. Indian sweets were presented to all, in mud *gumlas,* and covered with silver foil. This was also the time that the Christmas bonus payments were handed out to each of the servants and the clerical staff of the office. These payments were made from Estate funds, and the Nawab suggested that they be given out at Christmas time so as not to discriminate between the Hindu and Muslim festivals.

Once the children were safely tucked up in bed, Howard and Lydia sat on the veranda with their evening drinks, whilst jackals yip-yapped in the distance.

"Well, now that we've got Christmas out of the way, the next item on the agenda is Nawabsahib's visit," Howard said. "There's never a dull moment."

"For you, that is," Lydia said. She was always a bit aggrieved that whilst Howard always seemed to have plenty to do to occupy his time, she, conversely, had to actively look round for things to do. "Is he going to open the *Mela* this time?"

The Nawab's family had begun the *Mela,* the Panchpani annual fair, many generations ago, and it had become famous in the area for its cattle, elephant, and camel marts and for the shops, cinemas, and circus that it generated. It attracted multitudes of people from all around the country, who came to buy and sell their goods, and it was a great source of revenue to the Estate funds. The *Mela* season, which lasted for one month, was the busiest period in Howard's year.

"Yes," Howard said. "I'm planning on sending the Nawab's railway coach up the line to Kholagari, so he can travel down in it. It hasn't been used for years, and I thought it might be a nice gesture. I thought I might also arrange a band," he continued, "and give him some sort of reception at the station, with some of the old Panchpani residents there to meet him."

"I hope you're not going to engage one of those awful *foo-foo* bands," Lydia said. "You know, the ones that play at local weddings. Their playing is so awful, and they look so cheap and tatty."

"Yes, that's a thought," Howard said. "Perhaps I can have a word with the circus owner and see if I can't get his band. They're not too bad."

"What's the Nawab like?" Lydia asked. She had never met the Nawab and felt a bit apprehensive about his visit. "I hope he's not going to be too fussy."

"No, no. He's a very educated and affable fellow. Educated in England and all that. Of course, you know he has an English wife."

"Has he?" Lydia said in some surprise. "No, you never told me that."

"Ummm ... I'm sure I mentioned it sometime or other."

"Well, I certainly didn't know it." She felt a twinge of annoyance. It was typical of Howard not to keep her informed of anything that came to his knowledge. However, she did feel intrigued. "It is a bit strange for an Englishwoman to marry an Indian, isn't it?"

"Oh, a lot of the Indian aristocracy married Europeans," Howard said. "It was quite the thing to do in the days of the old East India Company. Of course, it was mainly well-to-do Englishmen marrying *begums* from royal Indian households; not so much the other way about, because there were scarcely any English memsahibs about in the early days."

"Do they have any children?" Lydia asked.

"Yes, a daughter—about Jamie's age, I believe. He's bringing both her and his wife on this visit, and his young nephew, I think."

Lydia looked at him in complete amazement. "How has all this been going on and I don't know anything about it?" The exasperation showed in her voice. "You seem to keep me in the dark about everything these days, I notice."

"I'm sorry, dear." Howard shrugged. "I thought you knew."

She exploded, "How am I going to know if you don't tell me! It'll be me who'll end up having to do all the organisation and make all the arrangements. If it had just been the Nawab it wouldn't have been so bad. But with a lady and children in the house, it will be a lot more *jehmela*, especially an Englishwoman."

"Domiciled European," Howard said.

"Same thing."

"No, not quite." He shook his head. "You know that very well, Liddy. She's not going to be one of those snobby English memsahibs."

"And how do you know that?"

Howard faltered. "Well, I must admit, I've never met the lady," he said. "I only met the Nawab that one time when he interviewed me for the job at his Alipore place in Calcutta. He didn't even mention that he had a European wife. I heard it through the babus in the office. But I believe she's from a Sing La family. Her father was a pharmacist. Ran his own business there for years and was a pillar of the community. Mattie and Pater remember him well."

"And they have a half-caste child."

"Ummm … I'm not sure if the Nawab looks on her that way," Howard said. "She's Muslim and all that. Generally speaking, Indian men tend to look at their children as Indian, even if they do marry a European woman."

"Why so?" Lydia said. "If she's half-and-half how can he say she's Indian?"

"Because," Howard said, "when Indian gentleman marry European ladies they generally adopt the child into their culture."

"And what happens if it's the other way around? You know, a European man and a native woman. What happens to the children then?"

"Well, in that case the wife and child are generally disowned by the Indian family."

Lydia was horrified. "Why?"

"Because she loses her caste," Howard said. "And when you lose your caste you are rejected by your community and become an outcast — a pariah."

"So, what you're trying to tell me is that not only do the British look down on the half-castes but the Indians do as well?"

"That's right."

"I don't believe it," Lydia said.

"Anyway," Howard said, "better not say anything about the Nawab's daughter being of mixed-race, or Anglo-Indian for that matter, to his wife. She may find it embarrassing or offensive."

"Why should she be offended? Anglo-Indian doesn't mean 'mixed' anyway," Lydia said.

"It does these days."

"How so?"

"Well, in the old days *anyone* born in India of British parents was called Anglo-Indian—people like Rudyard Kipling, for instance. *They* were the Anglo-Indians. Those with mixed blood were always called Eurasians, except that they changed all that at the turn of the century, and the Eurasians wanted to be known as Anglo-Indians too."

"Yes," Lydia said. "That's why as soon as we darker-complexioned people began to call ourselves Anglo-Indians you so-called British began to call yourselves Domiciled Europeans, just to be classed differently from us. Anyway ..." She tried to damp down her anger. "We've always called ourselves Anglo-Indians, because Papa told me that we were. He always told me that his great-grandfather was a soldier in the Horse Artillery and came out from England."

"Yes, that's probably true," Howard said. "It's more than likely that he married a native woman, as so many soldiers did in those days, because of the shortage of European women in the country. In fact, these unions were actively encouraged at one time. They didn't have the sort of discrimination in those days as they have today."

"Papa never said he had an Indian woman as his great-grandmother," Lydia snapped.

Howard sighed.

This was very much a taboo subject as far as Lydia was concerned, and was rarely, if ever, discussed. Lydia, despite her swarthy complexion, was unwilling to accept that she had any Indian blood.

"Well, perhaps she was Eurasian then," he said. "There were plenty of young Eurasian girls about in his day, but very few European ones."

"So if that's the case, according to you, we're Eurasian then? We've had all this bias before." She sighed. "I don't know why we have to put up with all this sort of prejudice just because we have a swarthy skin."

"Well," Howard said, "I don't know what's wrong with being called Eurasian. After all, it simply means a mixture of European and Asian. As you know, there were many Europeans here besides the British—the Dutch, French, Portuguese, and Germans for example, who inter-married with Indians, and, of course, there are many different types of Indians too. Take Dawa for instance. I'm sure he thinks more of himself as Nepalese than Indian."

"Why are you bringing Dawa into it now?" Lydia asked hotly. "Indians are all the same to me. What does it matter what part of India you were born in?"

"I'm simply trying to explain." Howard held his hands up. "That if it weren't for an all-embracing term like Eurasian, we'd have to use words like *Khasi*-Dutch, *Bengali*-German, or *Madrassi*-French. It would be a real hotchpotch."

"So we're hotchpotch now," Lydia said with heavy sarcasm.

Before he could respond, Dawa who appeared out of the shadows, interrupted the conversation. "'Frigerator *bund hogaya*," he said, grinning all over his face. It meant that their kerosene-powered refrigerator had run out of oil and stopped. Kerosene oil was a precious commodity and still rationed, so Lydia kept it locked away in the store-room off the dining room and doled it out to the servants as required.

She followed Dawa into the house and to the dining room, where the refrigerator was kept. She opened the padlock on the store-room door. Dawa pulled out a can of kerosene oil and began to re-fill the refrigerator. While he was doing this, Lydia chewed over what Howard had said. Was he trying to imply that she was half-caste—a *chee-chee*—simply because she had a slightly dark skin? She decided that, yes, he was. In the end it always boiled down to skin colour. She'd had this in the past when she was a primary school teacher. The better jobs always went to the fairer ones. Had she had a pink-and-white complexion, he wouldn't have dared to cast aspersions on her ethnicity. She was also furious with the know-it-all attitude he adopted when it came to India. He always seemed to have an answer and an explanation for everything. Grudgingly, she had to admit that he was much better informed about India and its culture—knowing all the festivals, traditions, and customs, than she was. He also spoke Urdu and Gurkhali fluently, not like her basic kitchen-Hindustani.

The more she thought about it, the angrier she felt, and by the time she got back to Howard, who was puffing contentedly on his pipe, she felt ready to confront him.

She stood directly in front of his chair, arms akimbo. "I don't know what you think I am," she said furiously. "Probably one of those *Chutney Mary* whores you may have had in the past. But I know what I am. An Anglo-Indian. Papa told me so. Not Eurasian, not hotchpotch, and definitely not *chee-chee!*"

Howard looked astonished at her outburst, with his gaping jaw and wide eyes. "I never said *chee-chee*."

"No, but you meant *chee-chee*. To you, all Anglo-Indians are *chee-chee*, like the prostitutes of *Karaya* Road."

"Oh, come on now, Liddy. There may be some Indian in all of us—who knows? You've heard the expression 'a bit of the old tar brush,' haven't you? There's always been a shadow cast over all of us country-born—even people with blue eyes and a white skin. That doesn't prove a thing. If we all dug deep enough into our past, who's to say what we'd discover, eh?"

The last sentence calmed her down.

She sighed. "I don't know, it's all so confusing and complicated. I don't even like to think about it sometimes. If only you could be one thing or the other, life would be so much more simple."

Howard got up from his chair and placed his arms around his wife. "I wouldn't worry about it, my darling. You know I love you dearly. I wouldn't have married you otherwise. It doesn't matter to me one bit."

CHAPTER 9

The following days were hectic ones for Howard. There were all the arrangements to be made for the *Mela*, the most important of which was the auction that took place. Merchants, traders, and contractors put in their bids for the various areas and plots of the *Mela* Ground—cinemas, shops, stalls, and the cattle, elephant, and camel marts. A large *shamiana* was erected in the grounds of Lal Kothi where Howard presided at his desk, surrounded by the babus of his office, whilst the bidders squatted down on carpets that had been laid on the grass beneath, and shouted out their offers. After the auction, he managed to get hold of the circus owner and arrange for the band, then he had to contact various government officials regarding health, sanitation, and safety and fire regulations. He also saw the station master of Panchpani to arrange the cleaning and checking out of the Nawab's railway coach before dispatching it to Kholagari Junction, where it would wait at a siding for attachment to the Panchpani train. This involved much tea drinking and *paan* chewing on the part of the station master, as he examined various timetables, and gave Howard numerous forms to fill in. Howard was anxious that the Nawab should not be delayed too long at Kholagari when his train arrived from

Calcutta, and that the timing of the Panchpani train should be exactly right.

The days passed and the erection of *Mela* stalls, shops, and cinemas was well underway, and Jamie, Frances, and the servants' children went to the back gate every day to see what progress had been made since the day before. The main event was the setting up of the enormous big-top for the circus which was the highlight of the fair.

As far as Lal Kothi was concerned, Lydia took over the domestic arrangements for the cleaning and tidying up of the Nawab's suite, and the planning of meals with Ishmael, being careful to avoid anything on the menu that might be offensive to the Nawab. Howard, meanwhile, got Abdul to take the Nawab's old black Daimler from the garage and give it a good wash and polish, and also to have his livery laundered. He also got Kaila to see that the Nawab's horses were freshly groomed. With the help of Dawa, he inspected all the shotguns and rifles in the gun-cabinet to make sure they were well-oiled and clean, as he expected the Nawab to do some shooting whilst on the Estate.

Finally, the day of the Nawab's arrival dawned, and Howard and the family, dressed in their Sunday best, left Lal Kothi for the station in the Ford, which Howard drove. The Daimler, chauffeured by Abdul, followed sedately behind. On the platform, a red carpet had already been laid out, and the circus band stood to one side, their brass instruments gleaming in the noonday sun. Though they were passable in their uniforms, Howard thought wistfully of the smart Gurkha Police Band from Sing La with their kilts, playing the old Scottish favourites so superbly on their bagpipes. The important merchants, officials, and prominent townspeople were gathered in little groups, and Howard was thankful that it had not been necessary to ask each and every one to be present at the reception, as word of the Nawab's impending visit travelled like wildfire, and anyone who thought he should be there, was there.

After a half-hour's wait, the train puffed into the station and came to a halt with a hiss of steam. The circus band struck up *It's a Long Way to Tipperary*, and the Nawab's coach stopped at precisely the point where the red carpet was laid out. The carriage door opened. Two children were the first to emerge, followed by the Nawab's wife—a slim, elegant lady with a peaches-and-cream complexion. The Nawab, a small, dark little man attired in an immaculate white suit and panama hat, alighted from the carriage next. Howard bowed as he greeted the Nawab and shook his outstretched hand. The introductions were made, with appropriate bows or curtseys. However, much to Howard's dismay, whilst Lydia was being introduced to the Nawab's wife, Eleanor, she remarked, "Why, my husband told me you had a little girl, not a little boy." She had mistaken the fairer-looking boy, with light curly hair, as their child, instead of the darker, more Indian-looking girl! Howard cringed at the *faux pas*.

However, the Nawab's wife just looked puzzled for a moment, then understood and gave a little giggle. "No, this is our daughter, Zerina. He's Ludoo, my husband's nephew."

They eventually came out of the station, after the townspeople had paid their respects, and when they approached the two cars, Howard tried to guide the Nawab and his family to the Daimler. Abdul, in his fine livery, held the car door open expectantly and gave a stately salaam, but much to his disgust, the Nawab insisted that he and his wife travel with Howard and Lydia in the old Ford, and leave the children to go in the finer car.

As they drove towards Lal Kothi, the Nawab said, "I'm overwhelmed at this fine reception. And my father's old coach — such a kind thought. We haven't travelled in it since dear Eleanor and I were first married. You really shouldn't have gone to all this trouble."

"It's my pleasure, Nawabsahib," Howard said.

"Please, do call me Mohi," the Nawab said. "All my friends call me that."

"Did you have a pleasant journey up, Nawabsahib ... ah, Mohi?" Howard asked.

"Yes, it was quite straightforward, and my secretary — Babu Lal — travelled up with us as far as Kholagari and took care of all the travel arrangements. He had to go on to Sing La though, to deal with my property affairs there. He'll be joining us here before we go down to Calcutta again."

"I hope you'll find everything satisfactory here," Howard said.

"Oh, I'm sure I will. We really should come down more often though," Mohi said. "I'm beginning to be known as an 'absentee landlord'." He gave a wry smile. "It's the climate, you see," he went on. "Panchpani can be so unhealthy at times, and my dear wife, much prefers the hills, don't you dearest?" He turned his head around and smiled at his wife.

"Oh, I don't mind really," she said, "although I do love Sing La and Mussoorie. I hope, Lydia dear, that you don't find the climate too oppressive here, especially in the summer. It must be terrible for you without electric fans and other little creature comforts."

"Well, we have the *khas-khas tatties*," Lydia said. "We keep these pulled down on the veranda during the hot weather."

These were screens of rough, sweet-smelling *khas-khas* grass which were erected across doors or windows. When sprayed regularly with water, the breeze filtering through was cool and fragrant.

"Yes, we use them in our Calcutta place too," Eleanor said. "And, of course, you have the *punkahs*, that is when the *punkah-wallah* doesn't fall asleep." She gave a little giggle.

"I can tell you an amusing little story about a *punkah-wallah*," Howard said.

"Oh, yes, please do," Mohi said.

"Well, there was this colonel who had a glass eye, and while he was sleeping on his *charpoy* one hot afternoon, he noticed that the *punkah* had stopped. When he went out onto the veranda he noticed the *punkah-wallah* had fallen fast asleep. He awoke the man and said, 'Look, this is my eye.' He took out his glass eye and showed it to the *punkah-wallah*. 'I am going back to rest now, and if you fall asleep again, my eye will be watching you, so have a care.' He placed the eye on a stool in front of the man, and returned to his *charpoy* only to wake up an hour later in a sweat, because the *punkah* had stopped again. He tip-toed onto the veranda to see what had happened. The *punkah-wallah* had fallen fast asleep, and had placed the colonel's *topee* over the offending eye!"

Mohi roared with laughter, and Eleanor and Lydia both tittered in the back seat.

They reached the main gates of Lal Kothi, which the durwan and one of the sepoys swung open. They were smartly attired in khaki uniforms and red turbans. The two men saluted as the cars passed through and crunched along the gravel drive. The children all tumbled out of the Daimler when it stopped, chattering and laughing. They ran towards the stables and out of sight, led by Jamie. The house servants paid their respects to the Nawab and his wife, then Howard led Mohi to the garden chairs on the lawn, under the shade of the two bottle-brush trees. Eleanor followed Lydia into the house while the servants unloaded the luggage.

"Would you like something to drink before tiffin ... ummm ... luncheon?" Howard asked.

"A few beers would be very welcome," Mohi said.

"And for the ladies?"

"Just some *nimbu pani*, please, for Eleanor. She doesn't drink much during the day."

Howard instructed Dawa, who went off into the house to get the drinks. He returned a few minutes later with some cold bottles of beer and the lime-juice drinks with ice. Lydia and Eleanor came back out of the house and joined Howard and Mohi.

"Ah, this is very good," Mohi said as he lifted his glass. "Cheers, everyone." He sipped the foam from the top of the glass and took a few gulps, then, opening his cigar case, he offered Howard one of his long black *cheroots*.

"I'll stick to my pipe, if you don't mind." Howard took out his pipe and kit, then lit a match and held it to Mohi's *cheroot*.

Lydia and Eleanor talked gaily to each other and giggled like two little schoolgirls. Howard felt relieved to see that they would get on well together.

"I hope you don't find the Panchpani Estate too much of a handful," Mohi said. "It's such a large area to cover, visiting all the villages and towns to collect the rents and taxes, and seeing to the needs of the people there."

Howard admitted to himself that the area was large. It covered about 750 square miles, and he was hard-pushed sometimes to get to each and every village himself. So, often he had to send one of the office babus in a bullock-cart, accompanied by a couple of sepoys, to represent him.

"I'm able to get around," he said. "Sometimes on horseback and sometimes in the Jeep. I don't find it too much of a problem." He hoped this half-truth would satisfy the Nawab.

"I'm grateful to you for arranging all the *Mela* affairs too," Mohi went on. "The Panchpani *Mela* is always such a complicated business. Is the opening ceremony tomorrow?"

"No, the day after."

"Oh good," Mohi said. "It'll give us a day to do a bit of shooting—perhaps a few wild duck for the dinner table tomorrow?"

"That'll be fine, Nawabsahib … ah, … Mohi."

The children raced back from the stables, flushed and out of breath. The little girl, Zerina, sidled up to her father and said, "Oh, Papa, Jamie has such a lovely pony called Gingernut. Oh please, Papa, do get me a pony too?"

"But, Baby," he said, "we're in Calcutta most of the time, and what will it do here when you're away? Who'll look after it and take it out for rides?"

"Jamie says he will." She turned to Jamie. "Didn't you, Jamie?" She looked at her father again, her eyes pleading.

"And we can come here again next winter, can't we, Papa? I'd love to have a pony for my very own."

"We'll see." Mohi laughed. "Perhaps we can find a nice one for sale in the *Mela*. How's that?"

"If Zerina's going to have a pony, I want one too," Ludoo said.

"You'll have to ask your father about that," his uncle replied. "He might not consent to you having one. You'll have to write him a letter about it, then we'll see."

"That will take too long," Ludoo said, with a sullen glint in his eyes and a pout on his lips. "I want a pony *now*."

"Now, Ludoo dear," Eleanor said. "Listen to *Cha-Cha* and write to your father. I'm sure he'll agree." She smiled at Lydia. "Children!" she said.

"Oh, then if I'm going to have to write to *Abba* for permission, I don't want one," Ludoo said, still in a sulk. "It's always Zerina who gets everything, and I'm left out."

"You know that's not so, Ludoo dear," Eleanor said. "We always try to be very fair. It's just that *Cha-Cha* can't very well get you a pony unless your father says you can have one."

Jamie touched Ludoo's elbow and offered, "You can ride Gingernut."

"No, I don't like your pony," Ludoo said. "He's too fat."

"Now, Ludoo dear," Eleanor said. "You mustn't be rude. Apologise to Jamie, at once." She tried to sound stern, but Ludoo stalked off into the house, and Eleanor looked at her husband in despair. "Get him a pony, Mohi dear," she said. "Otherwise he'll never be content."

CHAPTER 10

The next morning, the household rose early. Mohi, smartly attired in breeches, a shooting jacket, and wearing a wide-brimmed hat, was already waiting for the others to join him downstairs. After they breakfasted, Howard led him to the gun cabinet, and the Nawab selected the Purdy shotgun. "It was my father's favourite gun," he said, handling it affectionately. "Not tailor-made for me, of course, but nevertheless it will suit."

Howard chose the double-barrelled Greener, which he often used, for himself.

The *mahout* was sent for, and Howard gave him orders to have the elephant made ready for the shoot. Jamie and Ludoo were to accompany Mohi and Howard, whilst Frances was to entertain Zerina. "Come upstairs," she had said, taking Zerina by the hand, "and you and Cissy can play with my paper-dolls."

The elephant, Panpathia—literally meaning *paan* leaves, which shape its ears resembled—arrived a half-hour later through the side gate, her feet throwing up little clouds of dust.

Ludoo was terrified of the animal. He cowered behind his uncle.

"Come on," Jamie said, standing directly in front of Panpathia, who had come to a stop. "She's as gentle as anything. There's nothing to be scared of—look." He said something to the *mahout*, and the man commanded the elephant. She wrapped her trunk gently round Jamie's waist, lifted him high into the air, then just as gently lowered him onto her back. "There, you see?" Jamie shouted to Ludoo, still hiding behind his uncle in terror.

The *mahout* gave Panpathia another order, and the elephant knelt down on her front legs, then folded her back legs, until she reached a seated position on the ground.

Howard waited for Mohi to climb onto the animal, which had a thick mattress thrown across its back and tied securely with rope, but the Nawab said, "Please, get on first, Howard. I'll just try and persuade little Ludoo here that there's nothing to be afraid of."

After much coaxing and cajoling, Mohi managed to get his nephew onto the elephant's back, and climbed up after him.

On an order from the *mahout*, Panpathia lumbered to her feet.

"Hold on to me *Cha-Cha*," Ludoo wailed. "Don't let me fall off!"

They went through the gate, Panpathia's tail swinging, Dawa—carrying the shotguns,—Jubra, and Blackie—barking, all followed on foot.

"I do hope Ludoo will be all right," Eleanor said anxiously. "He's such a nervous child."

"Oh, I'm sure he will," Lydia said.

"He's inclined to be rather delicate too," Eleanor went on, "and gets tired out so easily. I hope this jaunt won't be too exhausting for him."

"He does look a bit pale," Lydia said, "or is that just his fair skin? He's such a pretty little fellow."

"Yes," Eleanor agreed, "almost too pretty for a boy, really. He gets his light complexion from his mother, you know. She was a begum from the House of Oudh. Of course," she continued, "Ludoo is only his pet name. His proper name is …" she thought for a moment, "… Mansooruddin, I think."

"Isn't 'ludoo' a sort of Indian sweetmeat?" Lydia asked.

"That's right. One of those dry, round, yellow ones. His father called most of his other children after Indian sweets too. Ludoo's younger brother is called, *Pera*."

Eleanor giggled.

They walked along a pathway in the extensive grounds. It skirted the flowerbeds then meandered through various shrubs and trees, some of which had been introduced from Australia by a landscape-gardener from that country, when Lal Kothi was first being built.

"Ludoo lives with us, mostly," Eleanor said. "His father wants him to be brought up in an English-speaking household." She looked at Lydia and said in a confidential tone, "I think though that Mohi's brother really wants Ludoo to marry Zerina when they grow up, so that the Estate can be kept in the family."

"But they're first cousins," Lydia said. "Can that be right?"

"Oh." Eleanor gave a little smile. "In Indian families, first cousins often marry, especially Muslim ones."

Lydia thought this very odd. She had always been told that marriage between first-cousins often caused birth defects. "Are you in favour of this?"

"Well," Eleanor said, "Mohi and I have often discussed what happens when Zerina reaches marriageable age, and we've decided that she can choose whoever she wants to marry. It won't matter to us whether it's an Englishman, if she so wants, or an Indian, since being of mixed-race she has the blood of both running in her veins. We're certainly not in favour of any arranged marriage, like with Ludoo, for instance."

"Do they get on together?" Lydia asked.

Eleanor sighed. "No, not really Lydia, dear. They tend to quarrel a lot, like brother and sister, really. I don't think their temperaments are very compatible."

"I suppose if they don't marry, then Ludoo's father will be very aggrieved."

"Yes." Eleanor nodded. "He's always thought of me as something of an alien—you know, a European coming into his family—and he's afraid that if Zerina marries someone else, particularly a Britisher, the Estate—which has been in their family for generations—will be divided up and fall into the hands of foreigners."

They came up to the main gate, and crossed the gravel driveway. The pathway continued on the other side, and they walked along it, towards the tank that was screened off from the rest of the compound by thick bushes.

"How did you meet your husband?" Lydia asked.

Eleanor gave a little laugh. "Well, it's quite a funny story. You see, when we all lived in Sing La, our family used to go to St. Mathew's Church every Sunday morning. Coming back around the Mall, we used to pass this Indian gentleman, riding by on his chestnut mare. He always used to raise his hat and wish us the time of day. Well, it so happened that I advertised in the *Sing La Times* that I taught the piano, and one day this dark stranger turned up on our doorstep and applied for lessons. Anyway, to cut a long story short, he never learnt to play, and instead we used to sit on the settee, talking and holding hands. We were soon deeply in love, and, after seeking Papa's permission, one day he proposed. Of course, I accepted immediately, and we were married soon afterwards, in Calcutta."

"Did you have to change your religion?" Lydia enquired, "I mean did you have to be married in a mosque?"

"Oh, no dear," Eleanor said, "Mohi would never have dreamed of making me change my faith. He's very open-minded that way, and not really an orthodox Muslim at all. No, the Registrar married us at Mohi's Alipore home. It was a civil wedding. Of course, Zerina is Muslim — you know, for the sake of the Estate and everything, although this is virtually in name only. She hardly knows anything of the Muslim religion at all."

"But didn't you meet with any opposition from your family? — I mean getting married to an Indian gentleman and all?"

"Strangely enough I didn't," Eleanor said. "Papa, Mama, and my brother and sisters, all took to Mohi instantly. I don't think they really looked on him as Indian at all. You see, Mohi never had much of an Indian upbringing. His father died when he was a child and his mother, the old Begum, married again. Their stepfather was an out-and-out scoundrel, and the British government feared for the boys' safety. So both he and his brother were taken out of their mother's custody and placed under the guardianship of English tutors, appointed by the Court of Wards. Then they were sent to England for their education. But they continued under the guardianship of their tutors until they attained majority. So, you see, Mohi is really quite English under his dark skin."

"And his brother?" Lydia asked. "How did he react to his elder brother's marriage to you?"

"Well, frankly ..." Eleanor looked sad. "His brother never really took to the English as Mohi did. His tutor was very strict with him, and he didn't like boarding school in England at all. So, when he became of age, he wanted to pick up his Indian roots again, marrying an Indian begum and all. I feel though, that he's never really approved of me, although their mother, the old Begum, was very kind whenever I visited her home in Calcutta, showering me with gifts and jewels. She used to call me *'Puree ke Rani'* which means Fairy Princess. To make matters worse, she never took to the brother's wife at all. I used to feel awfully embarrassed when I visited her, and she made her Indian daughter-in-law stand up all the while I was there—almost like a servant."

"So most of the prejudice came from Mohi's brother then," Lydia said.

"Yes, that sounds strange, doesn't it? But, we get on well enough, socially that is, and he leaves Ludoo in our care."

"But for a purpose." Lydia pursed her lips.

"Yes, I suppose that's true. He wants them to grow up together so that they can become fond of each other." She looked at Lydia with her placid, ocean-blue eyes. "I hope, Lydia dear, you don't mind me telling you all this. You see, Mohi is rather defensive whenever the subject is raised, and he always tries to assure me that his brother's very fond of me, so I don't talk to him much about it."

"Oh, no. I appreciate you taking me into your confidence," Lydia said. "I only hope you didn't mind me asking you so many questions. I didn't mean to be inquisitive."

"That's quite all right, Lydia dear. I suppose a mixed marriage like ours does tend to raise some curiosity, especially these days."

Mohi, Howard, and the boys returned from the shoot just before lunch. Ludoo in tears, and Mohi doing his best to comfort him. Eleanor asked what had happened, and Howard explained that they had run into a red ants' nest hanging from a low branch of a mango tree on their way back. They had all been bitten to an extent, but Ludoo had had the worst of it. Eleanor hurried the wailing Ludoo into the house to apply some TCP onto his bites, and Lydia and Jamie followed her. The shoot had yielded a half-dozen or so wild ducks, and Jubra took these into the kitchen to give to his father, to prepare for the table. Howard and Mohi seated themselves in the garden chairs and Dawa brought them cool bottles of beer.

"Ah, just the thing after a hot morning's shoot. Cheers." Mohi gulped down his beer. "I hope I'm not depleting your supplies?"

"Oh, no. There's plenty more where that came from," Howard said. "I replenished our stocks quite recently from Sing La."

"Yes, it's a tragedy that Panchpani has nothing to offer by way of alcoholic beverages, and one has to obtain these from outside. But there's no need to worry, I brought a few cases of beer up with me from Calcutta, and there's also a case of Johnny Walker. I'll ask dear Eleanor to see these are placed with your supplies."

"That's very kind of you, Mohi, but there's no need."

"My pleasure," Mohi said. "One can hardly live in Panchpani without a drink. That would be too cruel."

"Oh, but they've actually opened a liquor shop in the bazaar quite recently. Of course, it's only the Indian made stuff, like Hayward's whisky Rosa rum and Carews gin, but it does in an emergency."

"Ah, that's good news. There was no adverse reaction to the opening of this shop, I hope?" Mohi enquired.

"Well, some of the locals weren't very happy about it," Howard said. "The town being mainly Muslim and all. But I think they've more or less accepted it now."

"I suppose the towns-people must think rather badly of me and my drink," Mohi said with a wry grin. "I'm not a very good example of a Muslim."

Howard recollected that all through the morning's shoot, he had seen Mohi whip out a hip-flask in a flash of silver. Quickly taking a swig, he would screw the cap back on and replace the flask in his hip pocket. It happened so quickly and naturally, that he hadn't thought much of it at the time.

Eleanor and Lydia came out of the house and joined them. Ludoo clung onto Eleanor's skirts. Jamie followed behind.

Howard asked Jamie. "Did you get bitten much, son?"

"Just a bit, Dad." Jamie displayed some of the red blotches with pride. "But they're not as bad as wasp stings."

"Oh, take me back to Calcutta, *Cha-Cha*," Ludoo wailed. "I don't like this place."

"Come, come, Ludoo," Mohi said. "What will your father think if he hears you talking like this?"

Ludoo looked at his uncle anxiously. "You won't tell him, *Cha-Cha*, will you?"

"No, no, of course I won't." Mohi gave his nephew's curly head a pat. "But you must try and be a little more brave. Look at Jamie here. He doesn't seem to be afraid of anything."

"Oh, but I am," Jamie said. "Of snakes!"

"And with good reason," Mohi said. "The kraits are among the worst, though not, perhaps, as fearsome-looking as the cobras with their hoods extended."

"Yes, the kraits are deadly but more placid, I think," Howard said. "We had quite a fright recently when the cowherd awoke the household one night in great panic. He had returned home to find a krait coiled beside his sleeping infant son."

"Goodness! What happened?" Eleanor said.

"Well, they managed to remove the sleeping boy without disturbing the snake," Howard said, "and then, of course, they killed the snake, which was a bit of a shame."

"The compound is simply *crawling* with snakes," Jamie said, adding to the theme. "You can see their discarded skins hanging over the trees and bushes *everywhere*."

"Jamie!" Lydia said sharply.

"Oh, but it's true," Mohi said. "That's why we have so many mongooses running around the compound. My father introduced them specially to control the snake population."

"Yes, we watched a fight between a cobra and a mongoose once," Howard said. "Not one of those staged performances the snake charmers put on. This was for real—near the tank. Don't you remember, Jamie?"

"Yes, Dad. And remember the time that cobra tried to get into the hen house, and we found it the next morning threaded through the chicken-wire like a boot-lace?" He rushed into an explanation. "You see, this cobra was trying to get into the chicken-run through the wire mesh, but then something must have scared it and it tried to get out again, so it went through another hole in the mesh." He paused for breath. "So it became stuck. It tried to get back in again then out, until it weaved through the chicken wire. Of course, it was dead when we found it in the morning."

Ludoo let out a wail of terror. "Take me away from here, *Cha-Cha*. I'll be bitten by a snake next."

CHAPTER 11

The opening ceremony for the Panchpani *Mela* took place the next morning. The Nawab, suitably attired in Indian dress—*kurtha-pyjamas*—and wearing an *achkan* and an astrakhan cap, addressed the crowd in his faltering Urdu from a podium erected outside the back gate of Lal Kothi that led into the *Mela* ground. After a short speech, prominent members of the local townspeople garlanded him, and then he cut the ribbon at the entrance of the *Mela* ground, declaring it well and truly open. Refreshments of tea and Indian sweets were served to Mohi, Howard, and their families under the shade of a *shamiana*. The children tucked into a delicious feast of *rossogollas*, *jalebis*, and *gulab-jamuns* with great relish. Invitations to the circus, shows, and cinemas were handed out to the Nawab, which he graciously and politely accepted.

In the evening, after the children had gone to bed, the adults sat on the veranda with their drinks. However, the raucous music that emanated from the *Mela* ground disturbed the usual peace and tranquillity of the evening. The circus band played *Show Me the Way to Go Home*, and had to vie with loudspeakers that continuously blared out screeching Indian music. Besides the music, additional noise came from the generators that provided the circus and cinemas with electricity. Cooking smells from the eating shops mingled with the smell of cow-dung, and cattle urine polluted the air, and drifted in the direction of Lal Kothi. Fortunately, however, the veranda of the house faced away from the *Mela* ground, so the music and hubbub was somewhat muted.

"It wasn't very wise on my father's part to have Lal Kothi built so close to the *Mela*," Mohi said with a slight wince to show his regret. Then he took a sip of whisky.

"Well, I suppose in his day it wasn't quite so noisy," Howard said.

"Yes, that's true. It was mainly a cattle fair, and they didn't have all the cinemas and the circus to add to the noise and confusion."

"Was it your father who started the *Mela*?" Howard asked.

"Oh, no. It was long before his time — his great-grandfather, I think."

"So, how long has your family owned the Estate, then?"

"For many, many years now," Mohi said. "I think about four hundred or so."

"As long as that?" Howard was incredulous.

"Yes, I have the history written down somewhere," Mohi said. "But as best as I can remember, my original ancestor came out from Persia leading an Iranian army to help restore the Mogul emperor, Humayun, back onto the throne of Delhi."

"My Indian history's a bit sketchy," Howard said. "Was the Mogul emperor displaced from his throne at that time?

"Yes." Mohi took another sip of whisky. "By a very fierce Afghan warlord, Sher Shah." He took out a cheroot and lit it. "Anyway, Humayun asked for assistance from the Shah of

Persia, who sent Iranian armies to India to help restore him back onto the throne. One such army was led by my ancestor, and once the emperor was in power again, he sent my ancestor to this area to clear it of the Bhutia tribes that occupied the region."

"You mean the hill tribes were as far down south as Panchpani?"

"Yes, indeed," Mohi said. "They were quite a wild sort of people too, and there was a lot of plundering of wayfarers going on, and complete lawlessness in the *Pargana*." He drew on his cheroot. "So, you see, the other inhabitants in the territory kept pleading with the Emperor for help and protection, and he finally dispatched my ancestor with his army, who drove the Bhutias back into the hills of Morang."

"So the territory was given to your ancestor as a sort of reward?"

"Yes, he was put in charge of the area and was responsible for maintaining the law."

"And things settled down?"

"Well, eventually," Mohi said. "It took some years to achieve and, naturally, a fort had to be established on the banks of the Mahanada, fully equipped with cannon. Then there were further conflicts with neighbouring rajas and warlords."

"I see," Howard said. "I've often wondered what that old ruin on the banks of the river was."

"Yes, it was abandoned and finally fell into decay—half washed away by the river now."

"Like the Old Palace, which the jungle is quickly reclaiming."

"Yes, that too." Mohi sighed. "Unfortunately, there has been a lot of neglect by past generations of the family, and a lot of family feuds and blood spilt. Of course, my brother and I are guilty of this neglect too. We should really be living on the *zamindari* and looking after the needs of the people, and with all due respect, Howard, not leaving it to be run by managers. However, despite all this, it is strange that for the past four-hundred years or so the *zamindari* has remained wholly intact, and not divided up. In fact, it is only now that the Estate is divided proportionately between my younger brother and myself."

A lull in the conversation brought silence, which only the sound of the circus band broke. It played *Lay That Pistol Down Babe*, with great gusto. Then Eleanor spoke. "I wonder what's going to happen with all this Gandhi trouble going on."

"Yes," Lydia said, picking up the topic, "I don't know why he goes on stirring up the Indians all the time."

"Ah yes, Mr Mohandas Gandhi," Mohi said. "We must not forget him. A wily old gentleman indeed!"

"Yes, he's become more active again recently." Howard lit his pipe. "And he's demanding Indian independence in return for supporting Britain during The War, though he had to be locked up for the last few years of its duration to stop his 'Quit India' movement."

"I remember that," Lydia said. "It was a very frightening time for us, what with all the troubles and unrest everywhere."

"It was the worst we've had since the Mutiny," Eleanor said. "It's no wonder they had to lock him up along with the other Indian Nationalists. How could England have coped with another mutiny and a world war going on at the same time?"

"And how is Britain going to cope now, I wonder?" Mohi added. "She has been completely bankrupted by The War, and pressure from America for the relinquishment of the British colonies is also being brought to bear. I feel that it's only a matter of time now before the Indian Nationalists get their way and the country gets home rule."

"Oh my goodness!" Lydia exclaimed, "I hope it will never come to that."

"In time it will," Mohi said. "It is just a question of when."

"How soon do you think?" Howard asked.

"Well ..." Mohi reflected a moment. "Every hundred years or so they say that something happens in India that changes the course of its history. In 1757 it was the Battle of Plassey, when the British annexed Bengal. Then in 1857 it was the Mutiny. So if that is anything to go by, it's likely that in 1957 India will achieve its independence. It may happen much earlier than that. But it is the Hindu-Muslim question that is the crux of the matter and the most difficult to resolve."

"Yes," Howard said, "the minority Muslims would never be able to live in a Hindu dominated country, despite Gandhi's struggles to knit the communities together."

"Then there is Mr Jinnah, the leader of the Muslim League, to consider," Mohi said. "He won't agree to a Hindu dominated India. He will opt for a separate Muslim state — which will mean dividing India up."

"I expect all this is going to take some years then," Howard said, "despite Atlee's optimistic promises. Anyway, that should give us some time, and I'm sure we'll still have a role to play in all this and afterwards." He glanced at Lydia, who looked at him apprehensively.

She said, "I can't understand how it is that a man like Gandhi, who looks so inoffensive, has managed to incite the Indian people to so much hatred against the British."

"Yes, it is quite amazing." Mohi nodded, and had another drink. "Especially seeing that such a person, who didn't really know India all that well, has managed to sway the minds of the native population. But, it *has* taken him thirty years of perseverance to get anywhere with his campaign."

"I must admit, I don't know very much about him," Howard said, "except when the papers report that he's begun one fast or another or has been thrown in jail again for some act of civil disobedience."

Mohi refreshed his and Howard's glasses from the bottle of Johnny Walker. "Well, as far as I know, he left India for England as a very young man where he studied law. Then he landed up in South Africa where his campaigns against the authorities there began."

"What made him agitate there?" Howard asked.

"I don't know for sure, but I believe he suffered some sort of racial prejudice. Somehow, this fuelled his sense of injustice, and he took up the cudgels on behalf of the Asian community there, who were very much repressed."

"But where did he get all his ideas?" Lydia asked. "Not in England, surely?"

"Oh yes." Mohi nodded a few times. "Very much in England—from various philanthropists and idealists he associated with whilst there. Heaven knows, I met enough of them in my time at Cambridge."

"But if he studied law in England and was then a lawyer in South Africa, why did he come to India parading in those ridiculous clothes—just a loin cloth and shawl, almost like a beggar?"

"To be able to appear poor and humble in the eyes of the Indian people," Mohi said. "Nothing wins their hearts more. You see, when the South African authorities finally got rid of him for his political activities there, he came back to India and became involved with the Indian Nationalists, whose party was in a bit of a shambles, to say the least. With him came his policy of *satyagraha*—his non-violent movement of protest, which seems to have caught the British off-guard, because they are totally unable to deal with this new form of non-cooperation."

"Surely they could have done something to stop him," Lydia said.

"Well, nothing seemed to work in his case." Mohi drew on his cheroot. "He is against all things material, which makes him a very dangerous and uncomfortable opponent indeed, because unlike most, he cannot be tempted with sensual pleasures, riches, or comfort, and is simply determined to do what he believes is right."

"Well, I suppose he's used to living without those, being in jail all the time," Lydia said.

"Yes," Mohi said, "and that is precisely the point. This just adds to his martyrdom and he can wear his scars with pride. With such a man, though you may torture him, you cannot gain any purchase on his soul." He took a swig of whisky, emptying his glass. "Another tot for you, Howard?"

"Oh no," Howard said, "I think I've had enough for one evening."

"But you don't mind if I do?" Mohi asked.

"Oh, by all means go ahead," Howard said. "I'll ask Dawa to get another bottle." He called out to Dawa, who miraculously appeared a moment later out of the shadows. "Another bottle of Johnny Walker," he said in Gurkhali, giving

Dawa the empty bottle to take away. "Are you ladies ready for another drink?"

"Not for me," Eleanor said. "The last drink I had has gone completely to my head."

"Are you sure?" Lydia asked. "Come on, have another gin and lemon with me."

"Oh, all right then," Eleanor said, giggling. "But don't blame me if I get absolutely blotto."

Howard instructed Dawa, "Gin and *nimbu-pani* for the memsahibs." He eyed the ladies and added wickedly, "*Burra* pegs."

They both squealed in protest, but Howard waved the grinning Dawa off to get the drinks anyway. He knocked the tobacco out of his pipe, and refilled it. "What do you reckon is going to happen to you, Nawab … ah, Mohi, if Gandhi gets his way and India does get its independence at the end of the day?"

Mohi shrugged. "Well, for small *zamindaris* like ours, which are part and parcel of British India, the Estate will probably be absorbed into an independent India. But there would be no place for us landed proprietors, especially if socialists like Jawaharlal Nehru are at the helm of affairs."

"You mean you would lose your land, after all these hundreds of years?"

"Quite likely, and probably our titles too."

"Has anything been done in consideration of all this?" Howard asked, with a worried frown.

"Yes," Mohi said, "they've been talking about it for years now. The Princely States like Hyderabad, Kashmir, and Mysore should be all right. They are not part of British India, and their sovereignty has been assured. After all, the British can only hand over power for the three-fifths of India under direct British rule, not the hundreds of independent Princely States."

"Yes," Howard said, "but of course, a Labour government is not very sympathetic to the cause of the Indian princes, and wouldn't really do very much to protect their sovereignty, if it ever came to that."

"I agree," Mohi said. "Conversely, they're very much in sympathy with the Indian Nationalists, who have often referred to the nawabs and rajas as being un-Indian, parasitic, and lackeys of the British. Not a very complimentary description, I must say." He took a swig of whisky, then refilled his and Howard's glasses again, despite the latter's protests. Howard poured some soda into his drink, noticing that Mohi was drinking his whisky neat now. However, this was having little effect on the Nawab, except that his heavy-lidded eyes drooped more noticeably.

"It's all so worrying," Lydia said. "I was just saying to Howard the other day that if ever the British left India, we would have to do so as well."

"Oh, I'm sure it wouldn't come to that," Eleanor said. "India's been our home for generations, and I hope for generations still to come." She placed her hand on Lydia's in a gesture of reassurance.

"Have you been to England at all?" Lydia asked.

"Yes dear, when I was still a child. Papa took both my brother and myself to put us into school there."

"Did you like it?"

"What, the school?"

"No, I mean England."

"I didn't like either very much, Lydia dear. I was most unhappy in the school, and so lonely and isolated in England after Papa left."

"I think I would have liked to have gone to school in England," Lydia said. "But my father could never afford it on the money he earned with the Railways."

Eleanor looked at Lydia and said earnestly, "Oh, I don't think you would have been very happy there, Lydia dear. The school Papa placed me in — I can't remember the name of it now — was supposed to be 'A school for the daughters of English gentlemen.' Well, the girls there certainly didn't behave as such. You see, they were expecting to see a dark-skinned girl from India, and I think they were thoroughly disappointed when they saw that I didn't fulfil their expectations, and so they took it out on me."

"What sort of things did they do?" Lydia asked. She sat forward in her chair and gave her full attention to Eleanor.

"Oh, all sorts of nasty, spiteful things. They rubbed jam onto my face for a start, then into my hair, and played all sorts of horrible, mean tricks on me. They were dreadful."

"My goodness," Lydia said, "wasn't there anyone you could complain to?"

"They would have called me a sneak then, and I really would have been in for it. No, you had to grin and bear it or keep a stiff upper lip. I had to do that for Papa's sake, seeing he had spent all that money taking me to England and all that."

"Didn't you have any friends or family that you could have turned to?"

"Only my uncle. He was a Yeoman of the guard at the Tower of London, and I would have to spend my holidays with him. To 'amuse' me, he would lead me on these conducted tours, and show me all the grisly places, such as the site where Lady Jane Grey had her head chopped off. Eventually, I could bear it no longer and wrote long, unhappy letters to Papa begging him to take me back to India."

"And what happened?" Lydia asked.

"Well dear, Papa was so distraught that he did come out specially to take me back. But since he was short of funds, he had to travel by a cheaper class on an Australian boat." She paused to sip at her gin and lemon, then gave a little laugh. "I remember him recounting his experience in the ship's dining room, where, sitting opposite, was a burly Australian with his sleeves rolled-up. Papa, always the essence of respectability, was as usual, in dinner jacket and tie. Trying to make conversation, he asked the man if he were a Mason. Papa, you see, was a high Mason at the Lodge in Sing La. The Australian just looked at him and said 'No mate. I'm a plumber', and with that, he stabbed at the meat on his plate!"

Everyone laughed.

CHAPTER 12

Although the *Mela* brought an air of festivity to an otherwise dull Panchpani, it also brought smells (the sanitation provided at the *Mela* ground was primitive at best), clouds of dust, and hordes of flies that pervaded everywhere. Flies even covered the white marble table-top on the veranda in a black blanket, to disappear magically when one waved a cloth or hand-*punkah*. Lydia, having exhausted her supply of fly-paper, took to coating sheets of newspaper with honey or Lyle's Golden Syrup, laying these out in strategic places to trap the wretched insects.

However, as far as the children were concerned, the novelty of the fair overrode these minor inconveniences, and the day after the *Mela*'s opening, Howard arranged for two stalwart *sepoys* to accompany the children on an excursion to the fair. They wandered around the shops and stalls, the *sepoys* pushing the crowds aside to allow the children access to, or a better view of, some entertainment or shop. Everywhere the children went, they were treated with special cordiality, and generally presented with gifts or free sweets. A special attraction fascinated and amazed the children — a show where everything was done with mirrors, and the exhibits were human heads joined to the bodies of reptiles or animals — a woman's head and the body of a cobra; a man's head and the body of a jackal. Even little Cissy, held up high on the shoulders of one of the *sepoys*, squealed in wonder and excitement, especially when the heads began to talk. They also visited the circus menagerie and watched the tigers and other animals being fed, then it was on to the elephant mart, Jamie and Jubra leading the way.

"I say." Ludoo scowled. "You shouldn't be walking beside your servant boy."

"He's not my servant," Jamie replied over his shoulder. "He's the cook's son."

"I don't care. He should walk *behind* us, not in front."

"Don't take any notice of him," Zerina said, catching up to the two boys, and taking Jamie's hand.

"And you, Zerina. You shouldn't be holding a boy's hand!"

She tossed her hair back and ignored Ludoo's remark.

"Let's walk together then," Frances said, aiming for diplomacy. "And we can all hold hands."

"I'm not walking beside a servant boy," Ludoo snapped, "and I don't want to hold hands with anyone."

"Please yourself," Jamie said. "Jubra's my friend, and he can walk alongside me if he likes."

Frances held Cissy's hand and ran up to the others, then Cissy took Jubra's, while Frances joined hands with Zerina. Ludoo walked behind, sullenly. They reached the section of the *Mela* where the elephants were kept for sale. There were a few dozen animals—amongst them some mature bulls and cows—but most were young and not fully grown. Stout ropes, attached to their hind legs, restrained all the elephants—all, that is, except the very tiny ones who did not stray far from their mothers. Ample supplies of sugarcane were kept nearby, and the children were allowed to help themselves to these. They held the sticks out to the animals, and the elephants curled their trunks around them and took them gently from the children's grasp. Ludoo, being much too afraid of the larger animals, went to the end of the row where some of the smaller elephants were kept. Separated from the others was a young animal, still a baby, apparently parentless. Like the larger ones, a tether wrapped its hind foot.

"I say, look at this small one," he called out. To show off, he teased the little animal by holding out a length of sugarcane, but pulling it back just as the little trunk reached out for the tempting morsel.

"Go on, let him have it," Jamie said.

"Yes, you shouldn't tease dumb animals," Zerina added. "Especially elephants, because they never forget an unkindness."

Ludoo ignored them and continued to taunt the baby elephant, now poking it with the stick. Jamie went up to him and tried to wrest it away, but before he could do so, Ludoo threw it at the animal, catching it on its back. In the struggle, Ludoo lost his balance and fell to the ground.

"I'll tell my Cha-Cha that you pushed me." Ludoo's voice quavered in shock.

"I didn't push you," Jamie said. "You fell. That's all."

Ludoo climbed to his feet, bent down slightly, and dusted the dirt from his knees. He hadn't noticed, but by this time the little elephant had picked up the stick of sugarcane. Its little eyes glinted wickedly, and all of a sudden it lashed out at the unsuspecting Ludoo, catching him a resounding whack on his backside. He howled in pain and surprise as the others, dumbfounded for an instant at the speed of the attack, burst out laughing.

"It's not funny," Ludoo wailed, rubbing his behind. "I'm going to tell Aunt what has happened, and that Jamie pushed me."

"It serves you right," Zerina said. "I'll tell Papa that you were teasing the elephant. And Jamie didn't push you. You fell."

"Let's not argue," Frances said in a conciliatory voice. "There's no need to tell anyone anything. Jamie, you shouldn't have tried to take the stick away from Ludoo. And Ludoo, you shouldn't have teased the little elephant. Let's forget it, and all be friends."

Ludoo sniffed. "Make Jamie apologise then."

"I'm sorry you fell," Jamie said.

"Say you're sorry you pushed me."

Jamie sighed. "All right, I'm sorry you fell while I was trying to take the stick of sugarcane away from you. How's that?"

"I still think you pushed me."

"Oh, leave it be, Ludoo," Frances said. "Jamie says he's sorry, and we're all sorry that we laughed, aren't we?"

"Yes," Cissy said. "But it was funny."

"We shouldn't laugh when somebody gets hurt, Cissy," Frances said.

"I'm sorry." Cissy looked and sounded meek at the scolding, as she bowed her head and hunched into herself.

"And I am too," Zerina said, more to support Jamie than to appease Ludoo.

"Make your servant boy apologise too," Ludoo said.

Jamie turned to Jubra and explained the situation. Jubra folded his hands and said to Ludoo "*Maaf kuro,*" which meant "I beg your forgiveness."

Ludoo grudgingly accepted the apologies and dragged his feet as he followed the others home.

But he was soon in trouble again a few days later, when the children tried to knock down some fruit from the wild plum tree that grew at the far end of the compound. They used long bamboo poles, and Ludoo accidentally disturbed some pods growing on a vine entangling the tree. These thick, bean-like pods were covered with fine, silky hairs. But Jamie and Frances were well aware that these seemingly innocent looking pods could produce a terrible burning itch if the hairs came into contact with bare skin. They nicknamed these 'itchy pods' and were always careful to avoid touching them. Worse still, when the pods were dried-up, the hairs became loose and rained down on you if the vine was disturbed in any way. The fine hairs filtered down and settled on the unsuspecting Ludoo. He howled in agony as the itching began, and desperately rubbed his face and neck. Of course, this only aggravated the condition and drove the fine hairs deeper into his skin.

"Get some cow-dung and rub it on him," Jamie shouted to Jubra, who hurried away to find some. He returned a short while later with a large, freshly-laid cow-pat, which he found on the roadside.

"I'm not having *gobur* spread on me," Ludoo wailed as Jubra tried to apply some of the cow-dung onto his face and neck.

"Come on, Ludoo. It's the only thing that'll stop the irritation," Frances said.

"Yes, it catches the hairs and soothes the itching," Jamie added.

"But it's *gobur*!" Ludoo tried to brush away Jubra's hand.

Frances remained firm. "Don't make such a fuss. It'll soon dry and then when you peel it off, it'll take the hairs with it."

"Take me to my Aunt," Ludoo said. "She'll know what to do."

"TCP won't help this time," Jamie said. "It's only cow-dung that'll do the trick. I know. I've had some of those itchy pods on me once."

Ludoo eventually relented. "Let me take my shirt off first," he said. "I don't want to get *gobur* on that." He pulled the shirt over his head, and Jubra spread the cow-manure on his neck and face in a mask. "Mind you don't get any on my lips," Ludoo told Jubra in Hindustani. When the job was finished, Ludoo looked something like a Negro minstrel, and Jamie had to turn away, shaking with laughter.

"Sit in the sun for a while," Frances said. "It'll dry quicker, and then you can start to peel it off."

"There's nothing funny about this," Ludoo grumbled. "I hope it happens to *you* next time." But he had to admit to himself, albeit grudgingly, that the burning itching had begun to abate. He turned to Zerina. "And you, Zerina, don't you dare tell Cha-Cha that I had *gobur* spread on my face."

"Cow-dung isn't dirty," Zerina replied. "The villagers use it all the time for fuel. It's not as if was dogs' dirt."

"I heard that it has antiseptic properties," Frances said.

"Don't you believe it," Jamie said. "It's like the story Dad told me about the time he had a sty in his eye when he was a boy. The Nepalese servants told him that the best thing to cure a sty was to find a hen and put its bum against your eye." He paused while Zerina bit her tongue at the rude word.

"What happened?" She giggled.

"Well," Jamie said, "he ran round the house all day chasing this chicken and when he caught it he blew the feathers aside and planted the chicken's bum firmly against his eye."

"Did it cure his sty?"

"No, his eye came up like a cricket ball the next day."

"I hope this cow-dung isn't going to infect *me*," Ludoo said, and anxiety laced his tones.

"Don't believe Jamie," Frances said in a soothing voice. "I bet Dad was telling stories anyway. He always does. There's no harm in cow-dung and it doesn't smell ... much."

CHAPTER 13

The evening finally came when the two families attended the Indian circus at the invitation of the circus manager. They were conducted to the very best seats the circus had to offer and served with cool, refreshing sherbets and delicious Indian sweets. The children marvelled at the trapeze artists as they swung high above the circus ring and performed daring feats; they held their breath as the knife-throwing expert flung his daggers at the scantily clad woman attached to a revolving wheel; they gazed in awe at the high-wire act as the performers balanced precariously on the tight-rope. Then there were the gymnastic feats on bareback horses, the performers—usually pretty girls—vaulting off and back on the horses' backs. The animal acts came next: the lion-tamer cracking his whip as the big cats—usually tigers—snarled as they obeyed his commands, and the elephants paraded round the ring holding each other's tails, then climbing up and balancing on incredibly small stools. All the while, clowns kept the crowd in fits of laughter with their slapstick and often-vulgar humour. One particular clown, who was dressed in a Charlie Chaplin get-up, went around kicking the other clowns in the pants and 'accidentally' lifting the skirt of female performers with his walking stick while bending down to pick something up. Mohi laughed outright at his antics, and Eleanor giggled. It was only Lydia who remained straight-faced, and she once glared disapprovingly at Jamie who was almost falling out of his seat with laughter.

But it was a wonderful show, especially for the children who, starved of entertainment, could talk of nothing else for days. All the servants and their children too were given leave to attend the performance the following day, Mohi paying for their admission, and for days afterwards Jubra and *Humni* and *Thumni* aped the clowns' antics to amuse the children whenever the opportunity arose.

The Indian cinemas, on the other hand, did not attract the children, even Ludoo and Zerina. To Jamie, who had been brought up on a diet of Buck Jones westerns and Tarzan films, Indian pictures, all bundled into a hotchpotch of songs and dances, action and drama, were 'silly,' and besides he found the dialogue hard to follow. However, again, the servants' children, and especially Jubra, would be at the *bioscope* almost every day.

Before they returned to Calcutta, the opportunity arose for Eleanor to have another confidential chat with Lydia. The families were out on a picnic at the ancient family burial grounds, near the old ruined palace. Lydia, Eleanor and the children had travelled in a bullock-drawn carriage whilst Howard and Mohi were on horseback. The whole cemetery was three feet high in tall, dried grass, pale beige in colour, with half-hidden tombs standing out grey and silent, as if through a pale gold mist. *Dhurris* had been spread out on a portion of grass that the servants had flattened down, and the families sat around and feasted on *singharas* and other delicious Indian snacks, washed down with hot tea from Thermos flasks. Howard and Mohi had gone off to do a spot of shooting in the surrounding jungle, and the children played hide-and-seek amongst the gravestones.

"Are all Mohi's ancestors buried here?" Lydia asked.

"I think most of them are, Lydia dear," Eleanor answered. "They all died quite young you know. I believe Mohi's father died in his early forties."

"That's very young," Lydia said. "Was there any reason for this?"

"Consumption. It's been the scourge of poor Mohi's family."

"Oh, that's terrible," Lydia said.

"Yes, I feel so worried about Mohi sometimes. He doesn't have a very strong constitution, you know, and his drinking doesn't help a bit."

"Does he drink all that much?"

"Yes, a bottle of whisky a day at least. You must have noticed, surely?"

"Well, it's difficult to keep count," Lydia said. She thought for a minute. "Isn't there anything you can do about it?"

"Oh, I've given up now," Eleanor said. "Once upon a time I used to try and hide his bottles but, uncannily, he was always able to find them even when I hid them in the most unusual places. Then I tried diluting the liquor but this was no good either. He would simply discard the bottle and pull another one out from somewhere, or send Babu Lal or one of the servants to get another."

"But he never appears drunk or anything," Lydia said.

"Yes." Eleanor nodded. "And when he's had enough, he just quietly goes to sleep. He's never, ever, misbehaved himself no matter how much he's had to drink—not once, in all the years I've known him. I hope, Lydia dear," she continued, "you don't mind me taking you into my confidence like this. I have so few friends in Calcutta now, and since dear Mama and Papa have passed away and my brother and sisters have all gone to England, I have nobody, really, that I can talk to."

"I'm privileged you've taken me into your confidence, Eleanor. The only one I have to share my confidences with is my elder sister, Abigail, in Calcutta. Both my parents are dead now too."

"I'm so sorry," Eleanor said. "It's always so sad when one's parents pass on. Do you see your sister often?"

"Only when we can manage to get down to Calcutta for a spell. She never married—my sister, and lives alone in a flat in Ezra Mansions. She used to be a nurse in the PG Hospital, but she's retired now. You see, she's several years older than myself. Actually, I'm hoping to see her again soon, once we've had Jamie admitted in school."

"You must miss the city life and all its gayety dreadfully, being stuck away in this awful backwater."

"I don't mind too much," Lydia said, "although I'll have to do something about Cissy's schooling soon. I've taught her all I can, and she can read and write a few simple words. But she needs to be in school with other children of her own age."

"Will that mean that you'll have to live in Calcutta, away from Howard?"

"Well, I haven't spoken to him about it yet, but I suppose I'll have to do so very soon. It will probably be Sing La instead, where I'll be closer to Jamie and Frances. But I do have more friends in Calcutta — and, of course, my sister, Abigail. Do you have many friends in Calcutta, Eleanor?"

"Not any really close ones, Lydia dear, just a few acquaintances like the Hamilton-Smyths, Mohi's racing friends. Alexander is quite a dear, but I'm not awfully keen on his wife, Veronica. She's very beautiful and all that, but she strikes me as something of a flirt. Of course ..." Eleanor brushed at a fly. "... we do have quite an active social life and meet quite a lot of people, but none of them very genuine, I'm afraid."

"Yes, it's so difficult to find any sincere friends these days," Lydia said. "But I've certainly enjoyed meeting you, and the talks that we've had."

"And I too, Lydia dear. You must come over and spend some time with us should you decide to make that trip to Calcutta. It's been so refreshing, meeting someone like yourself, and I'm sure we'll have lots of thoughts and ideas to exchange."

Howard and Mohi arrived back when it was almost sundown, the huge crimson orb hanging just over the horizon and silhouetting the goldmohur tree. The horses appeared to have been ridden hard, and Mohi looked pale under his dark skin whilst Howard seemed slightly shaken.

"Goodness, what on earth has happened!" Lydia exclaimed. "We were just about to leave without you."

"Tell you about it when we get home," Howard mumbled. He clapped his hands and shouted out to the children still playing among the gravestones. "Hurry up you kids! Get into the carriage, *now*! There's a leopard that prowls around here at about this time."

The children hurriedly clambered into the carriage, looking out of the windows nervously whilst the driver goaded the bullocks into motion, and the carriage lurched forward. They reached Lal Kothi when it was dark, for immediately the sun went down, a curtain of blackness fell over the land, and it was only after the children had all been put in bed and the grown-ups sat on the veranda with their drinks that Howard, at Mohi's insistence, recounted their story.

"Well, it was all a bit weird." Howard stuffed his pipe with tobacco. "We had only ventured a couple of miles from the old palace when Mohi and I noticed something quite odd. There was complete silence in the jungle, which, as you know is always alive with sound. We saw some game—a spotted deer—and Mohi took a shot at it. Nothing happened. The animal looked completely unperturbed, and made no attempt to run away or anything. Then I had a go—again, nothing happened, although it was at quite close range." He put his pipe in his mouth and ignited it with a match. "As you know, Mohi is an excellent shot and I'm no mean marksman either, so we simply could not understand why this deer, which by all accounts should have been lying dead on the ground, was going about its business chewing at leaves on a bush as if nothing had happened. Mohi took another shot, but we might as well have been using blank cartridges for all the good it did. A lot of sound, but no effect. Another odd thing—you know when a gun is fired in the jungle, all the birds in the vicinity—particularly the parrots—take off instantly, making a hell of a row? Well, this was different. The jungle remained as silent as a tomb."

"We were a bit concerned about the cartridges," Mohi said. "I thought that perhaps they may have been duds. But Howard fired at a green coconut hanging from a tree and it shattered. So there was nothing wrong with the ammunition."

"I fired at the deer again with the other barrel," Howard said, "with no results. We looked at each other and wondered if this was really happening? It was the same with all the other game we encountered, firing at easy targets but to no avail. It was at this point we decided to return to the cemetery." Howard drew on his pipe.

"So what happened then?" Lydia asked. "To delay you so much, I mean."

"Well, it was as we were approaching the old palace from the other direction that we noticed a beautiful black stallion standing directly in our path, snorting and pawing the ground. It was a magnificent animal, a pure Arab thoroughbred we thought."

"Yes, it certainly wasn't a horse that had escaped from the *Mela* or anything," Mohi said. "They have nothing like that there, and nobody in Panchpani owns a horse of that quality."

"Our horses came to an abrupt halt," Howard went on. "Then this black stallion neighed, and with a sort-of toss of its head, as if beckoning our horses, cantered off towards the jungle. Our horses followed, and there was nothing Mohi or I could do to stop them. They seemed to have mouths of steel and simply would not respond to the reins. They just followed this stallion into the jungle as if under some sort of spell, and there was nothing Mohi or I could do about it."

"It was dark in the jungle," Mohi said, "and as we went deeper and deeper we could only catch an occasional shadowy glimpse of the animal through the vines and creepers."

"Then we came into a small clearing," Howard said, "and the black stallion stood directly in front of us, pawing the ground and snorting, and you know, in that jungle gloom, I could swear that its eyes glowed as red as fiery coals."

"My goodness, how frightening!" Eleanor exclaimed.

"Yes, we were both petrified, I think." Howard glanced at Mohi. "Our horses came to a stop and we just stood there, while this animal—or whatever it was—glared balefully at us."

"In fact, I was completely paralysed—by fear or something else," Mohi said. "Was it the same with you, Howard?"

"Absolutely." Howard nodded two or three times. "Couldn't move a muscle, not even to turn to look at you. I don't know how long we stood there. Time itself seemed to have stopped. But then we heard the faint cry of a peacock, and that seemed to break the spell. The stallion, with one last look at us, turned and dissolved into the jungle, and our horses and we seemed to come back to our senses, and they took off like bats from hell to get out of that jungle. And that, my dear ladies ..." He knocked out his pipe. "... is why Mohi and I were so late getting back."

"You're not telling a load of yarns again," Lydia said, with a trace of suspicion in her voice.

"Cross my heart and hope to die," Howard said. "It's all perfectly true. Mohi can vouch for the story."

"Yes, it really was a very strange experience." Mohi swigged down his whisky. "One that I don't believe I will ever be able to explain. Perhaps it has something to do with the belief that one should never do any *shikar* on a Thursday."

"Is there some sort of superstition about this, Mohi?" Howard asked.

Mohi nodded. "Yes, I remember my father telling me something about it when I was a child. I'd forgotten until now, but this strange experience has brought it back to mind."

"Well, I'll certainly remember it." Howard laughed. "No shooting on Thursdays from now on!"

CHAPTER 14

The arrival of the Nawab's secretary, Babu Lal, from Sing La, heralded Mohi's impending return to Calcutta. He landed up unexpectedly at the gates of Lal Kothi in a cycle-rickshaw from the station. A small, short gentleman, with a nut-brown complexion and a bald head, he was the epitome of the traditional Bengali gentleman, dressed in an immaculate white *dhoti* and *khadi* shirt, a black waistcoat, and patent-leather slippers. A pair of steel-rimmed spectacles with thick lenses completed his get-up.

"This is my faithful and trusted friend, Babu Lal," Mohi said. "He's known me since I was a boy."

"Yes, I've worked with Nawabsahib's family for many, many years now," Babu Lal said as he shook Howard's hand limply.

"Well, I'm very glad you're here," Howard said. "Perhaps you'll be kind enough to go through the books when you've rested enough?"

"Oh, there is no hurry for that," Mohi said. "There will be plenty of time tomorrow. I'm sure all the accounts are in order anyway, and won't require much checking."

"I'll see to it that my head babu takes you to the office first thing in the morning then," Howard said, a bit abashed at his thoughtlessness. "He knows more about figures than I do anyway. Would you like a drink of sorts, Babu Lal, and something to eat?"

"Just some tea, thank you very much," Babu Lal said. "It has been a long and thirsty journey, and I have already eaten on the train."

"Does he have any special dietary needs?" Howard enquired anxiously when he and Mohi were alone.

"Oh, just some simple fish or vegetable dish, with rice or *chapattis*," Mohi replied. "But he won't eat at table with us. He has these peculiar conventions, you see. He feels that it is disrespectful to sit with me at mealtimes, and he would be embarrassed. So, if it's not too much trouble, I would be grateful if you'd have his food served separately. He also likes to eat with his fingers, and he feels this is bad manners in company."

"He has no qualms about his food being prepared by a Muslim cook or anything, has he?"

"Oh no," Mohi said. "Despite being Hindu, he's not terribly caste-conscious that way. It's just that he has these funny ideas of respect. He won't even drink in front of me—although I'm sure he enjoys a tipple on the quiet. It's just his way, and I have to respect his wishes."

Another of Babu Lal's conventions, Howard was to learn, was that he seemed to adopt European dress when he was on official duty, for on the day of the Nawab family's departure, he wore a slightly ill-fitting suit, which he did not look entirely comfortable in.

Mohi had insisted that Howard and his family should not trouble to see them off at the station, and that their leaving should be without much fuss or ceremony. "Babu Lal has already made our First Class reservations at Kholagari on the way down," he said. "So, there's no need to make any special arrangements for our journey or anything."

Howard took this to mean that the Nawab didn't wish to use his own coach to Kholagari from Panchpani station. During their stay, he had become more aware of Mohi's modesty and felt slightly guilty that he had made special arrangements to greet the Nawab and his family on their arrival. He was sorry Mohi was leaving. He'd enjoyed his company immensely, and Lydia had got on so well with Eleanor. The children would miss Zerina, though he wasn't so sure about Ludoo, who seemed the only one pleased to be leaving.

There was just a simple farewell at Lal Kothi, and *salaams* and smiles from the servants who stood beside the car in a little group. Babu Lal had arranged for each and every one of them to receive a small gift of money, as a token of the Nawab's appreciation. Now Mohi, Eleanor, and the two children squeezed into the back seat of the old Ford, while Babu Lal got into the front, and with waves of goodbyes, Abdul drove through the gates of Lal Kothi and on toward Panchpani station.

CHAPTER 15

Jamie trudged up the steep, windy road on the way to his first day at Turnbull's. He felt a bit apprehensive as to what sort of reception he would receive at the new school, being a new boy and a day scholar at that! He was also sorry that he'd missed the opening day in the first week of March, because his mother had developed a bad bout of flu, and their departure for Kumsong had been delayed by a couple of weeks. The first few days at school were always a bit more relaxed, and one didn't stand out so much as a new boy, because there were other new boys who felt equally strange, so one usually chummed-up with these first, before making friends with the others.

Frances had been luckier. Her father had driven her up earlier to Kholagari from Panchpani, and she had joined the school group there, which arrived on the train from Calcutta.

In a way, Jamie regretted now that he was starting as a day scholar. At first the idea had appealed to him, but now he felt it would have been better to have bitten the bullet and gone in straight as a boarder. But his mother had been insistent. It wasn't, he thought, that Lydia wanted to molly-coddle him, but rather that she wanted some company, perhaps, during her one-month-long stay at Kumsong. They'd arrived a few days earlier, and Lydia had taken Jamie up to the school to meet Mr Stalkey, who he disliked from the start, with his thick, round glasses and 'Mr Punch-like' nose. He didn't think much of the school either. Its long bungalow-type building and rather ramshackle appearance was a far cry from Fern Hill's much more impressive clock tower and grey stone, ivy-covered walls.

He rounded a bend, and Queen's Hill came into view—its long white building and turreted roof standing out starkly against the cryptomeria-covered hillside behind. He paused at the gate and thought of Frances, somewhere in that building, happy in class with her friends. He really envied her. Why, oh why, did Fern Hill have to close down? He'd been happy there. He wasn't at all sure about Turnbull's. And had heard the boys there were a tough lot. Still, perhaps he might meet up with some of the old Fern Hill boys again, so would have some friends at least.

The road, wooded above and below, flattened out above the Queen's Hill gates, and he followed it along until he turned a bend, which brought the Turnbull's junior school above, and the chapel below, into view. He looked up and saw a line of small boys assembled at the perimeter of their playing field. Immediately they caught sight of him, they began chanting:

"Donald Duck, Donald Duck—quack, quack, quack, quack. Donald Duck, Donald Duck—quack, quack, quack, quack."

Then they pelted him with stones. Some of them fell harmlessly around him, but one caught him on the leg. He decided to ignore the chanting and the stones. The connection with Donald Duck was probably to do with his name, "Donaldson," because any information about a new boy spread like wildfire through school. He dodged the stones and hastened his step until he reached the main gate, out of reach of the stone-throwing but not the chants, which now turned to insults. Once he'd crossed the deserted playing field of the main school building, he made his way to Mr Stalkey's office, where he had been told to report.

"Enter," a voice barked after Jamie had knocked hesitantly on the door. He turned the brass door-knob and entered the room where Mr Stalkey sat at his desk, blowing his nose in an enormous handkerchief.

"Ah, Donaldson," he said. "Got here at last, have you?" He sprang from his chair, stuffing his handkerchief into his pocket. "I'll take you round to Standard IV and introduce you to your class-master, Mr Rose. He placed his hand on Jamie's shoulder and steered him down the long, wooden corridor until he reached the door of the classroom. Every head turned to look at them as they entered.

"This is James Donaldson," he said, "and this is your class-master Mr Rose." Mr Stalkey turned round and addressed the class. "Donaldson is starting here as a day boy for the time being, but will be boarding with us soon. I hope you are all going to make him feel at home and very welcome here at

Turnbull's." He beamed at Jamie, and with a nod to Mr Rose, whooshed out of the classroom.

Mr Rose was a short, plump, Anglo-Indian gentleman with a bald head and horn-rimmed spectacles. "You can have the desk in the corner." He pointed in the direction. "We're doing English literature at the moment and studying 'The Jungle Book' stories. Since you don't have a copy, you can share with Jacobs at the next desk."

Jamie ambled over towards the vacant desk, which he noted was in the darkest and dingiest corner at the back of the classroom. The chubby, wavy-haired boy with glasses at the next desk looked up at him, and wiggled up the seat to make room. He pushed his battered copy of "The Jungle Book" towards Jamie, who squeezed in beside him, half-on and half-off the seat.

Jamie had read "The Jungle Book" umpteen times. It was one of his favourites, and he was glad he would be in familiar territory with *Mowgli, Baloo, Bagheera,* and *Shere Khan.*

Mr Rose directed the boys to read passages in turn, each standing up at their desk and reading aloud to the class.

After the last boy had finished, Mr Rose looked in Jamie's direction. "Donaldson," he said, "would you please read the next passage for us?"

The next passage was the story of Rikki-tikki-tavi, the mongoose. This immediately brought back to mind the strange incident at Panchpani when, one night, his bedroom was invaded by a swarm of mongooses. They'd run around the floor and all over the bed. He was in a panic when one tried to run up the inside of his pyjamas, and he yelled out to his parents. But before his father could get to him, the mysterious visitors scampered away through the window.

Jamie got to his feet, picked up the book from the desk, and read, "*Early in the morning, Rikki-tikki came to early breakfast in the veranda riding on Teddy's shoulder, and they gave him banana and some boiled egg; and he sat on all their laps one after the other, because every well-brought up mongoose always hopes to be a house-mongoose some day and have rooms to run about in, and Rikki-tikki's mother (she used to live in the General's house at Segowlee)* ..." He read the last word carefully, trying to get the pronunciation correct, "*... had carefully told Rikki what to do if ever he came across white mice .... er ... I mean ... men.*" He flushed with embarrassment.

A titter arose from the class.

"That'll do!" Mr Rose said to the class in a severe voice. Then, more gently, to Jamie, "Thank you, Donaldson. Your reading is quite clear and precise. Only be careful to distinguish between mice and men." He added this last remark with dry humour.

Another titter arose from the class.

"Jacobs," Mr Rose continued, "take Donaldson to the book repository at the mid-morning break so he can have his own text books, and after that to the stationery stores. I'll excuse you if you're both a little bit late for the next lesson."

"Yes Sir," Jacobs said, eager. He looked at Jamie and again gave a shy smile. His large, prominent ears glowed with pleasure at this new responsibility.

Jamie was familiar with the recycling system for school text books. It had been the same at Fern Hill. At the start of the school year, one was issued with the text books that the previous year's class had finished with. These were usually well-battered, ink-stained, and scribbled upon. One was lucky if the cover wasn't missing or a few pages torn out. Usually, you could manage to bag a decent copy if you were fast enough. But being a school late-comer, all the decent copies would have gone by now. At least the stationery would be new.

When the bell sounded for the mid-morning break, Jamie followed Jacobs, who led him importantly down the dark corridor to the school's office, pestering him with questions all the way—"What was your last school? Why are you here as a day scholar? What does your dad do?" In return, Jamie found out that Jacobs's first name was Aaron, that this was his first year at Turnbull's, and the grub was terrible!

Aaron handed the form Mr Rose had given them to the office babu, who scrutinised it, and then filled the order for the new stationery—exercise books, pencils, a pen holder, G-nibs, ink tablets, erasers, a ruler, blotting paper, etcetera, etcetera.

Then he took the boys to the book repository and pulled out the necessary text books from the shelves. As Jamie had suspected, they were all worn and tatty.

On the way back to the classroom (the bell announcing the end of the mid-morning break had already sounded ten minutes ago), Aaron announced, "I say, I have to go to the bogs. Do you mind, Jamie? — I hope you don't mind me calling you Jamie. All the boys here are supposed to be called by their *surnames*, so we can only call each other by our *first* names in private — so, what I mean is, do you mind, Jamie, waiting for me outside the bogs until I've finished?"

"All right," Jamie said, "as long as you don't take too long."

"No, I'll only be a minute. I say, do you have any *bofkag* on you?

"Bof-what?"

"Bofkag. Boff paper." When he saw Jamie still looked puzzled, he said "Toilet paper — you know, to wipe your arse on. They call it *bofkag*, here."

Jamie reached into his pocket and took out a wad of toilet paper that his mother had given him from the roll in the bathroom earlier in the morning. "Better take some with you, darling," she had said. "You never know. They may not have any in the school." He had grumbled a bit at the way she fussed, but relented and put the wad in his pocket. He now handed this to Aaron, who examined it briefly before stuffing it in his pocket.

Heavily laden down with books, the boys made their way past Class IV, down the passageway, then a right turn at the end along the veranda until they exited at the back of the school building that banked onto the hill. A flight of narrow stone steps and a long covered walkway led them up to the school lavatories. Here, Aaron unloaded his share of books onto Jamie, who held them between chin and arms.

Aaron looked anxiously into the dank and vacant lavatory before entering. Jamie waited outside in the slightly tainted air, his arms aching from the weight of the books. It seemed ages before Aaron finally emerged, wiping his glasses on a snotty handkerchief. "I say, thanks for the loan of the *bofkag*. The boys stole mine, you know."

"What for?"

"For gambling with," Aaron replied. "They use it as money for gambling with. I say, can you bring me some more from home?" He hooked his wire-framed spectacles round the back of his protruding ears, and off-loaded some of the books from Jamie.

"I'll try."

"Try and bring me some Bromo, though," Aaron said. "Or anything in a packet. Nothing else will do. It *has* to be in a packet. The roll stuff's no good for anything, except wiping your arse on. Bromo's the thing everyone wants. They use it like money."

"Do they gamble playing cards?"

"Cards, Ludo, anything. Even stag-beetle fights. I say, can you get me some?"

"I think we only have the roll stuff."

Aaron looked disappointed. "Well, I suppose that'll have to do. At least I'll have something to wipe my arse on until matron gives me some more."

"Don't they have any in the toilets?" Jamie said, a little surprised. At Fern Hill the lavatories were always adequately supplied with toilet paper, though not the fancy ones in packets that Aaron wanted.

"Not here," Aaron said. "Matron rations it out to you, and it gets pinched or used up because of the gambling, and then you have to scrounge around for a few sheets, unless you win some."

"Do you gamble?"

"Yes, sometimes. When the other boys let me in to a game. But they cheat and I always lose. That's why they let me into a game, because *they* cheat and *I* lose."

They walked back to the classroom, Aaron chatting all the way, and when they reached the door, entered. Everyone looked up at them, and Mr Rose glanced at his watch. "Jacobs," he said, looking and sounding weary. "When I said that I would not mind if you were back in class a little late, I didn't mean that it would give you licence to dally on the way."

"I had to be excused, Sir," Aaron said.

"Yes, I know. We saw you and Donaldson going up to the lavatories." He gestured to the tall windows at one end of the classroom that looked directly on to the khud and the covered walkway to the lavatories. "I appreciate that you may have wanted to go to the bathroom," he continued. "But you could have let Donaldson return to class with his books."

"He needs someone to hold his hand, Sir," one of the boys said. The others tittered.

"Quiet," Mr Rose said. "Anyway," he addressed this to Aaron, "I'll let it go this time. But in future when I send you on an errand, don't dally. Go back to your desks now, and you, Donaldson, may put your books away."

At lunch break, one of the teachers assembled all the boys on the playing field for hand inspection, and those whose hands weren't clean enough for the teacher's satisfaction were sent hurrying to the washroom while the rest waited impatiently for their return. Finally, they formed into a line and trooped into the school building, and down the dark corridor that led to the dining room. It was large and gloomy, with tables arranged across it in long lines. Bearers, in rather bedraggled uniforms, stood at the head of each table, waiting to serve their hungry diners. The boys took their places at the tables, standing behind their wooden chairs, and a hush descended upon the room while Mr Stalkey, standing at the teachers' table at one end of the room, led the boys into singing grace:

> *"Thank you for the world so sweet.*
> *Thank you for the food we eat.*
> *Thank you for the birds that sing.*
> *Thank you God for everything."*

Then all hell broke loose as the boys pulled back chairs noisily and sat down. The bearers, animated into action, hurried over with platefuls of food, which they dumped down in haste. Jamie eyed his plate. There were a few tablespoons of red-looking rice, which smelt faintly of decaying teeth, and which even Blackie would have turned his nose up at, a dollop of thin, watery curry with a few lumps of tough-looking meat and overcooked potato, and more thin, watery dhal with a few strands of worm-like onions floating in it. Jamie agreed with Aaron's remark. The food *was* terrible. However, Aaron attacked what was on his plate with great gusto, even asking Jamie if he could have his potato if he didn't want it.

Jamie pushed his plate towards Aaron. "You can have it all."

"Thanks," Aaron said, with evident gratitude. "I don't mind your *jhoota*."

"It's all right. I haven't touched it," Jamie said, a little annoyed.

"But I don't mind. Even if you have. Honestly. The others don't give me anything." He kept his voice low while he grumbled. "Even if they don't want it. They'd rather have the servants in the kitchen eat it than give it to me."

"They don't eat leftovers. The servants, I mean," Jamie said.

"Don't they?" Aaron looked disbelieving, with his wide eyes and pursed mouth.

"No," Jamie replied. "They have their caste. Hindus and Muslims won't eat leftovers of other people's food."

"They won't eat *jhoota*?"

"No."

"Well, *I'll* eat *jhoota*. I don't mind. I say, can I have your banana?"

Jamie handed the overripe banana that had been dumped before him over to Aaron.

"I say, you're going to be awfully hungry not eating anything." Aaron peeled the banana then stuffed it into his mouth.

"I had a big breakfast," Jamie said.

"What did you have?" Aaron asked, his eyes big and eager behind the lens of his glasses.

"Corn flakes, bacon, and eggs, with toast and marmalade."

"Gosh." Aaron said in awe. "Of course, I can't eat bacon, being Jewish and all. But marmalade! I say, can you bring me some toast and marmalade tomorrow?"

"I'll see."

"Promise that you will, Jamie. And the Bromo."

"All right," Jamie said. His shoulders sagged with weariness, while he contemplated how he was going to smuggle a bit of sticky marmalade and toast into school the next day.

Aaron beamed at him. "You're a good friend, Jamie. I like you. I think we're going to be good friends, don't you?"

After lunch, they followed the other boys on to the compound outside the school building which was popularly known as the "Upper Flat," and where the boys congregated to spend the rest of the lunch break. Aaron chatted incessantly and Jamie only half-heard what he said. He noticed a group of senior boys talking and ambled over to them with Aaron in tow. He recognised one of them from Fern Hill—an older lad who he didn't know very well. He stood outside the group, hoping he would be recognised. The boy turned his head and glanced at him. "Oh, hello Donaldson," he said in an offhand manner. "You landed up here too?" Then he turned back to the group and continued his conversation.

"Hey," another pimply-faced youth said. "Don't you have a sister at QH, the one who knows Maureen Kingsley—the one with the nice tits?"

The rest of the group sniggered and guffawed with laughter.

"I don't know her," Jamie said.

"But your sister does," the boy said. "Tell your sister to tell her that I'll be sending her a love letter."

More sniggers and guffaws.

"I haven't seen my sister."

"Tell her when you do then. You can give her the letter to give Maureen. You're a dayboy aren't you? You pass the school gates on your way back home? You can slip the letter to her then."

Jamie mumbled something unintelligible.

"What's that? What did you say? You'd better take my letter," the boy continued, then added in a threatening voice, "otherwise I'll screw your balls off!"

"He doesn't have any!" one of the others said and laughed.

"You mean he *won't* have any by the time I've finished with him," the pimply-faced youth said.

"You're a real idiot, Fanshawe," one of the other boys said and laughed. "I don't know why you have such a stiff cock for Maureen Kingsley anyway. Pauline Dunaway has far better tits any day."

The group argued about the merits of the Queen Hill girls' breasts while Aaron tugged at Jamie's sleeve and said, "Come on, Jamie. Don't talk to this lot. I think there may be some more of your friends from your old school if you look around. Did you make many friends there?"

"I made some," Jamie said as they walked away from the group. "But no one in particular."

"So you didn't have any best friend?"

"No."

"I'd like to be your best friend if you want me to," Aaron said. "I haven't made any friends over here."

"Why not?"

"They don't like me because I'm a bit ..." He hesitated. "Well, because I'm a bit ... well, you know ... a bit ..."

"Fat," Jamie said. He didn't mean to sound brutal, but the encounter with the group of boys had left him edgy.

"Well, not exactly fat," Aaron said "... just a bit sort of chubby. You don't think I'm fat do you?" His voice was pleading.

Jamie looked at him. He had to admit that Aaron wasn't exactly fat—a bit chubby faced and round of body. Also, he wasn't an unattractive boy. He had a pleasant face and wavy hair, neatly parted in the middle.

"Well, perhaps not fat," he said hoping his voice would sound more kind, "but a bit on the plump side. But don't worry about it," he said hurriedly, "lots of people are fat. Even animals. You should see my pony Gingernut. Now, he *is* fat, and my *syce* says it's because he eats too much and doesn't get enough exercise."

"My mother says it's my glands," Aaron said, face gloomy, but then perking up. "You have your own pony?"

"Yes, Gingernut."

"Where?—Here?"

"No. On the Estate my father manages—Panchpani."

"Don't know the place," Aaron said. "Is it in the plains?"

"Yes, about sixty miles from Kholagari."

"Ah, Kholagari. You know, one of the boys here ran away from school and they caught him at Kholagari."

"What happened to him?" Jamie asked, amazed how quickly Aaron could change the topic of conversation.

"He was flogged," Aaron said, then added darkly, "Publicly."

"What do you mean?" Jamie asked.

"What? Publicly? It means the Headmaster summons everyone to the school hall and the boy is beaten publicly in front of the whole school."

He gave a lengthy and graphic description of how it was done; how a table was placed on the middle of the stage; the headmaster's explanation of why the boy was being punished; how the poor victim was brought onto the stage accompanied by two senior boys; how he was bent over the table, with one of the senior boys holding his arms stretched across the table; how his trousers were yanked down; how the headmaster applied the thin rattan cane in measured, deliberate strokes on the poor unfortunate's bottom; the yells and pleas for mercy by the victim. Aaron warmed to the theme as he noticed the look of utter disbelief grow on Jamie's face. "I'd like to run away too, if I could. But they always seem to catch you and then you're for it."

"I take it you don't like it here at Turnbull's," Jamie said.

"I don't like it one bit," Aaron said. "The other boys are always picking on me because I'm Jewish. ... You don't mind that I'm Jewish, do you?"

Jamie shook his head. He didn't know much about Jewish boys except that they were circumcised like Muslim boys.

"You know what they did to me when I first came here, Jamie? They held me down on my bed in the dorm and pulled my pyjamas off and painted by balls with red ink. Then they shoved a peach stone up my arse, and it really hurt. Then they put stinging nettle under the sheets at the end of my bed, so when I got in my feet got all stung. Then they're always flicking me with wet towels in the bathing rooms when I'm all wet and naked. It's a bit better now, but they still pick on me when they can. I hadn't made one friend until I met you, ... and you a new boy and all."

Jamie mumbled something, which he hoped would sound sympathetic.

"So you see, though I would like to run away if I could, if I get caught it's a public caning in front of everyone, and that's why I can't run away—ever. It's just too humiliating, and I couldn't stand the pain."

Jamie had a fleeting vision of Aaron bent over the table, his chubby pink bottom exposed, a look of utter terror on his face, and dismissed it with a shake of his head. In all his years at Fern Hill, seldom was a boy ever caned, and never in public. In fact, many a time if a boy were sent to the Headmaster's office, he was often let off with a prayer for repentance and a fistful of peanuts. Here it seemed things were far more harsh and Draconian. His dislike for the new school increased by another notch.

Afternoon classes droned on. The boys were more torpid after their midday meal and not as inclined to direct their remarks in his direction, so he could concentrate more on his lessons. History followed Geography, then the whole class trooped up to the Chemistry Lab (which he afterwards learned was called "Henshaw's House of Horrors"), where Mr Henshaw gave a demonstration of how to make hydrogen gas from zinc and sulphuric acid. Then it was back to the dingy classroom, for the final lesson, Algebra. He was glad when one of the boys was sent out to ring the school bell, which dangled from a rickety and rusty framework of iron scaffolding at the back of the school building, popularly called "the bell tower." This duty seemed privileged, and the ringing of the bell signalled the end of school for that day.

Aaron accompanied him to the end of the top flat and the school gate, where he stopped and said, "I can't come any further with you. The rest is out of bounds. How lucky you are to be going home to a nice tea. We'll only get weak tea and some dry bread."

"Yes." Jamie was glad he was going back home — or at least to the cosy boarding house — and that he didn't have to remain a prisoner in that dingy school building like poor Aaron. He dreaded the thought now of being admitted as a boarder.

Aaron offered his damp little hand to Jamie, who shook it.

"See you tomorrow," Aaron said. Then, as he ran back towards the school building on his chubby little legs, he turned round and shouted, "And don't forget the toast and marmalade ... and the bofkag."

CHAPTER 16

"Why on earth do you want to take your umbrella to school on such a nice morning, darling?" Lydia asked as Jamie prepared to leave Eagles' Crag for school the next day.

"It just *might* rain, Mum," Jamie said.

Lydia pulled the net curtains of the bedroom window aside. "I doubt it. There's not a cloud in the sky, and you can see right down to the plains this morning." The vista revealed the vast Indo-Gangetic plain stretching into the horizon like a vast ocean. "Anyway, take it if you must. And, oh! Could you give this little letter to the school durwan at the Queen's Hill gate to give to Miss Neale? It's to ask her to let Frances and her friend out for the weekend."

"Okay, Mum," Jamie said and slipped the envelope into his coat pocket, which held a packed jam sandwich in greaseproof paper, which he had persuaded his mother to ask Mrs Sheehan for, on the pretext that the school food was awful and he might be hungry at lunch break. "All right, darling. Just until you get used to it then," Lydia said.

He had also been successful with the toilet paper when he asked his mother if she had some with her. "Can't you take some from the roll in the bathroom, darling?" she had said, with a hint of puzzlement. So Jamie had to explain that all the boys were regularly issued with packets of Bromo paper as none was provided in the lavatories. "You had better take a packet then and keep it in your desk." She handed him a box of Jeyes from her suitcase.

So armed with these supplies for Aaron, Jamie set off for his second day at Turnbull's.

He stopped at the gate of Queen's Hill and had to call out to the moustached and turbaned *durwan,* who looked at him suspiciously when he saw the envelope in Jamie's hand.

"I cannot take *chitties* for the *missybabas,*" he said, shaking his turbaned head. So Jamie had to explain it wasn't for any schoolgirl but for the Headmistress, Neale Memsahib, which seemed to satisfy him.

He continued on to Turnbull's. The junior boys had lined up on their playground above the road and chapel to wait for him. But he was well prepared this time, and when the stones rained down, he simply opened his umbrella and they skipped harmlessly off the fabric. Frustrated, four little boys ran down the pathway to the school gate to plague him further, but Aaron stood there, ready for them, with his hockey stick.

"Leave Donaldson alone," he shouted, "or I'll bash you with this." He brandished the hockey stick in a threatening manner. "And, you're out-of-bounds, anyway."

The boys stopped in their tracks and looked at him with doubt on their faces. Then, grumbling and hurling a few insults, they turned back.

"They're little bastards," Aaron said, "especially that one." He pointed to one who was shouting 'Humpty Dumpty and his new palsey-walsey Donald Duck—quack, quack.' "He's the ringleader."

"Yes, and they're too little to fight," Jamie said as they walked away out of earshot.

"I say, did you bring the *bofkag* and the marmalade and toast?" Aaron asked with obvious anxiety.

"Yes, I have them here." Jamie extracted the sandwiches from his coat pocket. "Only, I couldn't get the marmalade and toast you asked for, but I have some jam sandwiches for you."

"That's even better." Aaron beamed. Then, seeing the square packet of toilet paper that Jamie took out from under his pullover, he said "Gosh! A whole packet! And Jeyes! That's the next best thing to Bromo! Aren't you going to keep some for yourself?"

"I'll ask you for some if I need it," Jamie replied.

"Don't know how long I'll have it," Aaron said with a glum face. "I've lots of debts to pay." He hid the precious pack under his coat and opened the packet of sandwiches. "Yum ... these are scrumptious," he said through a mouthful of sandwich. "I haven't had any jam for ages and ages." He finished the sandwiches before they reached the school building.

Jamie had made up his mind that he would disengage himself from Aaron's company today and try and make friends with some of the other boys, who had largely ignored him the day before because, he felt, of Aaron's constant presence. Aaron was an unpopular boy—either because he was fat or Jewish, or indeed both—and keeping company with him all day again would cramp his style. But try as he might, Aaron hung to him like a limpet. So he was still with him at lunch break when the pimply-faced youth, Fanshawe, approached him.

"I say, Donaldson," Fanshawe said in a more civil tone, "you haven't forgotten my letter, have you? I have it all written out." He pulled a rather crushed envelope from his blazer pocket.

"You'll have to deliver it yourself," Jamie said. "I'm not carrying letters for anyone."

Fanshawe glared at him, but without the support of his cronies he felt less sure of himself and just mumbled something like, "Cocky little bastard," before going off.

"You were quite right to refuse to take his letter," Aaron said. "You can get into very serious trouble for that, and besides there're quite easy ways to get letters to the Queen's Hill girls by bribing one of the bearers. He just wants to save a rupee."

"What do they want to write these letters to the Queen's Hill girls for anyway?" Jamie asked.

"To arrange meetings in the woods," Aaron said.

"Why?"

"To smooch and do rude things."

"What sort of things?"

"Rude things, you know ... sexy things."

"What do you mean, sexy things?"

"Well, you know ... kissing and touching, or even putting their things into girls' things." He looked at Jamie's nonplussed face. "Gosh! Don't you know *anything*, Jamie?"

Jamie shook his head.

"Don't you know where babies come from?"

"Well ... from your Mother's tummy."

"And how does it get into your mother's tummy?" Aaron asked.

When Jamie looked rather vague and uncertain, Aaron said, "What about cats and dogs?"

"Oh, that's easy." Jamie said. "They mate."

"Well, it's the same thing. Boys and girls mate."

Jamie felt shocked. He knew animals mated, and had often observed Blackie mounting and getting stuck to another dog. He had even noticed cows and bulls engaged in this act in the fields. But people, he thought, were beyond all that.

"Yes," Aaron went on, "it's called 'fucking.'" He said the word in a lowered tone. "And that's what boys and girls do together—they fuck. Gosh. You are green, aren't you?" He smiled and looked superior. "And that's not all," he went on. "When they're not fucking they're frigging—pulling on their things and leaving a sticky white mess everywhere—on the toilet seats, on their sheets, and pillows—everywhere. It's disgusting. You see that boy over there?" Aaron nodded in the direction of two boys sitting on the perimeter wall.

"Who? The boy with glasses?"

"No. The one sitting next to him who looks a bit Burmese."

"Yes, well what about him?"

"Well," Aaron said, "he gets other boys to suck him off, and if they don't he bashes them up. They're all sex mad," Aaron said with a glum look. "It's all they ever seem to think about, except food. And since it's not so easy to get to do it with girls here, they use boys instead."

"What do you mean?" Jamie said, puzzled.

Well … if they can't do it with a girl they'll do it with a boy — with each other. Do you get it?"

Jamie shook his head.

"Gosh. You *are* green," Aaron said. He sounded exasperated. "What I mean is, when they can't stick their cocks into a girl's pussy, they stick it into a boy's arse! Do you get it *now*?"

He couldn't have been more explicit, and Jamie was again shocked. "You don't mean … ?"

"Yes, that's what they do."

"I don't know how you know all this," Jamie said with disbelief in his voice. "I'm sure you're pulling my leg and making it all up."

"No, I'm not." Aaron said. "I see what goes on, Jamie." His eyes looked wise and owlish behind his thick lenses. "They leave me alone and think I don't understand anything, but I see *everything* that goes on — how one boy creeps into another's bed in the dorm at night, or when they go into the bogs together. They do it whenever they can."

Jamie shook his head again. He too had indulged in a bit of sex play in Fern Hill with other boys, but this was just showing your things to each other and perhaps touching someone else's, or having peeing competitions, but these activities always left him with a deep sense of guilt. He just thought it was secret things boys sometimes did; never girls or grown-ups. They were far too prim and proper to indulge in anything so vulgar or debase. He remembered the time, when he was very small and his pants were too tight and he wanted to go for a pee, he had run up to his mother with his hand clutching his penis. She'd been seated with a friend who was darning something or other. When she noticed him she cried in a shocked voice, "Jamie! How *dare* you touch yourself in front like that." Her friend reached into her needlework basket and grabbed a pair of scissors, and threatened to cut his little member off.

"Some boys like it though," Aaron continued, and gave a knowing wink. "They call them pansies or nancy-boys, like that boy over there." He pointed out a pretty-looking boy of about fifteen who habitually brushed back his flaxen forelock with a casual hand. "They call him Peach-Bottom, and I know he does it and likes it, especially with that boy over there." His finger pointed now to a slightly older boy of more masculine appearance and a prominent Adam's apple. "Sometimes they hold hands when they think nobody's looking. They're a pair of homos all right!"

Jamie grudgingly admitted Aaron had a wealth of knowledge about these matters far in advance of his years, and which, until now, had been a closed book as far as he was concerned. Things made a lot more sense now. Things he had half-noticed and words he had half-heard — words like "fuck," "frigging," and "pussy." He knew enough to recognise that they were bad words — words you wouldn't dare use in front of your parents, teachers, and grown-ups, but until now he'd never known what they really meant.

"Of course," Aaron went on, and he now had Jamie's full and rapt attention, "most of them really prefer girls. They just do it with boys when there're no girls about, and those ones are not *really* homos. But, sometimes, their nancy-boy gets quite jealous if they flirt with a QH girl. Then there's an awful row."

"I don't know how they can fancy soppy girls and want to do these disgusting things with them anyway," Jamie said. "It's sickening."

"We're too young." Aaron said, "We don't *get* these feelings older boys have towards girls, and if they don't get to do it, their balls swell up and burst or they go mad!"

Jamie could see some logic in this—he supposed it might be like dying to go for a pee and your bladder would burst if you couldn't. He had also once seen a Calcutta beggar with simply enormous balls—so big that he had to carry them in a cart between his legs that his little son wheeled. And as for this going mad thing, he had heard of elephants going *musth* if they didn't mate. His father had to shoot one once in the *Mela* when it went *musth,* and when Jamie had asked what *musth* meant, his father said it meant to go mad with love. But he still had some unanswered questions.

"I still can't understand why a girl should let a boy stick his thing into her anyway. Surely it must hurt?"

"Oh, they don't worry about the hurt, and it's the only way she can get a baby," Aaron said. "And you know how girls love babies." Jamie had a mental image of Frances bathing her doll or cooing to Cissy when she was younger. "So they let them do this to them because they want a baby badly, and the baby is inside the white sticky stuff the boy squirts into her."

"Then why aren't the QH girls having babies all the time if they let the boys do it to them?" Jamie asked.

Aaron sighed in exasperation. "Because they can't get babies *all* the time. It's only at *certain* times they can get a baby. And if they don't get a baby their pussies bleed."

"They bleed from their pussies?" Jamie said, aghast, and using this word in its new context for the first time in his life.

"Yes, their pussies bleed. But they put a sort of wadding between their legs to catch the blood—they're called sanitary towels—so that it won't drip into their knickers or dresses."

Another piece in the jigsaw of the mysterious sex-world of adolescents and adults clicked into place—a hitherto unexplained item 'sanitary towels'—pads of cotton-wool encased in gauze that he had glimpsed on one occasion when he accidentally looked inside the large, navy blue box labelled KOTEX in his mother's wardrobe. He knew that girls wore these between their legs, because he had come into Frances's room unexpectedly one day when she was still half-undressed, and noticed this wadding through the thin material of her knickers. Also, this explained the baffling blood in the toilet bowl when it hadn't been flushed properly. He had once asked his mother what this was and she told him, "Daddy had a very painful pile this morning, darling, and it must have burst."

Jamie couldn't fully comprehend everything Aaron had told him. It seemed so unbelievable that Jamie challenged him and asked where he had acquired such a wealth of knowledge about these sexual matters. But Aaron became evasive and only said that a much older boy in his last school used to talk to him and a group of younger boys and "educate them in sex." But there were still some unanswered questions. ... Nevertheless, he had enough to think about and try to absorb on the way home.

He experimented with an unexplored pathway that cut down the hill below the lower playing field, which avoided passing beneath the Junior Boys' School and the consequent taunts. He hoped this would bring him to the road where Eagles' Crag stood. It led through the dark woods with trees festooned with stag moss.

So this was what grown-ups did to make babies, and if what Aaron explained were all true, this was how he, Frances, and Cissy had come into the world. He tried to imagine his father and mother naked on the bed, and like two dogs—his mother on all fours and his father pumping away at her from behind like Blackie, then getting stuck together, back-to-back—his father calmly filling and lighting his pipe while they were still in this position. The thought was too shocking to contemplate. Of course, it made sense now why his thing became rigid—so that it was stiff enough to put into a girl. He had meant to ask Howard about these awkward and strange erections, but could never pluck up the courage to do so. In any case, his father would have probably fobbed him off with some unlikely explanation.

CHAPTER 17

The next few days passed uneventfully, and soon the weekend arrived when Frances was expected home from school. She came with Maureen Kingsley in tow, for whom Lydia had sought permission to take out over the weekend, and the plans were to spend it in Sing La. The old Chevrolet taxi Lydia had ordered from the Kumsong taxi rank arrived to pick them up at Eagles' Crag, and they all bundled in. Tulassa, released from her charge for the weekend, and who was to be dropped off at Kumsong station, carried Cissy on her lap in the front seat, while Lydia, Frances, Maureen, and Jamie all squeezed into the back. The car trundled down the steep road, and the driver kept the vehicle in neutral gear to save petrol, relying on his brakes to negotiate the sharp bends. They reached Kumsong station, and Tulassa took her leave with *salaams*, no doubt looking forward to her free weekend. Lydia got in to the front seat with Cissy on her lap, so there was more room now for the three children, and they proceeded along the Tonga Road towards Sing La.

Jamie looked forward to the break. Since leaving Fern Hill he'd had little in the way of entertainment, and Lydia had promised there would be a visit to the Plaza, and tea at Peliti's, and it was enough just to leave dull and boring Kumsong for a much more lively town. Frances and her friend seemed thrilled about the trip as they chattered away excitedly. Jamie could hardly help glancing at the two small mounds that stuck out of Maureen's school pinafore, guessing that these were the "nice tits" Fanshawe fantasized over, and perhaps saw or touched. He wondered vaguely if she was bleeding from her pussy. Since his conversations with Aaron, Jamie looked at the world in a new light, and he couldn't stop these mental images that seemed to jump out at him like the pages of one of Cissy's pop-up books. He tried desperately to blank these images out, but they kept coming up.

They arrived at the Sing La taxi stand, and a couple of stalwart coolies took charge of their suitcases. Lydia had decided upon "Snow View," since it was located closer to the town and far less expensive than the "Himalayan Hotel." They walked up the road paraded by shops and up to the hotel above. The name of the hotel certainly lived up to its reputation, and from the hotel balcony a wonderful vista of the snowy range greeted them.

The same evening, the promised tea at Peliti's materialised and Jamie gorged himself on cream cakes, sparing a guilty thought for poor Aaron. He had considered vaguely of asking his mother if she could have taken Aaron on this trip as well as Maureen, but plans had already been made and there had been no time. It wasn't that he particularly *liked* Aaron, but he felt extremely sorry for him—trapped like he was soon going to be, in awful Turnbull's. *Meet Me In St. Louis*, with Judy

Garland and Margaret O'Brien, at the Plaza, followed the scrumptious tea—although he would have preferred the Tarzan movie screening at the other Sing La cinema. The next day provided a visit to the zoo with its fine collection of Himalayan animals, including a red panda, and The Natural History Museum, with its display of stuffed animals of the region in glass cases, and shelves of beetles, butterflies and moths, and pony rides up to Beech Hill and *Gidarpahar* (the Hill of Vultures), with Lydia leading briskly on her horse, Telephone, and the rest lagging behind. Jamie wished it were Gingernut he was riding and not this sluggish nag, which seemed to want to pause and chew on every available blade of grass on the hillside.

All too soon, the trip ended and it was back to trudging up the hill to school, armed with mackintosh, gum-boots, and umbrella for any unexpected cloudburst that could come down in torrents at any moment. Jamie paused at the gate of Queen's Hill to deliver a letter to Frances that his mother had given him earlier. He had told her that the *durwan* was suspicious of boys delivering letters to the QH girls and you could get into trouble for it, but his mother had waved it aside with, "What utter nonsense! Surely a mother can write a letter to her own daughter if she wants to!" Fortunately, the *durwan* was nowhere to be seen, and although he couldn't see Frances, Maureen spotted him and ran to the gate.

"Is that a letter for me?" she enquired as she saw the envelope.

"No, it's from Mum to Frances. Can you give it to her?"

She looked disappointed, but took the letter from Jamie. Just then, the *durwan* appeared unexpectedly round the corner, and though he looked suspiciously towards them, didn't say anything. Jamie continued on to school.

The next few days passed without event. The usual round of Maths, History, Geography, Science, English, etc., etc., had the boys cooped up in the dingy classroom with Mr Rose and his dry sense of humour. Jamie talked with other boys in the school, but Aaron still clung on to him whenever possible and seemed to talk sex at every opportunity. It wasn't until a few days later that a small boy entered the classroom and said something to Mr Rose.

"Donaldson," Mr Rose said, "Mr Stalkey wants to see you in his office."

The other boys looked at each other, and Jamie got up from his desk and made his way to Mr Stalkey's office, wondering what on earth he was being summoned for.

"Enter!" a voice barked when he knocked on the door apprehensively.

Mr Stalkey glared at him from his desk as he entered his inner sanctum.

"Ah. So here's our little *dak-wallah*."

"Sorry, Sir?" Jamie stood before Mr Stalkey's desk, unsure of what Mr Stalkey implied.

"Yes, sorry you'll be, Donaldson," Mr Stalkey said, "when you hear what I have to say. You've been seen delivering letters to the Queen's Hill girls."

"Only one to my sister Frances from my mother and. ... Oh, yes, one for Miss Neale, earlier."

"Don't dare lie to me, boy," Mr Stalkey snapped. "You were *seen* giving a letter to one of the girls by the school *durwan* the other day."

"But that was for my sister."

"LIES! LIES! LIES!" Mr Stalkey thumped his desk to emphasise each exclamation. "You were seen giving it to ..." He at looked at the paper on his desk, "to ... a, ... to ... a ... Maureen Kingsley," he finished.

"But that *was* for my sister—from my mother," Jamie said. He felt unhappy—he was in a lot of trouble now.

"NO IT WASN'T!" Mr Stalkey yelled. "It was from Fanshawe ... to this ... to this ... to this girl." He picked up a letter from his desk and waved it in an accusatory manner. "I have it here, with a letter from the Headmistress, Miss Neale."

Jamie's heart sank into his boots. "I didn't take it, Sir," he said, a quaver in his voice.

"Yes, you *did*. This is the evidence right here."

"It could have been one of the bearers, Sir ... that delivered the letter, I mean, Sir," he said, remembering what Aaron had said about the transfer of letters between Turnbull's and Queen's Hill through the school servants.

"How *dare* you accuse the servants," Mr Stalkey roared, "when you were seen in the *act* of delivering this letter." He waved it again at Jamie. "Do you know what trouble you have caused? Do you know that both this girl and Fanshawe are under the threat of expulsion?"

Jamie's face flushed, but he stayed silent.

"Do you know what filth was written in this letter you delivered? Do you? Hey?" He looked at Jamie. "Your face is evidence of your guilt, Donaldson. I can always tell when a boy is lying to me. Now, I am going to punish you, and punish you severely for what you have done, and for lying to me on top of that."

A great cloud of doom descended upon him. Whatever he said, there was no way Mr Stalkey would believe him. He was for it. He was going to be caned — and for something he hadn't even done.

Mr Stalkey rose to his feet. "Take your jacket off and hang it on the hook." He indicated a small hat rack standing near the door, and Jamie numbly obeyed.

"I normally cane a boy over his trousers," Mr Stalkey said, "but owing to the seriousness of your offence, Donaldson, I will cane you on your bare buttocks." He went to the cabinet mounted on the wall, then selected a thin and wicked looking cane from an array of other such implements. "Lower your pants and underpants, and bend over the desk."

Jamie fumbled with the buttons as he undid them, then lowered his shorts, and they fell around his ankles. He pulled his underpants down to his knees, and bent over the desk as ordered.

"Now, Donaldson, I'm going to give you eight cuts of the cane, and I hope it will be a lesson to you not to carry messages to the Queen's Hill girls for other boys." He flipped up the tail of Jamie's grey flannel shirt to expose his naked bottom.

Jamie waited in anticipation. He didn't have too long to wait. A whine sounded when the cane cut through the air, then a crack, followed by another swish-crack in quick succession. He flinched. For a moment he felt nothing—just a numbness on his behind. Then the pain came—a searing sting and burn, like a red-hot poker being pulled across his flesh. He expected the other blows to follow, but instead the headmaster paused, then Mr Stalkey blew his nose vigorously, and all the while the burning of Jamie's backside increased. A slight delay as Mr Stalkey returned the handkerchief to his pocket, then whistle-crack, whistle-crack. Jamie bit into his lower lip to prevent yelling out.

"Not good enough for you, Donaldson?" Mr Stalkey said. "Shall we try something else?" He walked over to the cabinet. Jamie could hear the rattling of the canes as the headmaster selected a stouter and more robust instrument, which he tested by making a few swishes in the air. Jamie's backside was on fire, and this increased by the second.

"Perhaps this one will bring a better response from you, Donaldson," Mr Stalkey said.

Jamie's buttocks tightened in anticipation. Then it came — a slightly lower whine while the cane crashed down and bit into his bottom. This time he couldn't hold back a yelp of pain.

"Ah, we're getting somewhere now, aren't we, Donaldson? Not so brave now, eh?"

Another cut — harder this time. Mr Stalkey gave a grunt of exertion when he delivered it.

Jamie screamed in agony, and tears welled in his eyes.

"Aha! That one hurt, didn't it? But there're another two to go, aren't there, Donaldson? Or is it three? I hope you're keeping count."

"Two, Sir," Jamie said and moaned. Could he take another two? The pain felt worse than anything he had ever imagined or experienced. A hive of wasps descending on his bottom couldn't have been worse than this.

"Perhaps we ought to choose another cane for the remaining strokes, eh?" Mr Stalkey said. He walked back to the cabinet and again Jamie could hear the rattle of the canes. "Ah, yes! I have the very one here — one that's guaranteed to make even the toughest of my lads howl for mercy. It's been tested on the best of them — or the worst of them, to put it another way. It's the one I reserve for particularly troublesome boys like yourself."

Jamie caught a glimpse of the implement as Mr Stalkey walked back to his position behind him. The cane looked wicked — not pale yellow like the others, but a darker colour, and as thick as a man's thumb.

Whoosh-crack. The cane bit deep into his sore and tender flesh. Jamie yelled without shame this time. He had sought to be brave and not to give Mr Stalkey the satisfaction of driving him to tears, but they fell readily now. He just couldn't take the pain any longer. He raised one of his hands to cover his searing buttocks.

"Keep your hands on the desk," Mr Stalkey snapped. If Jamie caught the cane on his hand it could very well break his fingers. "Don't you *dare* try to protect your posterior, or I'll give you four more and call in one of the senior boys to hold you down!"

Despairing, Jamie returned his hand to its original position. The thought of the extra cuts and witnesses to his degradation was more than he could bear.

"Now, how many is that?" Mr Stalkey asked. "Was it six or seven? I've lost count."

"It was seven, Sir." Jamie sobbed.

"Ah, so there's just one more to go. I'll try to make it one to remember."

He lashed out. It was the mother of all cuts—the cane sang through the air and bit so deep into his flesh that he felt as though his bottom had split open. He howled, all vestiges of control gone—Mr Stalkey had won.

"You can stand up now, Donaldson." Mr Stalkey panted.

Jamie, tears streaming down his face, stood up and faced Mr. Stalkey. He pulled up his underpants and shorts. He could hardly see the buttons through his tears, as he did them up. The only satisfaction he had was noticing the beads of perspiration on Mr. Stalkey's forehead. He had won, but not easily!

"Well, I hope this has been a lesson for you, Donaldson," Mr Stalkey said, wiping his brow with his snotty handkerchief and sitting down at his desk. "You will appreciate that we at Turnbull's do not take lightly to any breach of our rules, and there'll be more canings to follow if you infringe them again. Reflect on your punishment and you will realise that it is all for your own good. That will be all. You're dismissed."

Jamie walked stiffly out of the dingy office, rubbing his injured bottom. The pain was excruciating now. He made his way to the lavatories, his vision blurred through his tears. Not surprisingly, Aaron was there to meet him.

"I say, did you get it?" Aaron said. "The cane, I mean."

Jamie nodded.

"What for?"

"He said I delivered a letter from Fanshawe to Maureen Kingsley," Jamie said, still in tears.

"You didn't, did you?" Aaron looked horrified.

"No, I bloody-well didn't," Jamie snapped, "but he didn't believe me."

"How many did he give you?"

"Eight."

"Eight? It's usually six."

Jamie shrugged.

"Is it hurting?"

"Like hell." He went to the washbasins, opened the tap and washed his tear-stained face.

"Better come in here." Aaron opened the door to one of the cubicles.

"What for?"

"I want to see," Aaron said, "the damage, I mean."

Jamie didn't feel particularly inclined to show his injured bottom to Aaron, but after all he'd been through, he hardly cared.

The cubicle Aaron selected had a tap fixed on the wall, with a rusty Quaker Oats tin underneath to catch the drips.

"Let's see," Aaron whispered once they were inside and had locked the door. "Better climb up on to the toilet seat though, in case anyone comes in and sees us under the door, or we'll be for it."

Jamie put the lid down on the toilet and climbed up. Then he dropped his shorts and pulled down his underpants.

"Bloody hell," Aaron said in a voice full of awe. "He really gave it to you, didn't he?"

Jamie craned his neck to view as much of his bottom as he could. He couldn't see properly, but could just make out the red and purple wheals across his backside. They stung like billy-o, and there was a thin watery fluid oozing out.

"Gosh," Aaron said, tracing one of the welts with an ink-stained finger. "He cut across the others with that one. Did he use the bum-buster for that?" He tried counting the strokes. "Did you cry?"

Jamie nodded, but he had to grudgingly admit to himself that he felt a sense of triumph that he had weathered the storm and had been able to take all that Mr Stalkey threw at him, albeit with yells and tears. He recalled briefly the sweat on Mr Stalkey's brow. He hadn't given in easily. It was the first proper beating he had ever had in his life. Howard had never beaten him ever. There had been threats—"*One day I'll give you a thrashing you'll never forget,*" but it had never materialised. Sometimes his mother had slapped him on the bottom for small misdemeanours, but they had never really hurt and she had probably hurt her hand as much as him. He had never been included among the few canings at Fern Hill, but he had read plenty of books about schools in England where the boys were thoroughly thrashed by their masters and prefects, with graphic illustrations of boys bending over desks, their trousers stretched so tightly across their bottoms that you could imagine they had no trousers on at all. And then there were all the spankings in various comics — the boy over his father's knee while he whacked him with a slipper or strap. So he had felt left out in some ways.

"I'll put something cool on it," Aaron said, wetting his handkerchief under the tap.

"No, leave it be," Jamie said. He had no inclination for a wet and snotty handkerchief to be applied to his wounded bottom!

Aaron shrugged. "It's up to you if you want it to burn. I'm only trying to help," he said.

Gingerly, Jamie pulled up his underpants and shorts while Aaron opened the door of the lavatory and poked his head out to see if the coast was clear, then they exited the toilets.

Every head turned to look at them as they entered Class IV. Two boys sitting on neighbouring desks exchanged knowing glances. Mr Rose was writing something on the blackboard. He glanced at them, and continued with his writing. Jamie and Aaron returned to their desks, and Jamie sat down only to spring up immediately with a quick intake of breath. Some of the boys who had experienced Mr Stalkey's cane, looked at him sympathetically, and returned to their lesson books. Jamie gritted his teeth and determinedly sat down. The pain this caused was incredible, and hot tears welled up in his eyes and dropped onto his open exercise book, smudging the ink.

"Donaldson's crying, Sir," one of the boys said. Mr Rose turned away from the blackboard and looked at him over his glasses. "Get back to your studies, Turner," he said. Then he returned to his writing, his glasses at the end of his nose as he copied some text onto the board from a book in his hand.

Later, as he walked along the aisle throwing exercise books of corrected homework onto the boys' desks, he paused at Jamie's. He leaned over him and said quietly, "Did Mr Stalkey cane you?"

Jamie nodded.

Mr Rose closed the open book on Jamie's desk and said in a gentle voice, "Better go to matron. She'll put some ointment on your cuts. Then you can go straight home."

Jamie rose gratefully from his desk. He was in no mood for studies and just wanted to get out of school. He lifted the top of his desk and put his books and pens away, and with a "Thank you, Sir," he left the classroom. No way was he going to see matron. He would go straight home.

CHAPTER 18

Lydia failed to notice anything unusual in Jamie's behaviour that evening, except perhaps that he pecked at the food on his plate at dinner time, and seemed rather preoccupied and uncommunicative. She did notice he limped a bit and winced if he sat down, but children were always bruising and hurting themselves, so she didn't pay it much heed. However, the next morning, he had a slight fever, so she kept him home. Only the day after, a Saturday, when Frances was home from school for the weekend, did she hear what had happened. Frances, her eyes agog, told her all about the scandal that had broken out at Queen's Hill involving her friend, Maureen—how a letter, from the Turnbull boy, Fanshawe, had been found under her pillow by Matron, and the turmoil that followed.

Jamie, clad in his pyjamas and lying on his tummy in bed reading *The Coral Island*, perked his head up.

"And they thought Jamie was involved," Frances said, "or, that's what they said at first. But later they found out it was one of the Turnbull bearers who delivered the letter through one of the QH servants."

Jamie groaned. Despite her son's reluctance, the ordeal of his caning all came out under Lydia's intensive questioning. She coaxed him into lowering his pyjamas sufficiently to enable her to inspect his injured backside, and both her and Frances drew their breaths in sharply.

"My God!" Lydia said. "Is this what that monster did to you?"

She went up to see Miss Neale that same morning.

"I'm so sorry Mrs Donaldson," Miss Neale said, "that our initial investigations led to your son's implication in all this. But you see, our *durwan* HAD seen him delivering a letter to Maureen Kingsley. We know now that this was a letter from you to your daughter, but I had already written to Mr Stalkey by then, and he acted rather hastily. You see, Mrs Donaldson," she continued, "this is why we have to be so strict about the delivery of letters coming through the postal services only, and then being vetted before they are given out to the girls."

Lydia felt a twinge of guilt at this mild admonishment, recalling Jamie's reluctance to deliver her letter to Frances.

"But these servants have their own clandestine method of getting the odd letter through, despite our best efforts to prevent it. Of course, I have been assured by Mr Stalkey that the offender will be sacked immediately."

"Yes, double punishment for the same crime," Lydia commented, grim faced.

"Unfortunately so. And then there are the children involved to consider. We don't know yet what that action will be. But I hope we can count on your discretion about this matter, Mrs Donaldson. Girls will be girls, and boys will be boys, and they're at that difficult age."

Lydia was quite appalled by Miss Neale's apparent acceptance of these disgusting antics that were going on. Jamie, she was determined, would be withdrawn from Turnbull's forthwith, but what about Frances? Would she be safe with all this nonsense going on between the children of these neighbouring schools? Lydia hadn't been told what was in the letter, but she suspected the worst from these lascivious adolescent boys.

She left Miss Neale and made her way, in a determined frame of mind, in the direction of Turnbull's to confront Mr Stalkey. Like Jamie, she had never liked him, and after seeing what he had done to her son, her dislike had turned to detestation. She didn't find him at his cottage above the chapel. His wife told her that he was at his office in the school catching up on some paperwork. When she reached his office, she didn't even bother to knock on his door—she just twisted the handle and barged right in.

Mr Stalkey, foraging through some papers, looked up at her aghast.

Before he could recover his equanimity, Lydia strode over to his desk and, leaning over it, shouted, "You *beast* of a man. How *dare* you thrash my son for something he didn't do?"

Mr Stalkey stared at her, dumbfounded. Lydia glowered. Surely he'd expected some comeback from her. After all, Jamie was a day-scholar, and his family would, of course, come to know about his punishment. It was "safe" to punish the boarders. They were isolated during the school year, and beatings were often forgotten by the end of term—in fact it was likely they never mentioned it to their parents at all. Lydia, furious, demanded an explanation concerning the punishment of her child, and an unjust one at that.

"I have come directly from seeing Miss Neale," Lydia said in angry tones, "and she has told me all about these *disgusting* letters from *your* boys being delivered by *your* servants to the girls at the Queen's Hill School."

"Ah, yes ... a most unfortunate incident ..." Mr Stalkey looked to have recovered his composure somewhat.

"And that you should *dare* implicate my son in all of this and beat him for it without a proper investigation is absolutely *disgraceful*! Have you seen what a state he is in—all black and blue?"

"Ah, yes ... I'm terribly sorry ... but he *was* seen delivering a letter."

"Yes, a letter—one from me to my daughter. *Not* a filthy one from one of your boys."

"But what was I to think?" Mr Stalkey asked.

"You should have *waited* until Miss Neale had completed her investigations before you went ahead and punished my son."

"Ah, yes ... I admit I acted a bit hastily," Mr Stalkey said, an unhappy expression on his face. Of course, he couldn't uncane a boy, but Lydia wanted an apology at the very least. "And he *denied* it, when you questioned him, didn't he?"

"Yes, but I thought he was telling lies."

"My son has been brought up *not* to *lie*," Lydia said, furious. "You should have checked your *facts* before you went ahead and thrashed him ..." She spied the cabinet on the wall, and the rack of canes through the diamond-shaped glass panes, "... with one of *these*." She wrenched open the cabinet door and pulled out one of the canes.

Mr Stalkey cringed in his chair as she waved the cane at him — the coward was fearful she would strike him.

"How would you like a taste of one of these yourself — you, you *brute*."

"Now ... now ... have a care," Mr Stalkey said. His voice shook. "Control yourself, Mrs Donaldson! Control yourself!" He cringed further back into his seat.

Lydia looked at him — his face pale, his eyes wide and terrified behind his thick glasses. For a moment she felt tempted to give him at least one whack, but his words returned her to her senses. Instead, she vented her anger on the cane, snapping it across her knee and throwing it across the office, where the pieces bounced off the wall and clattered to the bare wooden floor.

"I think you are overreacting to all of this, Mrs Donaldson," Mr Stalkey said, his voice still a bit shaky. "You will understand that administering punishments to the boys at school is one of my more unpleasant duties as Headmaster, and I take no joy in it, I assure you. In your son's case I admit I was rather harsh with him, but at the time the punishment seemed to fit the crime."

"There *was* no crime."

"Ah ... yes, admittedly so. But I will try to make it up to the boy by apologising for my hastiness and misjudgement, if that's any consolation."

"It is certainly *not*," Lydia said. "And I doubt if you will have the opportunity, as I am withdrawing him from your dreadful school immediately."

"There is really no reason for that," Mr Stalkey said. "James was just beginning to fit in nicely, and I'm sure he will settle in if he is admitted as a boarder."

"Well, I'm not leaving my son in your school to be further bullied by the likes of you. Besides," Lydia continued, "this wickedness between your boys and the Queen's Hill girls is disgusting and unhealthy, and I am in two minds about withdrawing my daughter from Queen's Hill too."

"Oh, I hope you will decide not to do so, and I hope this incident will go no further, Mrs Donaldson," Mr Stalkey said, apprehension showing in his voice. "Your confidence and discretion will be very much appreciated. After all, the reputation of our school is at stake."

"Frankly, I don't give a damn," Lydia said. "It's up to you and Miss Neale to sort out what is happening, and put an immediate stop to it. Meanwhile, I am withdrawing Jamie, and will consider what to do about my daughter."

With that, she turned on her heel and stalked out of the office, slamming the door shut after her. A group of boys wandering aimlessly on the playground, looked at her curiously, and one whispered to the other—"Donaldson's mother."

When she returned to Eagles' Crag, Lydia told Jamie and Frances about the interview she'd had with Miss Neale, and the furious row with Mr Stalkey.

"You needn't worry about going back to that awful school, darling," she said to Jamie, who groaned at the scene his mother had caused. *Why, oh why did Frances have to open her bloody mouth?* he thought. He still hated Mr Stalkey and Turnbull's, and smarted over his unjust punishment, but he also felt he was copping out of the situation, and would rather that the whole incident be buried and forgotten, and he return to school as normal. In an odd way, he felt as though he had passed some sort of rite of passage—like in the story he'd read about a young African warrior venturing out to kill his first lion and gaining his manhood. He felt that the other boys at Turnbull's would treat him with much greater respect, now that he had weathered the storm and survived his ordeal.

"And as for you, young lady," Lydia said, addressing Frances. "I want you to stop being friendly with that Maureen

Kingsley. I think she's a bad influence on you, and there're other matters I want to speak to you about privately. Do you understand?"

"Oh, Mum!" Frances cried. "She's my best friend. How can I suddenly stop being friendly with her?"

"You'll understand when I talk to you," Lydia said, her voice firm and final. "I don't want any nonsense now. Otherwise I'll take you out of Queen's Hill too."

"But you *can't*, Mum," Frances said.

"Oh yes I can," Lydia said. "I can see the nuns at St. Teresa's Convent on Monday to admit you there, if need be."

"But that's RC and our rival school in Kumsong, Mum," Frances cried. "You won't put me there, surely?"

"I will if I have to," Lydia said. "At least that's located far enough away from the loathsome youths of Turnbull's, and the nuns will maintain some sort of discipline."

Frances broke into tears. "All right, Mum, I promise," she sobbed. "I promise to break off my friendship, with Maureen … I mean. But please let me stay on at Queen's Hill. Please, Mum."

"All right darling—if you really mean it. And we'll have our talk when I walk you back to Queen's Hill tomorrow evening."

Jamie felt a wave of satisfaction that Frances too was getting some of the flak for blabbing her mouth off to her mother. If she had only kept quiet, none of this would have happened, and life, however grim, would have carried on as normal. He knew now what the "talk" was going to be about—sex! How much did Frances know? Probably a lot more than he did, having Maureen Kingsley as a friend. He felt annoyed now that he had been so naïve and blind all these years to all that was going around about him, and felt a sense of gratitude towards the "all knowing" Aaron Jacobs. However, he couldn't imagine his mother being as explicit in her talk with Frances as Aaron was, especially where the "bad words" were concerned. Another thing he regretted was that he wouldn't be seeing Aaron again—not even to say goodbye. It wasn't that he had any particular liking for the boy, but he felt sorry for him, and had a mental image of Aaron looking out for him vainly from the playing field, and missing him when he didn't appear. Poor Aaron. Regretfully, too, he would miss the conversations and the knowledge he gained from them. There were still so many unanswered questions.

But if Jamie thought he'd seen the last of Aaron, he was grossly mistaken, because on the night before their return to Panchpani, he heard an urgent tap-tapping on the window-pane. It was a filthy night with rain lashing down, and gusts of wind howling through the rafters. At first, he thought it might be a branch or twig rapping against the window-pane. Lydia, lying down in bed smoking a cigarette and reading a novel, looked up from her book. "What on earth is that?"

Jamie, clad in his pyjamas, got out of bed, went to the window, and peered out into the dark. What he saw amazed him—the white and frightened face of Aaron looked in through the glass.

"Gosh!" Jamie exclaimed, "It's my friend Aaron, from school."

"Good God" Lydia said. "What on earth is he doing here?"

Jamie rushed into the bathroom and opened the back door that led out into the narrow pathway outside. The wind almost blew the door off its hinges, as a drenched and bedraggled Aaron entered, dripping puddles of rainwater onto the bathroom floor. "I've run away from school," he said.

CHAPTER 19

They sat round the blazing coal fire that Lydia had stoked up from the glowing embers in the grate. Aaron, stripped of his wet clothing, which had been put to dry on the clothes-horse, and clad in Jamie's dressing gown, sipped a mug of hot cocoa that Tulassa had brought him from the kitchen. Little Cissy lay fast asleep in her cot in the corner.

Aaron had poured out his troubles—how unhappy he was at Turnbull's with the beatings, bullying, bad food, and the fate that awaited him if he were returned to school.

Lydia listened sympathetically, undecided in her mind what she was going to do with this wretched, unhappy child. To take him back to school the next day was out of the question. The taxi to take them to Kholagari, would be arriving early in the morning to pick them up, and she was determined that she would not take Aaron back to Turnbull's and into the clutches of that brute of a headmaster. No, she decided, it would be better to take him back with them to Panchpani. She could always explain that they had seen Aaron wandering about lost at Kholagari Junction, and that she had no choice but to proceed with him to Panchpani. Mrs Sheehan, the boarding-house keeper, was away in Sing La for a few days, and there were only the servants about, so there would be no witnesses to this deception. She would write to Aaron's mother once they were back in Panchpani, and it could then be decided what was to be done. She was confident that once his mother learned how unhappy her child was at Turnbull's, she would arrange for his return to Calcutta, and not send him back to this awful school.

She explained her plan to the two boys, and was gratified to see Aaron's chubby little face light up in relief and gratitude.

"Now, you boys better get off to bed. You'll have to share with Jamie, Aaron. Do you have any pyjamas you could lend him?" she said, addressing her son.

"Don't think they'll fit him, Mum," Jamie said.

"Never mind then," Lydia said. "He'll have to sleep as he is in your dressing gown."

She went in to the bathroom, and Jamie and Aaron climbed into the single bed.

"I really *had* to run away, Jamie," Aaron whispered, "when I heard you wouldn't be returning to school. I was *really* looking forward to you coming in as a boarder and us being friends. You were the only friend I had, and I missed you."

"Well, it wasn't my idea," Jamie said. "It was Mum's. ... What did the boys say about my caning, and what happened to Fanshawe?"

"The boys? Oh, they said that you must have been really tough to take that sort of beating. And Fanshawe? Mr Stalkey decided not to expel him, but to give him a public caning. You should have seen the way he yelled and howled for mercy!"

Jamie recalled his own caning, and felt the welts on his backside flare up again.

"What happened to the girl, Maureen, your sister's friend?" Aaron asked.

"Don't know. Haven't seen Frances since. They don't cane girls — publicly, I mean, do they?"

"Shouldn't think so," Aaron said. "It wasn't her fault really — it was Fanshawe's. They'll probably let her off with a warning, or at worst she'll be expelled."

A low level of pandemonium ensued the next morning when it was discovered Aaron had wet the bed, and peed all over Jamie in the process. Aaron, his face flushed with embarrassment was almost in tears. Lydia remained unruffled. She said, "Never mind, dear. These things happen." Tulassa washed out the sheet and the rest of the wet clothing.

"I say ... I'm ever so sorry, Jamie," Aaron mumbled.

"It's all right," Jamie said, determined this was the last time he was going to share a bed with Aaron.

They breakfasted, and then the taxi arrived to take them to Kholagari.

CHAPTER 20

Howard met the train when it steamed in to Panchpani Station. Lydia, Tulassa, and the children emerged from one of the carriages. He went up to greet them, giving Lydia a perfunctory peck.

"Good God. Who is this?" he asked in surprise, when he noticed Aaron.

"This is Aaron. One of Jamie's friends from Turnbull's," Lydia said in a sweet voice, and with a rare smile. Then, addressing Aaron, she said, "And, Aaron, this is Jamie's father, Mr Donaldson."

"But what on earth is he doing here?" Howard had received Lydia's letter from Kumsong, telling him that she had withdrawn Jamie from Turnbull's, and when they would be returning to Panchpani. But she had made no mention about this strange little boy in her letter. He took Aaron's damp little hand and gave it a weak shake.

"I'll explain to you later," Lydia said.

She did when they reached home, and were comfortably seated on the veranda, now shaded by the cool and fragrant *khas-khas tatties,* drinking tea.

"My God!" Howard exclaimed, when he had heard Lydia out. "That's kidnapping. We could very well be arrested and prosecuted for that."

"And who's going to find out?" Lydia said, her voice inviting no argument. "Who's to know that we didn't find him wandering about at Kholagari Junction?"

"They'll say you should have taken him to the local *thana*."

"Then I'll tell them that we would have missed our train."

"They'll still call it kidnapping," Howard said, his shoulders sagging with gloom. "You've really behaved most irresponsibly, Liddie."

"Call me irresponsible, if you like," Lydia said. "But you're a fine one to talk. What would you have done in such a situation?"

"I would have taken him back to school."

"To be publicly thrashed by Mr Stalkey?"

Howard shrugged. "If need be. Boys at school know the rules, and expect to be punished if they break them. I received my fair share of the cane at school, and it didn't do me any harm."

"Well, after I'd seen what that brute had done to Jamie, there was no way I was going to send that poor child back to face a similar and humiliating punishment in front of the whole school. I think these sorts of beatings should be outlawed."

"It's all part of the discipline," Howard said. "Otherwise there would be no control."

"And what do you think about your son being thrashed for something he didn't do?"

Howard shifted in his seat, and fidgeted. "Yes, that was a bit unfortunate, but he'll survive. He wouldn't be the first boy to be caned for something he hadn't done. It often happened ... at least in my time."

"Well, I'm glad I have withdrawn him from that awful school. I don't know how you could have suggested it in the first place."

"It was probably better in my time ... things must have slipped a bit, especially the food. ... Anyway," Howard continued, "we had better think of what to do now. We'd better let the boy's mother know where he is, and that he's safe. She must be out of her mind with worry. Do you have her address?"

"Yes, I got it from Aaron on the train. She can't know her boy is missing yet. Mr Stalkey wouldn't have had the time to inform her. He'll probably wait for the boy to be caught then tell her about it — that is, if he thought it necessary to tell her at all!"

Howard called out to Dawa and indicated, with a scribbling gesture, that he needed some writing implements. Dawa hurried away and returned with a pad and pencil, which he handed over to Howard with a smile.

"Better send her a telegram." He pondered for a moment then wrote:

"YOUR BOY SAFE WITH FAMILY. RAN AWAY FROM SCHOOL. LETTER FOLLOWS. DONALDSON AT PANCHPANI."

He showed it to Lydia, who nodded with approval. Then he wrote down the address from the back of the envelope Lydia gave him. He tore the paper from the pad and handed it over to Dawa with instructions to take it to the Post Office for immediate despatch, and gave him some change at the same time. Dawa salaamed, and just before he left them, Howard said, as an afterthought, "Ah ... do you think we ought to let Mr Stalkey know as well?"

"No," Lydia said, and pursed her lips. "Let him sweat over it. As long as we've informed the boy's mother, that should put us in the clear."

"I hope," Howard said.

"Well, I don't want him turning up here and hauling Aaron back to school. If that were the case, I would have sent him back in the first place."

Howard shrugged in resignation. "Well, now that we've got that out of the way, what are we going to do about Jamie? You've pulled him out of Turnbull's and we now have to think of an alternative school. What do you suggest we do?"

"I think I'll take him down to Calcutta and put him in school there."

"Where? St. Xavier's?"

"No. I thought The Lytton School for Boys would be the best. They have a better class of boy there, not like the disgusting Turnbull's lot." She threw an accusing glance at him.

Howard ignored the look. "As a boarder?"

"No—a day scholar."

"What? You want to leave Panchpani and live in Calcutta?"

"Well, what is there for me to do here?" Lydia said. "I'm fed up with the dull routine and having none of my family or friends here. At least in Calcutta there'll be Abigail."

Howard remembered Abigail, Lydia's eccentric elder sister who had worked as a nurse in the Calcutta General Hospital. He sighed. "Well, Liddie dear, you must do what you must. But it's a bit unfair on me, you know, having to live here all by myself."

"You hardly notice that I'm here at all," Lydia said, "you're so wrapped up in your work."

"That's unfair, Liddie. You don't know how much I missed you—and the children, when you were in Kumsong. And that was only for a few weeks." He didn't mention his abstinence from sex. During her absence, he'd had to resort to masturbation, as there were no local women who could have offered him any "pleasure," and Panchpani did not boast of a whorehouse of any sort—not that he would have wanted to avail himself of native women anyway. He had far too much respect for them, and his own reputation to consider. It had always been the case, right from his adolescent days, when Pater had warned him not to fraternise with the pretty Nepalese tea coolies. There were many planters who did, however, and illegitimate offspring from these liaisons had to be absorbed by an orphanage in the Sing La district. So masturbation was the only relief, and it was always Veronica who featured in his thoughts as he indulged in this solitary and boyhood activity.

Lydia shrugged. "Well, there's no life for me here, Howard, as you very well know. Panchpani is such a backwater. I don't want to live the rest of my life in the *Mofussil*, and in such an unhealthy climate, with nothing to do and all day to do it in. I need friends and family and some sort of social life."

"What about me?"

"You have your job. Besides, you can always come down to Calcutta and see us. It will give you a good excuse to get away from Panchpani from time to time."

"It won't be the same," Howard said, "and I can't leave everything up in the air while I'm gallivanting off to Calcutta every now and again."

"Well, you might need to see Mohi about something."

"I don't think the Nawab will take very kindly to me leaving my duties and responsibilities just to see my family. But of course, if necessary, I will take advantage of the opportunity if and when it should arise."

"That's settled then," Lydia said.

"When do you want to leave?"

"In a couple of weeks, I expect. Let's see what response I have from Aaron's mother. I could take him down to Calcutta with us. It'll save her having to come up all the way to Panchpani to collect him."

"What makes you think she'll want him back with her? She might want him to go back to Turnbull's."

"You're so blind, Howard!" Lydia said. "What mother in her right mind would want to return her child to school when she knows what will happen to him if she does?"

"Mr Stalkey could make some concessions."

"But he *hates* Turnbull's anyway. She'll be a cruel kind of mother if she wants to return her child to that sort of school where he is so unhappy. Besides, when she hears what I have to say about the disgraceful goings-on between the Turnbull boys and Queen's Hill girls, that should decide her."

"You could be right," Howard said.

"I'm *sure* I'm right."

CHAPTER 21

The next few days of this unexpected school break passed happily for the boys, especially for Aaron. He had never experienced the Indian countryside, and new sounds, smells, and sights excited his senses. The weather was hot—unlike the rain and cool mists of Kumsong—and the boys, with Jubra, frolicked naked in the tank, shaded by its surrounding trees and bamboo thickets. Then there were rides on Gingernut and *Panpathia*, the elephant, whenever the *mahout* cared to take them out on these excursions. On one such occasion, they went to Ahm Bagh where the mangoes were ripening on the trees. Here, they encountered a wild boar that came charging out of the undergrowth straight towards them. The *mahout* immediately commanded the elephant to a halt. Then, as the black, snorting beast approached to within striking distance, *Panpathia* swiped at it with her great trunk and sent it up the field, rolling over and over. The boar staggered to its feet, charged again, and received the same treatment as before. Its final attempt seemed rather half-hearted—presumably fed up with being the ball in this bizarre game of cricket—and, with a defiant snort, it trotted back into the jungle.

The boys were quite shaken by this experience, but the *mahout* seemed unperturbed. But he did warn the boys not to mention this incident to *Sahib* and *Memsahib*; otherwise, no further elephant rides would be forthcoming!

The sun had settled low in the sky when they returned to Lal Kothi. They found Howard entertaining a Mr Cyril Harrop, the Deputy Commissioner of the district, who had come on one of his routine visits. He was a small, weaselly man with thinning hair and a small, ginger moustache, which he tugged absently from time to time. Jamie had met him before, and on the last occasion, Mr Harrop had given him some stamps. He hadn't liked him very much, or the way his watery, red-rimmed eyes seemed to follow him about. He liked him even less when Mr Harrop had invited him to sit on his lap whilst his father had gone into the house to get some papers. He looked at Mr Harrop's bare knobbly knees and hairy legs poking out from his khaki shorts. He didn't really want to, but Mr Harrop had been kind enough to bring him the stamps, and besides, it was rude to disobey grown-ups. He walked over to Mr Harrop and sat down as directed. Mr Harrop hugged him closely, and whispered in his ear, "Won't you give your Uncle Cyril a little kiss?" He felt the wet tongue lick his ear, but worse, he felt Mr Harrop's hand shoot up the leg of his khaki shorts. He grabbed at the hairy wrist—alarmed at this abnormal behaviour on the part of an adult, and looked at him in astonishment, but Mr Harrop simply looked away.

Just then, Howard appeared on the veranda waving some papers. "Found them," he called.

"Good," Mr Harrop said, behaving as if nothing had happened.

Now here he was, slumped in a deep cane chair, with a gin and tonic in his hand, while Howard told him about a particularly troublesome leopard which was terrorising one of the local villages.

"I'll have to shoot it," Howard said, and he looked glum at the thought. "It's already killed two goats, and the village women are too frightened to go to the *nullah* to collect water. We don't want an incident of a baby killed, or the thing might turn man-eater if it finds easy prey."

"Well, I'd certainly like to come with you when you do go," Cyril Harrop said. "Never really bagged a cat, though I've been on a few hunts."

"I usually like to go alone on foot," Howard said, "and it's not exactly a hunt, with beaters and the rest."

"How do you do it?" Mr Harrop said, "on foot, I mean."

"Well, I usually find a convenient tree in a small clearing, and get the villagers to slaughter a goat and tie it to the trunk a few feet from the ground, slitting its belly to expose the entrails. Then they build me a little blind in the bushes not too far away. The leopard, attracted by the smell of blood, usually comes prowling around at dusk. I wait in the blind and, when the leopard eventually gets to the goat, I get a clear shot."

"What if it's dark?" Mr Harrop asked.

"I have a powerful flashlight, which I shine on the animal a few seconds before I pull the trigger. The leopard usually looks directly into the beam for a few seconds, dazzled by the light, and then I fire."

"I would really like to come with you," Mr Harrop said. "Is there any possibility that you would consider a daytime shoot?"

"Well, I suppose I could," Howard said, with obvious reluctance. "But in that case I would have to wait for news from the village of where the animal is—if it shows up—and take a few beaters to flush it out. We could go on the elephant, or in the Jeep. You'll have to be ready to move as soon as we get news."

"That I will," Mr Harrop said. "But would you let me have first chance of bagging it?"

"If you like," Howard said. "I don't like killing these animals anyway—especially a cat. I do it out of necessity rather than sport."

"Thank you, Howard. That's pretty decent of you. I'll await word from you then." He noticed the boys, and smiled weakly at Jamie. Then, glancing at Aaron, he said, "Who's this young fellow, now?"

"Oh, that's Aaron," Howard said. "One of Jamie's school friends. His mother wants him back in Calcutta, so Liddie's taking him down with her when she goes in a few weeks' time." He hoped the feeble explanation would work. It seemed to, for Mr Harrop didn't question him any further.

"Well, I'd best be on my way." Cyril Harrop rose from his seat. "I don't want to take up more of your time. And don't worry about giving me those papers yet. You can send them to me tomorrow by your servant boy." He nodded in the direction of Jubra. "And I can sign and stamp them, and send them back to you. Let me know about the leopard, though." He shook Howard by the hand, and went to pat Jamie on the head. Jamie shied away, despite his father's frown.

"Getting too big for petting, eh?" Mr Harrop said. He laughed with embarrassment, and gave Aaron's chubby cheeks a squeeze.

He and Howard walked away to where Mr Harrop's Jeep was parked.

CHAPTER 22

Lydia threw the sheet aside and got up from the bed. She and Howard had been making love—or at least, that's what he called it. She couldn't understand what this had to do with love. To her, it was just lust and carnal pleasure. That is what she had been taught. She had never forgotten the time when she was about eleven, and her *ayah* had taken her and her little eight-year-old brother to the park in Calcutta. An elderly Bengali gentleman, who asked the *ayah* if he could take the children with him and "feed them with sweets," had approached them. The *ayah*, being only a young, inexperienced girl and being given some *baksheesh* by the gentleman, had let them accompany the man, who held them by the hand and led them away. He had taken them to his house, and as soon as he had got them there, insisted that he should give them both a bath. The rest was like snapshots in her mind; he peeling off their clothes; his thick, brown thing sticking out from between the folds of his *dhoti*; he pouring water over her brother's head, so that it flowed down him and formed a little stream dribbling from his penis, as if he were urinating; he soaping her unformed breasts, then between her legs, his fingers feeling—probing. She and her brother had never told anyone. It was just, after all, a bath, and she was used to being bathed by servants and parents alike. But this wasn't like any other bath that they had had. It had something wrong about it. Something dirty. It felt just the same when Howard made "love" to her, his sweaty, hairy chest rubbing against her breasts, and his thick thing probing between her legs for entry. Dirty.

Lydia went to the chest of drawers, and took out a small cardboard box, which contained her douche, and took it into the bathroom and performed the ritual cleansing. She had to wash his sticky mess out of herself, and also had to be careful of not becoming pregnant again. Her menstrual cycle was carefully worked out so that no sex took place when during her fertile time. Howard didn't use condoms.

When Lydia returned from her ablutions, Howard said, "I hope you're not thinking of leaving me, Liddie, or anything like that."

"What nonsense," Lydia said and snorted. "Of course not. It's just this place and the sort of life I have here."

"Where are you going to stay? With Abigail?"

"No, she wouldn't have room in her flat, and besides, she and I wouldn't get on living together. She's far too eccentric and bossy. No, I'll probably stay at The Evergreens to start with, then I might look round for a small place."

"Nothing too expensive, I hope."

"No, Howard." Lydia sighed in exasperation. "Nothing too expensive. Besides, if you're worrying what all this is going to cost, I might look round for a teaching job in one of the Calcutta schools. I did complete my teacher training you know, so I'm not completely unemployable or dependent on your salary."

"Oh, that's good to know," Howard said with a trace of sarcasm in his voice.

"And there's Cissy to consider too," Lydia said. "She'll have to start in Kindergarten soon. I can't go on teaching her forever. She'll have to learn to mix with other children. We can't neglect her education either."

"I suppose you're right." Howard sighed, then continued, "Now that you've brought Cissy into the equation. I didn't think of that."

"No, you never do. It's always me who has to think about everything. You're always quite happy to go about, never seeing an inch before your nose, and leaving me to work out everything. I would probably have had to live in Calcutta anyway to put Cissy in school. Now that Jamie's situation has cropped up, it will be killing two birds with one stone. I'm glad in a way that it *did* arise. He would have been completely corrupted by those ruffians at Turnbull's, and he'll have some decent boys to mix with at The Lytton School, if they'll admit him. In fact, I think I'll try and persuade Aaron's mother to send him to the same school. It's nice that he has a decent little boy for a friend."

"Well, they certainly seem to be enjoying themselves here, including Jubra."

"I'm a bit worried about them mixing with Jubra too much," Lydia said. "After all, he is only a servant boy, and familiarity breeds contempt."

"Oh come on, Liddie," Howard said. "Jamie's been friendly with Jubra for years. Servants and *Sahib's* children always keep a sense of protocol, no matter how friendly they become. They have a mutual respect for each other, and never cross that borderline between familiarity and contempt."

"I don't know about that!" Lydia said. "I saw them playing most vulgarly after that time at the circus, with Jubra aping the activities of the clowns, and Jamie laughing his head off."

"I suppose there's no harm in that."

"I don't agree. I think Jamie is being influenced far too much by the behaviour of the servants' children, especially Jubra. I saw him blowing his nose the other day, not using a handkerchief but just his fingers like the natives do. I'll be glad when he's admitted into a good school."

"Well, hopefully it won't be long now that you've apparently made all your plans," Howard said, with more sarcasm in his voice. "But I don't think you need to worry. Jamie would never do that in school. It's just a case of *When in Rome* …"

CHAPTER 23

If it were any consolation to Lydia, the fact was that Jubra kept a significantly low profile for the next few days, and even failed to appear when the mahout offered the boys another jaunt into the jungles on Panpathia. It was only when Howard had news of the prowling leopard and asked Jamie to get Jubra to deliver a *chitty* to Mr Harrop informing him of this, that the boys sought Jubra out. They searched Lal Kothi's servants' quarters in vain, but finally spotted him in the distance, sitting on the wall of Lal Kothi's compound looking out vacantly over the *Mela* ground. Jamie shouted out to him and waved the scrap of paper in the air. Jubra looked towards them, but didn't make any effort to get down from the wall and go up to the boys.

"What's the matter with him?" Aaron said.

"Dunno," replied Jamie, "he's been acting a bit odd these last few days, keeping away from us."

When they reached Jubra, Jamie said, "Donaldson sahib wants you to take this *chitty* to Harrop sahib. It's about the leopard that has been seen prowling round the village again."

Jubra's empty expression immediately turned to one of alarm.

"Oh, Jamie baba. I cannot."

Jamie was a bit surprised. It was not usual for Jubra not to want to carry out a task, especially since it was for his father.

"Why not?"

"Oh, Jamie baba. Please do not ask me. I cannot." There was anguish in his voice.

"Wonder why he doesn't want to run an errand for my dad." Jamie said to Aaron.

"Dunno," Aaron said. "Haven't you noticed that he's been acting a bit strangely ever since your dad sent him with those papers to Mr Harrop's office the other day?"

Jamie had to admit that he had felt a little apprehensive when his father had summoned Jubra to give him the papers to give Mr Harrop, taking into account the advances Mr Harrop had made towards him in the past. But at the time, he couldn't really think up a good enough reason for his father *not* to send Jubra, and so he said nothing.

"Is it that you do not wish to go to Harrop sahib's office?" Jamie enquired of Jubra.

Jubra nodded.

"Why not?"

"Please do not ask me, Jamie baba."

"Why? What's the matter?"

"Please leave it be." Then he added feebly, "I am not feeling very well."

"What's the matter?"

Jubra shook his head. "I do not know."

"Would you like me to tell my father so that he can send you to the doctor?"

"No. Please Jamie baba, do not tell your father."

"I think Mr Harrop has done something to him," Aaron said.

"What?"

"Don't know. Perhaps he's buggered him. I didn't like the way he kept looking at you that day. I think he's a fucking pervert."

"What do you mean 'buggered'?"

"Stuck his thing in his arse," Aaron said with his usual brutality.

"You mean ... ?"

Aaron nodded.

"Did Harrop sahib do anything to you the day you took those papers to him?" Jamie asked of Jubra.

"Please, do not ask me, Jamie baba. I am so ashamed." A big tear rolled down his cheek.

"Yes," Aaron said, "he's definitely been sodomised by that dirty bastard!"

"Did Harrop sahib try to touch you in any way?" Jamie said, and when he saw Jubra's puzzled expression, added, "To touch your *lowra*?"

Jubra hung his head. "I cannot say, Jamie baba. Please, do not ask."

"I think you're right," Jamie said to Aaron. "Mr Harrop *has* done something to him. But I don't think he's going to say any more."

"Did Harrop sahib put his *lowra* into your *chutar*?" Aaron addressed Jubra. Not mincing his words and using the crude Hindi equivalents for penis and anus, seemed to shock Jubra into a positive admission. He looked at them and nodded, and another tear slipped down his cheek.

"Where did this happen?" Jamie asked.

"In his office," Jubra said and snivelled. "He locked the door and sent the *durwan* away. He made me do other things as well. Bad things. Oh, Jamie baba. I am so ashamed."

Jamie patted Jubra's shoulder, and turned to Aaron. "Shall I tell my dad?"

"Won't do any good," Aaron said.

"Why not?"

"He's a big, important man and a government official. Who'd believe a poor servant boy anyway?"

Aaron was probably right. Nevertheless, he would have to think up an excuse for Jubra as to why he couldn't deliver the *chitty*.

"I suppose we'll just have to leave it be, then." Jamie said.

"Nothing else to do. I didn't like that Mr Harrop. I sort of knew that he was a homo."

"But surely grown-ups don't behave that way?" Jamie said.

"Oh yes they do," Aaron said. "Some of them anyway. We had a master once—not at Turnbull's, but in my other school—who fancied some of the boys, and he sometimes used to 'touch them up.' But he was discovered and kicked out, although it was all kept very hush-hush."

At that point, Jamie decided to confide in Aaron and tell him about the incident with Mr Harrop.

"So you *knew* he was a homo," Aaron said. "Why didn't you warn your dad?"

"I couldn't tell my dad because I have never discussed these sorts of things with him, and he wouldn't have believed me anyway."

Aaron shrugged. "You're probably right. Anyway, I hope that dirty pervert gets his deserts someday."

"How?"

"Perhaps he'll catch VD and his cock will drop off."

"What's VD?"

"Venereal Disease. You catch it when you go with whores," Aaron said.

"Well, perhaps that's why he has boys instead, like poor Jubra."

"Hope he gets his deserts anyway," Aaron said.

CHAPTER 24

News of the leopard spread like wildfire, and the next day a crowd of villagers gathered in Lal Kothi's compound, together with beaters, sepoys and, of course, Mr Harrop with his Jeep and .303 rifle.

Howard busily tried to organise everything, and the boys stood beside him while he shouted and waved his hands about. Eventually, everything seemed to settle down. It was decided that they should take the two jeeps—Howard's and Mr Harrop's—the old V8 Ford, which could accommodate whatever villagers and sepoys remained. Also Panpathia, who would provide a safe place for the boys, as it was most unlikely that a leopard or other wild cat would attack anyone on an elephant. It had taken Jamie and Aaron a good deal of time to persuade Jubra to accompany them on the shoot, because of Mr Harrop's presence. After a lot of cajoling and coaxing, Jubra finally agreed to go, with the assurance that he would be with Jamie and Aaron all the time on the elephant, and would have no contact with Mr Harrop, whatever. These assurances and the temptation of not missing this great event eventually swayed Jubra, and he agreed to accompany the boys.

Lydia and Cissy stood on the steps of Lal Kothi and waved them goodbye as the procession of three cars exited the main gate, with the elephant and rest of the party following on foot.

The five miles to the little village, along a rough cart track, made for a bumpy ride. The motor vehicles travelled at a snail's pace so that Panpathia and the villagers on foot could keep up with them. As soon as the procession reached the collection of mud huts which made up the village, a crowd of villagers ran out to greet them — the men all armed with *lathis*, and the women carrying their babies on their hips, and followed by their naked children looking on with great curiosity at all the *tamasha*.

A couple of excited villagers led Howard and Mr Harrop, together with Dawa and a couple of sepoys, whilst the boys sat behind the *mahout* on Panpathia a little way behind, and had a first-hand view from their high vantage point.

The leopard, which had been prowling round the neighbourhood earlier in the day, now apparently sheltered in a bamboo clump that fringed the clearing, so Howard arranged for some beaters to skirt round to the back and flush the leopard out. They didn't have long to wait, for after a few minutes hullabaloo from the beaters, the leopard came out into the clearing, spitting and snarling. It was too far away for a clear shot, but when it came within range, it took refuge behind a small bush in the centre of the clearing, and all that could be seen of it was part of its tail sticking out.

Cyril Harrop, standing a few feet in front of Howard, already had his rifle to his shoulder.

"Wait on," Howard shouted. "Wait until the beaters scare the cat out. Then you'll get a clear shot."

But Mr Harrop wasn't going to wait for that. He fired into the centre of the bush.

What followed was almost too quick for the eye to follow. The leopard charged out of its hiding place and made straight for its antagonist, Mr Harrop. Before he or Howard could fire another shot (Mr Harrop was in the line of fire anyway), it was upon him. Over and over they rolled in the grass, Mr Harrop screamed as the leopard went for his throat. Everyone looked on, helpless. It was impossible to shoot the animal while it and Mr Harrop rolled over and over. The only thing that Howard could do was strike the leopard on the back of its head with the barrel of his rifle whenever the opportunity presented itself. This happened on at least three occasions, and eventually the leopard looked up, and saw a *sepoy* nearby poised with his *lathi,* and probably now thinking that this was its provoker, it leaped up from the stricken Mr Harrop and clawed the poor fellow right down his face with a single stroke of its paw. The poor man fell to the ground writhing in agony, and it was then Howard raised his rifle to his shoulder and shot the animal dead.

The dazed and shaking Mr Harrop, his khaki shirt and shorts ripped and covered in blood, was helped to his feet by Howard and Dawa, and bundled into Howard's Jeep. The injured sepoy, screaming and holding his torn and bleeding face in his hands, was lifted up by two sepoys and placed in Mr Harrop's Jeep, and both vehicles sped off towards Panchpani, their tyres kicking up a hail of stones and dust.

The boys, from their vantage point on top of Panpathia, had a clear view of all that had happened, and although shocked at the speed of it all, did feel that it was all Mr Harrop's fault, as any experienced *shikari* would never risk firing at an animal unless he was certain of his aim, for there's nothing more dangerous than a leopard or other wild animal, when wounded.

Jubra stayed silent throughout the whole incident, and when one of the boys finally spoke, it was Aaron.

"Is there a hospital in Panchpani?"

"No. There isn't," Jamie replied. "The nearest hospital is in Kholagari. I expect Dad will have to take Mr Harrop there, although Sing La would be better, because they have a good hospital there for the tea planters."

"Don't know whether he would survive the trip," Aaron said. "He looked badly mauled."

"I feel sorrier for the *sepoy*," Jamie said. "Did you see his face? It was all torn open and the flesh hanging down. I doubt if he's going to survive."

"Yes, he was pretty bad, poor fellow," Aaron said. "But I'm not sorry for that bastard Harrop, after what he did to Jubra, and it was all his own fault anyway. Looks as if he got his just deserts after all."

As it transpired, Aaron's predictions *did* come true, for although Mr Harrop survived the journey — not to Sing La, but Calcutta by special ambulance coach — septicaemia set in, starting in the region of his genitals, which had been badly clawed by the leopard's hind legs. He died within a week of being admitted to hospital. The poor unfortunate *sepoy* though, was never sent to hospital but died the following day.

CHAPTER 25

Pleasure filled the days that followed for the two boys and Jubra, who had now returned to his former self, probably due to the fact that his abuser, Mr Harrop, was out of the way. One day, Jamie suggested they should visit the old ruined palace and look down the well for the supposedly buried treasure. When they approached Jubra about the plan, he was apprehensive. "Do not go there, Jamie baba. It is a bad place full of *djinns* and snakes."

Jamie knew full well that his parents would disapprove, as Howard had often warned him about the place, fearing that the crumbling walls would come crashing down on anyone venturing into the ruined and collapsing building. But they would stay in the vicinity of the compound, as it was only the well Jamie was interested in, so he reckoned that that should be okay.

Jamie instructed Kaila to get Gingernut saddled and ready for the ride, and Jubra and Aaron borrowed two bicycles from the office babus. They followed the path to Ahm Bagh in the vicinity of the palace—Jamie trotted briskly on Gingernut, and the two boys followed on their bicycles. They reached the palace compound, and Jamie dismounted from his pony, who immediately set to grazing on a patch of lush grass, while Aaron and Jubra propped their cycles against one of the crumbling walls. They approached the well, and looked down. Their reflections floated on the dark and silent water when they leaned over the low wall surrounding the well. Tree roots grew all the way down from the top in a tangle.

"We need a long bamboo pole," Jamie said. "Then we can dip it into the well and prod around to see if we can find the box of treasure." He looked around and spied a clump of thick, tall bamboos growing in a patch a few yards away. "Jubra, see if you can cut down one of those long bamboos."

Jubra had borrowed Dawa's *kukri*—a long curved Gurkha knife with a razor-sharp blade—as a possible protection against snakes. This he carried in its sheath around his waist.

Aaron peered into the dark depths. "Do you really think there's any treasure down there?"

"Mmm, there are stories about one of the Nawabs putting all the family jewels in a steel box and throwing it down the well when the palace was being besieged in the past, because all the jewels mysteriously disappeared, and nobody has been able to find out what happened to them."

"Gosh. We'll be rich if we find it," Aaron said.

They continued to peer down the well, while Jubra hacked away at a thick thirty-foot-tall bamboo growing in the clump. They waited, sitting on the wall of the well while Jubra hauled the bamboo pole, and trimmed off the branches and leaves that sprouted from it. Eventually, it was finished. The three of them lowered the pole into the mouth of the well, and when it dipped into the water, prodded about.

"Gosh, it's deep," Jamie said. "I can't feel the bottom yet."

"Don't lean too far over," Aaron said, "or you might fall in."

Jubra called out in alarm. "Don't move, Jamie baba."

Despite the warning, Jamie turned his head. About four feet away from him, a black cobra—its hood extended—reared up hissing, its forked tongue flicking in and out of its mouth. Jamie froze. The one thing he feared most, was snakes.

Jubra, standing a short distance away, edged slowly towards Jamie, holding the *kukri* in his hands. He interposed himself between Jamie and the snake. The cobra reared up higher, swayed, and hissed threateningly. Jubra lashed out with the *kukri*, aiming for just below the cobra's head, but the snake dodged the blow and struck. It caught Jubra on his right leg, and buried its fangs deep into his flesh.

"Aiiiieee." Jubra screamed as he tried to shake the snake off, but it was too firmly attached. Then it let go, and sped off into the deep grass at lightning speed.

Jubra sat down on the ground, clutching his leg and writhing in agony.

"Get my dad, quick," Jamie shouted to Aaron as he held Jubra. He raised the leg of Jubra's pyjamas and could see the marks of the two fangs, now reddening as the poison spread.

Aaron dashed for his bicycle. "I hope I'll be able to find my way back," he yelled and he raced off on the rattling machine.

Jamie held Jubra in his arms. He had seen films where snake bite was dealt with by cutting into the surrounding flesh with a knife, and sucking out the poison. He did have his penknife in his pocket, but was hesitant to use this technique. A tourniquet might help, so he undid his belt and buckled it as tight as he dared above the site of the bite. He held Jubra in his arms, and noticed the boy's breathing had shallowed and his eyes glazed over.

"Oh, Jamie baba. I am going to die." Jubra moaned, and Jamie tried to comfort him by stroking his head.

It was a good half-hour before Howard roared up in the Jeep. By then it was too late. Jubra had already fallen limp in Jamie's arms.

CHAPTER 26

The death of Jubra cast a dark shadow over the days that followed. The whole household fell quiet and Jamie was profoundly depressed, not to mention the cook at the death of his only son. "He sacrificed himself for me," Jamie said through sobs, tears rolling down his cheeks, as Aaron put his arms around his shoulders in an effort to comfort the distraught boy. "He was my true friend and I'll miss him so much." An image of Jubra's smiling face flashed up in his mind.

However, plans had to move forward, and Lydia made arrangements for her and the boys' trip to Calcutta. It was good the boys would soon leave Panchpani, as a change of scene might help to take Jamie out of his deep depression.

Howard sent one of his clerks to the station, and he made reservations for First Class tickets, from Panchpani to Kholagari Junction, and from there onward to Calcutta. Meanwhile, Lydia packed her cases, and Jamie his tin trunk. Aaron just had a bag with the few possessions he had with him—mainly the clothing Lydia had had tailored up for him by the local *durzee*, seeing he had only the clothes he stood in when he sought sanctuary with them in Kumsong. She had written to Aaron's mother, telling her of the events and how unhappy her son had been at Turnbull's. Mrs Jacobs had responded, and expressed her thanks to Lydia, saying she'd had no idea how unhappy her boy had been at school and that she had written to Mr Stalkey withdrawing her son. Lydia had given Aaron's mother their proposed date of arrival in Calcutta, so that they could meet up at Sealdah station, and Mrs Jacobs could take charge of her boy.

Howard saw them off at Panchpani station where they boarded the train to Kholagari. It was only a two-hour journey, and they had a three hour wait to catch the train to Calcutta. They had a meal at the railway restaurant before boarding the train. The journey to Calcutta would be an overnight one, and they had a large compartment all to themselves. Tulassa accompanied them in the carriage, so that she could take charge of Cissy. Although Lydia had bought a Third Class ticket for her, it was customary for servants to travel with their masters or mistresses, and the ticket inspector, if he happened to inspect the tickets, could always be bribed with a ten rupee note.

Jamie chose the upper berth in the large railway compartment, and Aaron did likewise on the opposite side. Lydia shared a lower berth with Cissy, and Tulassa occupied the second lower berth.

Jamie loved these journeys on the overnight train as it jogged along the track with a rhythmic clickety-clack of the wheels that lulled him off to sleep. He awoke when the train slowed and crossed the huge Sara Bridge that forded the lower Ganges river, and the girders made a distinctive hollow sound when they swished past the shuttered carriage windows.

Then, at frequent stops at stations along the way, vendors would call out their wares, like *"paan; bidi;* cigarette" or *"garam cha."* Indian railway stations never slept at night, or if they did, awoke with the arrival of the next night train.

They arrived at Sealdah at eight o'clock the following morning, late enough to give the family sufficient time to wash their faces in the attached washroom and get ready for their arrival. The journey passed without incident, except when Aaron got a piece of soot in his eye, and Lydia had to pick it out with the corner of her handkerchief.

As promised, Aaron's mother was there to meet them. She opened her arms wide as he ran up to her, and she hugged him. "Thank you so much, Mrs Donaldson, for rescuing my son from that awful school," she said, with gratitude in her voice.

The coolies, in procession, carried the luggage on their heads, as they made their way to the taxi rank. The families exchanged goodbyes, and they boarded separate taxi-cabs.

"Goodbye, Jamie," Aaron said as they parted. "Thank you for being my friend." They shook hands in a grown-up fashion. "And thank you, Mrs Donaldson, for all your kindness and help." He gave her a hug, and she patted his head. Tulassa held Cissy up, and she planted a kiss on his chubby cheek.

All the taxis in the city were large American open cars, dating from the 1920s—usually Chevrolets, Studebakers, and

Fords—with a canvass hood, and usually painted a bright grass green or canary yellow. Khaki material always covered the upholstery inside, to protect the original leather seats.

The taxi made its way through crowded streets, the gutters littered with green cocoanut shells (with one end hacked off to drink the refreshing *daab* water inside), broken mud *chattis*, and other garbage. The Sikh driver continuously squeezed his bulb horn to make pedestrians move out of the way. The traffic on the road was congested with an assortment of wheeled vehicles—cars, trams, buses, horse-drawn *gharries*, push-carts, and rickshaws. Pariah dogs and stray cattle mixed in with the pedestrians on the pavements, though often wandered into the centre of the busy streets. Whenever the car stopped at traffic lights, beggars would come to the open windows, sticking their arms inside, their cupped hands waving as they begged for alms.

Once leaving the vicinity of Sealdah, which was the more squalid part of the city, they progressed to the cleaner and better parts, like Chowringhee and Park Street. Lydia had decided to lodge with Mrs Trutwin who ran a boarding house at the lower end of Camac Street, as this was located nearer to the school where Lydia intended to have Jamie admitted.

They reached the wrought-iron gates of the stately building, which the durwan opened for them, and the taxi-driver parked the vehicle beneath the porch supported by Doric columns. The large building had a grass tennis-court to one side and a gravel driveway. Mrs Trutwin came down the marble steps to greet them—a little old lady with her grey hair tied up in a neat bun on top. She showed them the large room on the second floor, which had a bright and airy feel. It had a high ceiling with a crazy-china floor.

The taxi driver and *durwan* followed them in, carrying the luggage. Outside the room, a long covered balcony looked onto a quiet lane that ran alongside the building, and over the wrought-iron railings was Auckland Square, with gardens surrounding a large tank—or reservoir as they were popularly known in India. The Lytton School lay beyond the gardens, and just a fifteen-minute walk through the park. Mrs Trutwin had thoughtfully provided a *charpoy* on the balcony where Tulassa could sleep, instead of being accommodated in the servants' quarters.

The Monsoon had well and truly set in, and although it had cooled the temperature of the city down, the air still felt hot and sticky. Lydia and the children were grateful for the electric fan, which hung down from the ceiling—a great improvement from the primitive hand-drawn *punkahs* that Lal Kothi had to offer—and relaxed on their beds.

Jamie loved Calcutta and all the entertainment this vibrant city had to offer. He looked forward to going to the luxurious, air-conditioned cinemas and seeing the latest films. Lydia, too, was grateful that at last she was in a bustling city and not stuck away in the confines of Panchpani, where she felt lonely and isolated. Here, at least she had some friends, and of course, Abigail.

Jamie went with his mother to the Lytton School and saw the headmaster, a Mr Mason, who showed them around. The building looked impressive and stately, with large grounds surrounded by a high wall. Jamie liked the large, bright, airy classrooms — so different from the dark and dingy ones of Turnbull's. The whole atmosphere was different. Whereas Turnbull's was isolated high up on the hill, this school was in a select part of a busy city, surrounded by life and gaiety. He was a bit disappointed that Aaron's mother had decided to admit her son back to St. Thomas's in Free School Street, where he had been happy before, but he hoped he would see Aaron from time to time. He had grown to like the boy and was thankful for all the sexual knowledge he had gained from him. He now realised how naïve he had been throughout all his years.

Lydia also had Cissy admitted to a small private school for little children in Camac Street itself, and with the education of the children arranged, applied for a teaching job in one of the girls' schools such as Pratt Memorial and the Loreto Convent. She hoped the extra income would help with the school fees and her accommodation for her and the children at Mrs Trutwin's. Not only that, but it would prove her independence to Howard. As for Jamie, on the advice of Mr Mason, he was to be admitted after the mid-term examinations in September, as it would not be fair to admit him now, and then expect him to sit for and pass the exams, after only a month or so at school. Lydia saw the logic in this.

She also contacted Eleanor on the telephone, and Eleanor was delighted that Lydia was in Calcutta, and invited them to her and Mohi's home in Alipore. Lydia only took Jamie with her, as Cissy was already attending Kindergarten. Tulassa would collect the child when it was time for her to return home.

Eleanor sent their black Bentley sedan to collect Lydia and Jamie from Mrs Trutwin's, and they made their way to Alipore, which was by far the most select part of the city, on the outskirts beyond the Victoria Memorial and near the Alipore Zoo. The palatial white marble building stood in extensive grounds, and Eleanor, Mohi, and Zerina met them at the entrance.

"I'm so very pleased to see you, Lydia dear," Eleanor said, and then kissed Lydia on the cheek.

Zerina greeted Jamie with great excitement, but then lowered the tone of her voice and said how sorry she was to learn about poor Jubra.

"How did you know?" Jamie asked.

"Jubra's father is related to one of our servants here," Zerina answered, "so that's how we found out."

"Where is little Ludoo?" Lydia enquired.

"Oh, he's gone back to his father," Eleanor replied. "He wasn't very happy living here with us and wanted to go back home."

Eleanor led them into their large and spacious drawing room where a huge crystal chandelier hung from the high ceiling, the crystals reflecting the afternoon sun and casting rainbows of colour around the room; oil paintings hung on the walls in gilt frames; a glass-fronted cabinet held an assortment of expensive bric-a-brac; the antique furniture exquisite and ornate; marble figurines stood on pedestals, and a grand piano graced one corner.

"I must introduce you to our friends — the Hamilton-Smythes," Eleanor said, as she conducted Lydia towards a couple seated on the sofa. "This is Alex," she said, and an elderly gentleman rose to his feet and shook Lydia's hand. "And this is his wife Veronica." Lydia noticed that the wife looked a lot younger than her husband. She didn't rise from her chair, but offered a white bejewelled hand to Lydia, looking at her through slanted green eyes and a curl of cigarette smoke.

"Lydia's husband, Howard, manages Mohi's estate at Panchpani," Eleanor said.

"Yes, I know," Veronica said. Then added with haste, "At least, that's what I understand."

"Do you, dear? Eleanor said, "I don't remember mentioning that."

"You must have," Veronica stumbled, awkwardness in her tone.

"Oh well, I probably did at some time or other," Eleanor said. "I'm afraid I'm getting rather forgetful these days. Now, what about some tea?"

"We won't be staying," Alex said. "We really just popped in at the off-chance of finding you at home."

"Don't rush off," Mohi said. "How about joining me for another whisky?"

"No, no. We'll really have to be getting along. I have to meet up with some race-*wallahs* at the Calcutta Club. I'm hoping to get some tips for the races on Saturday." He turned to his wife. "Come now, my dearest."

"Yes, my darling," she said in an affected manner. "But it was nice meeting you," she said with a drawl, addressing Lydia. Then she rose to her feet. Eleanor and Mohi accompanied them to the door.

"I can't stand that woman," Eleanor said when she returned to the room.

"Come, come, dearest," Mohi said. "It's unlike you not to like anyone."

"Yes, I know," Eleanor said. "It's just that she gets on my nerves, especially when she runs poor Alex down in front of company."

"Yes, she does go on about him a bit, which is somewhat embarrassing. Anyway, tea for all?" He summoned a liveried bearer and instructed him to serve tea, cakes, and sandwiches.

"You don't mind if I have a whisky instead?" Mohi asked.

Eleanor gave Lydia a quick knowing wink.

"Of course we don't mind," Lydia said. "It's a pity Howard isn't here to join you."

"How is he getting along?" Mohi asked. "I hope he doesn't find the Estate affairs too much of a burden."

"No, he loves his work. Did you hear about the awful tragedy of the shooting accident when a leopard mauled and killed poor Mr Harrop?"

"Oh no," Mohi said. "Please, do tell."

Lydia recounted the story while Eleanor poured the tea from her silver tea service, which the bearer had brought in on a tray. She didn't mention the incident about Jubra in case it upset Jamie, who had just bitten into a tea cake.

"Can Jamie and I go outside to play?" Zerina said.

"Yes, of course, baby," Mohi said. "But first of all, wouldn't you like to sing us a little song?"

"All right, Papa," Zerina said. "What one shall I sing?"

"Oh, any one you like." He poured himself a large Scotch from the bottle on the table.

Eleanor got up from her chair and went to the piano in the corner. Zerina followed, and stood beside, straight backed and prim. She whispered something to her mother, and Eleanor played *In My Sweet Little Alice Blue Gown*, and Zerina sang in her high childlike voice. They all applauded after she finished with a curtsey.

After that, she and Jamie ran out to play in the garden.

CHAPTER 27

The next port of call was a visit to Abigail, Lydia's sister who lived in a large flat in Ezra Mansions, on the 5th floor. The mansion had no lift, so they had to walk up five flights of steep steps, with Tulassa carrying little Cissy. They reached the top floor, which a large skylight on the roof of the building lit.

They rang the bell to her flat, and Abigail greeted them as she opened the door.

"Lydia, my dear," she said and pecked her sister on both cheeks. "I am so pleased to see you after all this time. And this must be James. My goodness gracious, how he has grown! He was only a toddler when I saw him last."

"I don't think you have ever seen little Cissy," Lydia said. "She wasn't born when we last met."

"Hello, my dear," Abigail said as she went to kiss Cissy, still in Tulassa's arms. The little girl shied away, hid her face, and hugged Tulassa tighter around the neck.

"My. She is a shy little thing isn't she?" Abigail said. "Come, come inside now." She led them into her large spacious flat.

An assortment of old-fashioned furniture—mostly glass-fronted cabinets that held china ornaments—filled the drawing room, which was rather dark and dingy, and had a cane sofa and two easy chairs, upholstered with a set of fabric-covered cushions. A large fridge occupied one side of the room, and a big Victorian walnut desk with a roll-down cover sat against one wall. Most of the furniture had a light covering of dust. Beyond the drawing room, a long covered balcony overlooked the streets below and the terraces of lower buildings that surrounded the tall mansion.

Abigail, a bird-like woman in her sixties, wore her slightly greying hair done up in a knot on top. Short and skinny, the bones showed up prominently on her face and arms. She wore a loose fitting cotton dress, with a printed floral pattern.

"I expect you are all hot and thirsty. Would you like a nice cold drink? I have Vimto and lemonade. Which would you prefer?"

"A Vimto please," Jamie said. It was his favourite cold drink.

"Just a glass of ice-cold water for me," Lydia said.

"And what about little Cissy? Would you like a cold drink, my dear?"

Cissy just hid her face again and clung more tightly to Tulassa, who laughed.

Abigail took some bottles out of the fridge and set them on the glass-topped coffee table. Then she took two glasses from one of the cabinets and filled them with the drinks. She handed the fizzy drink to Jamie and the glass of cold water to Lydia. "Would you like some ice in it?" she asked.

"No, it's just fine as it is."

"I'm sorry I don't have any alcoholic drinks to offer you."

"That's perfectly all right," Lydia said, knowing her sister disapproved of alcohol.

"And what's all the news then? I know there's not much in that awful backwater you live in."

"Well, there have been some things that have happened, which are a bit distressing." She filled Abigail in with the recent events—mainly about Jamie's treatment at school, her taking charge of Aaron, and the incident of Mr Harrop and the leopard. She only mentioned the subject of Jubra when Jamie had gone out onto the balcony to talk to Mr Jones, Abigail's parrot who was in a birdcage, the bottom littered with bits of fruit and nuts mixed in with bird-droppings. When she did, she spoke in lowered tones.

"I don't know why you live in the *Mofussil*," Abigail said. "What with all the snakes and wild animals. It's also so unhealthy, with malaria and such."

"Well," Lydia said. "I don't intend to continue living in Panchpani if I can help it." She discussed her plans with Abigail, who listened intently, with little bird-like jerks of her head from time to time.

Jamie re-entered the room.

"And how are you, my young man?" Abigail said.

"I'm a bit worried about him," Lydia said. "He hasn't been to the toilet for four days now."

"Oh really?" Abigail said. "I hope you have given him a laxative."

"Yes, I've tried everything. I gave him a large dose of Californian syrup of figs last night, but it hasn't worked."

"What the boy needs is an enema," Abigail said, with authority in her voice. "Would you like me to give him one?"

"Yes, that would probably do the trick," Lydia said. "If it's not too much trouble."

"It's no trouble at all, my dear. I've administered hundreds of enemas in the course of my nursing career."

Jamie looked horrified at this topic of conversation. He had run the course of these at different points of his childhood, but that was when he was very much younger. It was usually Lydia who administered these, but he'd had one in hospital before his tonsillectomy operation when he was eight.

"Do I really have to have one?" Jamie said, his voice full of apprehension.

"Yes, dear, I think you should. Aunt Abigail has plenty of experience and it won't take very long."

"I'll start to get things ready," Abigail said. "Come on into the bedroom, James."

He dragged his feet as he followed her in, and she busied herself with the preparations, spreading a rubber sheet on the bed. "I'll just go and prepare the enema." She made her way towards the attached bathroom. "In the meanwhile, lie on the bed on your left side and remove your pants and underpants completely."

Jamie suddenly felt a griping in his bowels. "Actually," he said, "I think I might need to go to the bathroom right now." He gripped his stomach.

Abigail perked her head up. "Oh, that's good," she said. "Go into the bathroom then, and see if your bowels will open. If not, we will proceed with the enema. And don't pretend that you have been if you haven't, because I'll soon know."

Jamie entered the bathroom and closed the door behind him. He dropped his pants and sat on the toilet seat. True enough, his bowels moved, and though he had to strain a bit, they eventually opened. He breathed a sigh of relief. Thank God he'd escaped the indignity of this embarrassing procedure in the nick of time. Perhaps it was the threat of an enema being administered by someone like Aunt Abigail that had prompted his bowels to open, probably in sheer fright. He caught sight of the dreaded equipment, which hung from a hook on the door by its enamelled can, with the tube and nozzle neatly curled up. He had seen plenty before, as it could generally be found in the bathrooms of every Anglo-Indian household in India. He wiped himself, and pulled up his pants and then tugged the chain of the flush.

"Did you have a good motion then?" Abigail asked, breaking off her conversation with Lydia as he exited the bathroom and re-entered the drawing room.

"Yes, thank you, Auntie."

"Oh, that's good. You feeling better now?"

Jamie nodded.

"Don't hesitate to bring him around if he gets constipated again," Abigail said with authority in her voice. "Children's bowels must be moved regularly."

Jamie made a mental note to avoid another visit to his Aunt Abigail if at all possible!

There was plenty to do in the busy city during this unexpected holiday. They had shopping sprees in the Sir Stuart Hogg Market, or the New Market as it was better known, in Lindsay Street. This was an enormous shopping arcade under one roof. It held hundreds of stalls, divided up into various shopping areas for flowers, jewellery, clothing, shoes, toys, fruit and vegetables, meat and fish, and cheeses — virtually everything from a sewing needle to a rhesus monkey, as there was a large section at the back that sold all types of animals, birds, and pets. Then there were huge department stores like Whiteaway Laidlaw and Hall & Anderson's — every bit as well appointed as any large London shop. There were also the big and expensive hotels like the Grand and Great Eastern, with their nightclubs and restaurants. Jamie liked Firpo's best, which overlooked the wide Chowringhee Road below, and the large *Maidan* beyond, and which served the most delicious vanilla ice-cream with a chocolate sauce in a silver jug to pour over it.

They had visits to the Alipore Zoo with its variety of exotic animals, both foreign and indigenous. The reptile house, with its various species of snakes, lizards and crocodiles, particularly attracted him. It was good to be able to see the snakes, which he feared the most, from behind the safety of their glass enclosures. The Botanical Gardens was another attraction, and he was enthralled with the Great Banyan Tree, the oldest and largest in the world. It had spread so much that over the years its dangling roots had planted themselves firmly into the ground beneath, and had become separate tree-trunks themselves, thus making the one tree into a mini-forest. They also had visits to the cinemas—"The Lighthouse," "Metro," and "New Empire." He particularly enjoyed *The Yearling, Anchors Aweigh,* and *Beau Geste,* as also the latest Bud Abbot and Lou Costello comedies, and of course the Tarzan films, which were usually screened at The Tiger Cinema, that showed many of the older films. Lydia wouldn't accompany him to The Tiger, as she said it was full of bed-bugs that lived in the woven cane seats and bit you on the backside or thighs at every opportunity. But Jamie was prepared to put up with this minor discomfort in order to see Tarzan and Boy swinging from tree to tree in the African jungles, or Tarzan fighting a crocodile.

So the days passed happily in the City of Joy, until the terrible events of August 16th, 1946.

CHAPTER 28

The end of the Second World War had left Britain in a position where she was virtually bankrupt, and Mohandas Gandhi made demands for India to be given Dominion Status in reward for their support in fighting the Japanese and Germans. Churchill had always opposed this, but with a Labour Government in place a year before, Clement Atlee was more sympathetic towards Indian demands, and talks began on giving India its independence from British Rule. However, despite the Hindus and Muslims having lived in comparative peace for hundreds of years under the Moghuls and British, the Muslim community became agitated as they did not wish to live in a Hindu dominated India. So Muhammad Ali Jinnah, leader of the opposing Muslim League, stirred up the Muslim community. He wanted the Muslims to have their own state so they could rule themselves, should India be given its independence by the British. This led to protests, and a *Hartal* (general strike) in Calcutta was called for on August 16th, where there would be a huge gathering of Muslims at the Ochterlony Monument at Esplanade. This day was to be called "Direct Action Day," and all shops, restaurants, and offices were to remain closed for the duration.

Although Lydia had seen accounts in the papers, there had been no forewarning of what was about to ensue. The day started peacefully enough, so she decided to take Jamie for a walk around neighbouring Auckland Gardens in the early afternoon. Everything seemed calm, and since all road traffic had been banned for the day, the streets were quiet.

On their way back, they found a small black-and-white abandoned kitten, mewing at them plaintively. Jamie picked up the little scrap and held it in his arms. "Can we keep it, Mum?" he asked. "The poor little thing is half starved."

Lydia wasn't very keen on cats, but seeing Jamie's pleading face, didn't have the heart to say no, so she agreed. After all, a little kitten would be company for Cissy.

It was only on their return to Camac Street, that Lydia and Jamie noticed that torn clothing, slippers and shoes, broken bottles and weapons like brick-bats, iron bars, and *lathis* littered the normally tidy road. Telephone poles had also been torn down, and patches of blood stained the road. But there wasn't a person in sight. When they reached the guest-house, the gates were firmly closed and locked. They waited outside patiently, then the *durwan* came up to the gate, followed by a very agitated Mrs Trutwin.

"My dears. My dears," she said, ringing her hands. "Don't you know what's been happening? The Hindus and Muslims are killing each other in a frenzy. I was half-expecting to see your heads cut off and impaled on the spikes of the gate."

"I—I didn't know anything," Lydia stammered. "But we did see signs of disturbances."

"Well, thank God you're home safely. Come in, quick."

The *durwan* unlocked the gate and let them in, then closed and padlocked it again.

The next day the papers were full of the news of the killings, and this continued for the next week or so. All in all, about four-thousand Hindus and Muslims had slaughtered each other. Graphic photographs showed hundreds of dead bodies lining the sides of roads, and being incinerated by large military lorries carrying flame-throwers. One photograph was particularly poignant. It showed a Muslim being stabbed and thrown down a manhole, his hands still held up in supplication. The British military had been called out, supported by Indian and Gurkha soldiers. Most of the troubles were in the north of the city, and areas like Camac Street were relatively peaceful. Lydia and the children were confined to the boarding house for a week. Fortunately, Mrs Trutwin had a well-stocked larder, so the family and the rest of the house-guests were reasonably catered for.

Lydia received a telegram from Howard the next morning.

"WORRIED ABOUT YOU WITH ALL THE TROUBLES IN CALCUTTA. AM COMING DOWN SOONEST. HOPE YOU ARE ALL SAFE. PLEASE WIRE BACK IMMEDIATELY — HOWARD."

He arrived six days later, when things had settled down. He, Lydia, and Jamie sat in wicker chairs on the balcony adjacent to their room, Howard with a drink of whisky at his elbow. Little Cissy sat on the floor at the end of the balcony with Tulassa, playing with the kitten which they had decided to call Fluff.

Howard took a gulp of whisky from his glass. "I felt in my bones that all this trouble between the Hindus and Muslims would flare up once we British started negotiations for Indian independence."

"We've never seen anything like this before." Lydia lit a cigarette. "We've had both Hindu and Muslim servants working together for years, and there's never been any trouble between them."

"Yes," Howard said, "and now the troubles are spreading to all parts of the country. God knows what will happen if India ever gets its freedom."

"What do you think will happen?" Lydia said. "And what will happen to people like us?"

"I don't really know." Howard took another sip. "It will probably end up in a bloodbath and India being divided in two—one part for the Hindus and the other for the Muslims. And as for ourselves, we might not be very welcome in India. They might have another Quit India movement, like they did in '42."

"What would happen in that case? Would it mean we would have to leave India and live in England?" Her tone held a slight hint of optimism.

"I Hope it doesn't come to that."

"Why? What's wrong with England?"

"Nothing's *wrong* with England," Howard said, "it's just that we British living in India have become thoroughly spoiled, with servants and such, and things would be very different and difficult there—particularly for women who would have to do all the housework themselves, for example."

"I don't mind a bit of work," Lydia said. "If it would mean getting away from these horrible Indians who are willing to slaughter each other at the drop of a hat. In fact, I'm beginning to rethink my plans for living in Calcutta. If all this bloodshed is to keep breaking out, it won't be safe for us here."

"Where would you want to live then?" Howard said with a scowl and a gruff voice. "In Sing La?"

"No, I was thinking more of Maflong. Papa took me there when I was a child. It is a lovely place and there are schools where the children could go. I'm even thinking of taking Frances out of Queen's Hill and away from those lascivious boys at Turnbull's. There is a very nice school for girls there, called Pinewood. Jamie could go to St. Vincent's. It's run by the Christian Brothers, but it shouldn't really matter being RC."

"Yes, I've heard of Maflong," Howard said. "It's the hill resort the Assam tea planters use. But wouldn't that be a bit far away from me?"

"It's only a twenty-four hour rail journey from Panchpani, so you could make brief visits." She took a sip of gin and tonic from her glass.

"Ummm. You've certainly been hatching plans."

"Well, I have to think of something," Lydia said as she stubbed out her cigarette. "But in the end I would really prefer it if we all went to England. Papa always wanted to take me to England and put me in school there so I could get a decent education."

"Well, this is a big change of plan," Howard said, knocking out his pipe. "I don't want to leave this lovely country, unless I am forced out, that is."

"We *will* be," Lydia said. "You mark my words. If India gets its independence they won't want us here. They hate us. We would be made much more welcome at Home." She used the term "Home" as so many Anglo-Indians did when referring to England. "Can't we at least send Jamie there for admission into a boarding school? I could take him and leave him there, or we could find some friends who he could travel with."

"Well, I'll have to think about it. In the meanwhile, what other news do you have? Have you met up with Mohi, Eleanor, and Abigail?"

"Yes, we saw Mohi and Eleanor, and met a couple there — the Hamilton-Smyths."

"Oh, did you?" Howard looked away evasively. "What did you think of them?"

"Well the husband seemed all right, but the wife—I think her name was Veronica—seemed a bit of a cat. And then we visited Abigail."

"How is she?"

"Her usual bossy self."

"Is she all right with all these troubles? Most of it was in the north of the city where she lives."

"Yes, I phoned her the other day, and she's fine."

When things had settled down in the city, Howard took Lydia to Firpo's. First they dropped Jamie, Cissy, and Tulassa off at The Metro to see a matinee showing of *The Wizard of Oz*. Howard gave Jamie the money for the tickets and a taxi back to Mrs Trutwin's after the show, then he and Lydia proceeded to Firpo's and entered the cool interior of the tea-room downstairs, with its array of tables and chairs, and hanging crystal chandeliers.

They both had afternoon tea, and when Lydia excused herself to visit the powder room, Howard felt his eyes being covered unexpectedly from behind, and a voice in his ear said, "Cooee. Guess who?" He turned around, startled to see Veronica standing behind him.

"My God, what are you doing here?" Howard said.

"Having afternoon tea like yourself, you silly thing."

"Is Alex with you?"

"No. It's only little old me, all lonely and by myself at the table in the corner."

"Well, you'd better not stay. Lydia has just gone to the Ladies room and will be back at any moment." Panic laced his voice.

"Yes, I've met her at Mohi's. Of course, she didn't know I knew you."

"Thank God for that!"

"Why? Are you ashamed of me?" She pouted, stubbing out her lipstick-stained cigarette in the ash-tray. "She's a dull thing," Veronica said, "like a little brown sparrow. No wonder you're bored with her."

"Yes, yes," Howard said, "and you're a bird of paradise. But you better get a move on. Look, I'll try and meet up with you." Desperation filled his voice.

"When?"

"What about the lobby of the Great Eastern Hotel tomorrow at about four? I'll think up some excuse to give Lydia."

"Very well, my darling. I'll see you then." She gave him a parting hug and blew him a kiss as she returned to her table. It was in the nick of time, as Lydia exited the Ladies room and returned to their table.

"Whose cigarette stump is that in the ash-tray?" Lydia asked with a suspicious glance, when she spied the cigarette butt.

"Oh, just a woman who was passing by the table. She didn't have an ash-tray on hers." He hoped the explanation would satisfy his wife. It apparently did as she didn't question him further, much to his relief.

Before Howard returned to Panchpani, he paid a call to Mohi's. He didn't take Lydia with him as he told her that it would be mainly the Estate affairs they would be discussing. He hoped that he would not bump into the Hamilton-Smyths during his visit, as that would have made the situation very awkward. He had, however, met up with Veronica at the Great Eastern as arranged.

"How frustrating it is, darling, to see you sitting there," she had said, "and not being able to have a good screw. You'll have to let me know somehow when you are coming down again so that we can arrange something."

Howard returned to Panchpani the following week. In the meantime, Lydia formulated her plans to take Jamie and Cissy to Maflong, accompanied by Tulassa. She made enquiries about the hotels there, and finally wrote to "Ferngrove Hotel" and booked a suite of rooms for themselves. Then she went to the railway office in Free School Street and booked their tickets. They left from Sealdah Station the following week. It was a straightforward journey to Amangaon, which they reached the following morning, then they boarded a ferry to take them across the wide Brahmaputra river.

The ride on the ferry thrilled Jamie, as it was the first time he had ever travelled on a boat. Actually, it was a float attached alongside a paddle-steamer, with a large dining area on the deck, where tables covered with tablecloths and stiff napkins in the shape of ducks were arranged. They breakfasted on porridge and ham and eggs, followed by a strong cup of coffee. After that, Jamie stood at the bow of the float and watched the porpoises diving in and out of the muddy water in the bow-wave of the ferry. Here, he got into conversation with a priest who stood alongside.

"Hello, young fellow," the priest said." He introduced himself as Brother O'Leary, and told Jamie that he taught at St. Vincent's in Maflong. "You know the Ganges porpoise is completely blind," he went on to say. "The waters of the Ganges and Brahmaputra are so sandy and murky that they have evolved with no vision." When Jamie told him that he was soon to be admitted to St. Vincent's, the Brother became quite interested, and told Jamie all about the school. Jamie felt more comfortable now that he had met the Brother, who seemed friendly and talkative. When they parted, the Brother shook Jamie by the hand, and said he looked forward to seeing him again when he joined the school.

The Brahmaputra was so wide in places that you couldn't see the opposite bank. When they eventually arrived at the *ghat,* taxi-cabs were available for the 45 mile journey through Gauhati and on to Maflong. They broke journey at Nongpoh for a welcome cup of tea. Poor little Cissy was sick in the car, and Tulassa held her head out through the front car window to throw up onto the side of the vehicle. They reached Maflong at about four in the afternoon, and the taxi took them straight to Ferngrove Hotel.

CHAPTER 29

Maflong was traditionally called "The Scotland of the East." It was located high up in the Khasi Hills of Assam, and it reminded the British of Scotland with its rolling hills covered in forests of Scots Pine. It had wide open spaces and meandering roads. An artificial lake stood in the centre of the town with a wooden bridge across. Unlike Sing La, it did not have precipitous mountainsides, and of course lacked the splendour of the snowy mountains in the distance. The climate was temperate and it neither became too hot in the summer nor too cold in the winter. But it could be rainy, as it neighboured the rainiest place in the world—Cherrapunji, and was prone to earthquakes. The local Khasi people were somewhat Burmese-looking, and the female member of the family was head of the household and the dominant personality in the marriage. They were mainly Christians—Roman Catholics, and far outnumbered the Hindus and Muslims, so it was unlikely there would be any communal trouble in the region.

The town boasted of two rather run-down cinemas, a few restaurants, a gymkhana club, a golf course, and also a racecourse. A number of shops and bazaars populated the town centre. The two main schools were St. Vincent's for boys, and Pinewood for girls. As Maflong bordered Burma, a lot of military activity had taken place in the area during the War, and dumps where lorries and other abandoned and partly destroyed army vehicles were deposited, littered the area. Also in the aftermath of the War, a host of American candies, like Butter Fingers, Tootsie Rolls, and Babe Ruth flooded the local shops.

Ferngrove Hotel seemed reasonably well-appointed. It consisted of a main building and various surrounding cottages covering a wide area of slopes, with connecting pathways. Like all the houses in Maflong, these were lightly constructed—lathe and plaster walls, whitewashed canvass ceiling cloths and corrugated iron roofs, as there had been a serious earthquake in 1897, where almost every building had collapsed and completely demolished the town.

Lydia had a fairly comfortable suite in one of the cottages. It boasted two bedrooms—one for the children and one for herself, with a small attached sitting room. A French couple, Madame and Monsieur Poirier who were rather finicky, insisting that all guests took their meals in the large dining room, managed the hotel. All children were expected to have their meal times separately. Lydia preferred her and the children's to be brought to the cottage by a bearer on a tray, so they could all eat together, as little Cissy was fussy about her food. However, the food was good and Continental. Lydia had grown rather tired of the curries most of the hotels regularly served. As far as Tulassa was concerned, although she slept on the floor of the children's bedroom, she took her meals with the rest of the hotel's servants, and also availed of the toilet facilities afforded to them. It was customary that Indian servants never shared the lavatories of the sahibs and memsahibs.

Over the days that followed, they engaged in walks around the locale to familiarise themselves with the roads, or taxi rides to various places of interest, like the Tussore Silk Farm, where mulberry trees were grown on surrounding slopes to feed the silkworms that were reared on wire-mesh beds covered with the leaves. They were conducted through the entire process of silk production from cocoon to moth to the spinning and weaving of the Tussore silk itself. This was of special interest to Jamie who was particularly fascinated by the large, dark enclosure that housed the enormous silk-moths. Poor little Cissy screamed her head off as these insects fluttered around her in the dark, so Tulassa had to take her out of the room.

The family didn't stay at Fern Grove for very long. It was too expensive, and Lydia didn't get on with the Poriers, so she looked around for cheaper lodgings, and eventually found one in Lai Mukhra which was about three miles distant from Maflong town centre, and at a higher elevation. It was also closer to St. Vincent's and Pinewood where she hoped she might get Frances admitted the following year. "Peach Grove" was a guest house run by a Roman Catholic priest of Indo-Portuguese descent, Father Da Silva, who had taken the vow of chastity but not of poverty, so was able to run this establishment, together with his sister and family. It comprised a large rambling central building, with a few cottages surrounding it. The grounds were extensive, with plum and peach trees, and a cement tennis court below. The food was of rather poor quality and the service at the dinner table sloppy, served by a bearer in an ill-fitting and rather dirty uniform.

A handful of guests resided there—mainly Anglo-Indian visitors from Calcutta, and a few permanent residents, which included an eccentric old lady, Miss Perkins. After dinner, they would retire to the drawing room, furnished with overstuffed sofas and easy chairs, for coffee and parlour games. An upright piano lived in one corner of the room.

Despite the general tattiness of this establishment, Jamie rather liked it, and once he had become acquainted with the other guests, participated in the after dinner games, and sing-songs at the piano. Miss Perkins, with arthritic fingers, played popular old-fashioned songs on the out-of-tune keys, singing in her high-pitched, cracked voice. His mother, on the other hand, did not enjoy the social activities, and retired to her bedroom in the adjacent cottage, where she had a small suite.

Jamie also chummed up with a little Indian boy called Ignatius, that Father Da Silva's sister, Mrs Xavier, had adopted. The Santhali boy had dark skin, and reminded Jamie of Jubra in a way, although he was a sad little creature in comparison, and treated more as a servant than an adoptive child. Mrs Xavier's own children also bullied him terribly, particularly her young son Rodrigo. Jamie became friendly with three brothers, the Fraser boys, who lived on Uplands Road leading up to the guest house, and who attended St. Vincent's.

Lydia took Jamie to visit the school, and the Principal, Brother O'Brien, saw them. Jamie did grumble to his mother, saying he was rather fed-up with all these different decisions concerning his schooling. He was rather unimpressed with St. Vincent's too, as it reminded him very much of Turnbull's in Kumsong. However, Roman Catholic Irish Brothers ran this institution, and Brother O'Brien seemed a cheerful enough person, as he showed them around the school. Of course, again it was only three months to the final examinations in November, after which the school would break up for another three months for the winter holidays. They were now into September, and Brother O'Brien advised that Jamie would have to study hard in order to pass the exams. "Perhaps he could get some extra tuition by engaging a private tutor to coach him," he said.

Of course, his mother's true intention was to persuade Howard to send Jamie to England for his schooling, so St. Vincent's would only be a stop-gap measure. In the meanwhile, he was aware that she'd determined to apply to some schools in England for a prospectus, which she would show to his father.

So, Jamie started at St. Vincent's the following week. Since he was already friendly with the Fraser brothers, the youngest of whom was in Jamie's class, he didn't feel so strange starting in a new school, and didn't have to run the gauntlet of the usual teasing that a new boy had to endure, as he had with the younger boys at Turnbull's. Also, most of the day scholars lived in Lai Mukhra, several on the same road that ran up the hill to Peach Grove, and they would all walk home in a group, leaving their friends off at various points, so Jamie didn't lack for friends or company.

He did feel sorry for little Ignatius though, and one day after returning home from school, he found the little boy tied by his hands and feet to a post, in the hot afternoon sun.

Jamie approached the boy. "What are you doing here?"

"Father," he said and sniffed, referring to the priest. "He gave me a beating and tied me up here because he said I stole four annas from his purse." A big tear rolled down his dusty cheek.

"But you didn't, did you?"

"No, I never did. But he didn't believe me."

"Can I get you anything? Some water?"

"Please, yes. I'm very thirsty. I haven't had anything to eat or drink all day."

Jamie hurried to the main building and asked the bearer for a glass of water from the dining room. As he was taking this to Ignatius, he bumped into Father Da Silva.

"Where are you taking that water?" the priest asked in a brusque voice.

"To give to Ignatius," Jamie said.

"No. He's not to have any," Father Da Silva said. "He is being punished." With that, he took the glass out of Jamie's hand. "And you are not to talk to him."

Jamie was astounded at the priest's harshness and cruelty. He could not understand how a supposed man of God could meter out this severe treatment. Another instance of the priest's cruelty was when Jamie noticed that a tatty pet parrot kept in a cage almost lacked a beak. When he enquired of the other Xavier children why this was so, one of them replied, "Oh, the parrot bit Father one day. So he shaved its beak off with his razor."

The Irish Christian Brothers were also strict disciplinarians and the boys would often get whacked on their hands in the classrooms with a formidable strap. One of the Brothers, Bro. Garrett, had a terrible fear of mad dogs, and often the school bell that was suspended from a tower, would be rung in alarm if a stray dog was found wandering on the playing fields. Bro. Garret would approach the animal with his shotgun, and as it stood wagging its tail, would blow its brains out. This fate would often befall some faithful pet that had followed its owner to school.

The Pasteur Institute was close at hand—the only one in India at the time. If your pet or a friend's dog ever bit you, you would wait for a few weeks and keep it under observation, then if the dog were to die suddenly, its brain would be taken out and sent to the Pasteur Institute for examination. If the analysis discovered the rabies virus, then the person bitten would have to undergo a course of painful injections in the stomach. However, if the dog were a stray, you would have to have the injections anyway.

Besides the Fraser brothers—Malcolm, Fredrick, and Brian—he soon got friendly with all the others in the day-scholar group. There were the two Berry brothers, the Wrigley brothers, the Weatherall brothers, and a very naughty boy by the name of David Monk, who was the chief instigator of all the mischief within the group. All the boys lived at different points along the Uplands Road that rose up towards Peach Grove, then flattened out in a long straight lane. They were a rough and ready lot, but likeable, and Jamie had never made so many friends at one time in his life. David Monk, who lived close by, would often come to play with Jamie after school. He had a very strict father, who would frequently give him bare-bottom canings, and David would show his wheals off proudly to Jamie, which brought back vivid memories of his own caning by Mr Stalkey.

On weekends, picnics would often be organised by the boys. It was usually to places like the Spread Eagle Falls or the Ward Lake, or even on the Maflong golf course. The boys took all the picnic stuff in haversacks, which consisted of things like spaghetti or baked beans, which they would warm up on a campfire, made from pinecones. On one such occasion, the Berry brothers took their two fox terriers, and when the younger boy, Peter, had to take a crap behind the bushes, the dogs followed him and rolled around in his excrement, much to the consternation of the other boys, who dispersed at the speed of lightning, climbing up trees when the dogs came running up towards them. They also made excursions to the local outdoor swimming pool near Crinoline Falls. All in all, it was a happy time for Jamie.

His mother was happy too, and she became a member of the Maflong Club and would often spend an afternoon in the reading room browsing through the latest issue of "The Vogue" or "Tatler," or the Indian society magazine "The Onlooker." Here, she met a French lady, a Mrs Deville who had a young son, Maurice, about Jamie's age. She was the wife of the local dentist and had a vivacious personality. Lydia preferred the company of Europeans rather than people from her own Anglo-Indian community.

Neither Lydia or Jamie were that keen on Mrs Deville, who pursued his mother's company. She often breezed in unexpectedly on visits. On these occasions she would bring her boy, Maurice, to play with Jamie.

"Ah—my Maurice ees so lonely. It ees so nice 'e has a leetle friend to play with—no?"

Like his mother, Jamie was not very keen on Maurice either. He was a small boy with a chubby face, dark straight hair and prominent ears, which would burn bright red if he were embarrassed. He had rather fishy grey eyes and large front teeth. He found the boy clingy and rather effeminate.

One day, Maurice invited Jamie over to his house. The large rambling double-storied house lay at the end of Uplands Road, and stood atop a hillock. It had vast, neglected grounds which tumbled down the hillside, with hedges, shrubs, and statuettes which poked up amidst the foliage. The house had numerous rooms and passages, decorated with African masks, assagais, and shields—procured no doubt when Mr Deville was in East Africa. He was the leading dental surgeon in the town and enjoyed a small but select clientele, mainly among the tea-planting community. Maurice sneaked Jamie in to the dental surgery, which was unoccupied, as it was a holiday and both Mr and Mrs Deville were out. The dentist's chair fascinated Jamie. He sat in it and Maurice showed him how to adjust it until it was in a reclining position. The object of Jamie's interest was a gleaming white human skull with equally white gleaming teeth, which sat atop a pedestal. The skull wore a mortarboard at a somewhat jaunty angle. The array of gleaming instruments of torture also held his attention, as did the dental posters on the wall, showing pictures of blackened gums and decaying teeth. It satisfied his morbid curiosity.

As it was a beautiful sunny day—the weather in India was always bright and sunny after the Monsoon—Maurice suggested they go berry-picking, and armed with a wicker basket they wandered down the hillside looking for raspberry bushes that grew around in profusion. The wild raspberries of the region were small, round, and orange in colour, and they soon had enough to quarter-fill the basket. Afterwards, they lay on the long grass on their backs, looking up into a blue and cotton-ball sky.

Maurice's moist hand took hold of Jamie's, and he said, "Are you feeling skittish, Jamie?"

"What do you mean—skittish?"

"Well, you know. Sexy."

He looked at Maurice and noticed a small lump in his shorts.

"We could go upstairs to my bedroom, you know," Maurice said, "and fool around."

"What do you mean?"

"Take our pants off and show our things to each other."

Jamie had rarely indulged in sex play with the other boys when he'd been at Fern Hill, and even Aaron, despite all his talk about sex, had never approached him in such a fashion.

"Then there are other things we can do," Maurice continued. "I'll show you. It'll feel really nice, and there's no one in the house, so we won't be disturbed." Then his tone turned entreating. "You do like me, don't you? I like *you* a lot."

Jamie lied, "Yes, I like you. But I don't feel like it, and I think I'd better be going home anyway."

A look of disappointment crossed Maurice's face, but Jamie rose to his feet. Maurice's ears glowed bright red. Jamie determined not to see Maurice again, if he could possibly avoid it, and made his way homeward.

The happy days continued into November. Jamie sat for the final school examinations and passed by the skin of his teeth. Lydia had employed an elderly gentleman, Mr Dewsberry, to coach him after school. A retired schoolteacher, he occupied a little bungalow beside the tennis court at Peach Grove. He lived in as one of the hotel's permanent residents. Jamie enjoyed his lessons with Mr Dewsberry, as the kindly old gentleman would take no end of trouble to explain things in answer to Jamie's many questions, and would refer to his library of books for any he did not know the answers to. He was also an excellent mathematician and helped Jamie considerably in this, his weakest subject.

Jamie celebrated his twelfth birthday in the first week of November, and Lydia arranged a party for him and all his friends in the drawing room of Peach Grove. She also invited Mrs Deville and, to Jamie's discomfort, Maurice. Mrs Deville had coached him into performing a little dance — the "Sailor's Hornpipe," and he did this tapping his toes daintily, dressed-up appropriately in a sailor's suit, while Miss Perkins played the piece on the piano. He sidled up to Jamie on the sofa when he had finished, and whispered, "Did you like it? I did it especially for you, and it took me ages to practice."

Besides Jamie's friends, Lydia had also invited some of the house guests, like Mr Dewsberry, and also Mrs Xavier and family. Of course, poor little Ignatius was not allowed to attend. All the party food and the birthday cake had been ordered from "Morellos," an Italian restaurant and confectioners. They played party games—like Dumb Charades, Pass the Parcel, and Irish Whispers, which all the adults alike participated in. All in all, the event was a great success.

Now that St. Vincent's had broken up for the school holidays, and winter approached, Lydia decided to take the children to Calcutta again. It was customary for people living in the hills to escape the colder climate and holiday in warmer climes, as the weather in the plains remained temperate and pleasant. Things had calmed down in the city, according to reports in the newspapers, and Lydia undertook to stay at the Evergreens Hotel in Sudder Street, as it was cheaper than Mrs Trutwin's and closer to places like the New Market. However, it was in a more squalid part of the city.

So, Lydia made the rail reservations and ordered a taxi to transport them to Pandu *ghat*, which lay on the banks of the river, to board the ferry for the journey across the

Brahmaputra, and to the connecting railway station on the opposite side.

She wrote to Howard and told him of her plans, and hoped he would be able to make another visit to Calcutta, at least for Christmas, and also told him to bring Frances down with him, as she would be on her three months' vacation from school.

CHAPTER 30

The Evergreens Hotel was a far cry from the posh Mrs Trutwin's. It lay at the slummier end of Sudder Street, comprised a four storied building in the front, a small building in the middle which housed the office downstairs and the kitchen above, and a double storied building at the rear, with rooms downstairs and a large dining room upstairs. A long cemented open passageway to the left connected all the buildings with a wall alongside, and a gateway guarded the entrance. A cheap and cheerful place, it usually accommodated people like the teachers from the hill schools on vacation for the winter holidays. Jamie was overjoyed to discover that the Fraser brothers were also spending their holidays with their parents at Evergreens.

He and his family stayed in a large room downstairs in the front building. It had a small ante-room attached, where Tulassa could sleep, and an iron-barred window that looked onto the busy street. Bold rhesus monkeys, sometimes carrying a baby on their back, would often peer through the iron bars, sometimes putting in a tentative hand imploring for food like a Calcutta beggar. Jamie would occasionally give them a banana or some peanuts. His mother warned him not to encourage these creatures, which could sometimes be aggressive and bite. Fortunately, the windows could be closed with wooden Venetian-blind shutters painted a dark green, and there were also glass doors inside that could be shut to keep out the noise from the street. All the floors of the rooms were paved with crazy china, and if you ever dropped an anna bit, it proved impossible to find. A doorway led out from the main bedroom directly onto the outside passageway.

Jamie's friends occupied a large suite on the top floor of the first building, which had a big sitting room and two bedrooms, to accommodate the family. Mr Fraser was a big, fair man with red hair, and his wife, a small darker-skinned lady with her black hair taken back in a neat bun. She looked somewhat Burmese in appearance.

The boys would often play on the terrace, climbing up a rickety spiral staircase that ran up the side of the building, and fly their kites. Jamie had little experience at kite-flying, but the Frasers were well-practised in the art, and soon taught him. High-flying kites dotted the skies above the city, and kite battles would often ensue. The first few yards of the kite-string would be coated in *manja* – a mixture of flour paste and powdered glass. This was required for cutting the string of another kite. The rest of the string would be very long, and wound on to a spindle called a *latai*. This controlled the kite in the sky, and for sending it up or allowing it to dive downwards. Great kite battles would take place over the city, and once a kite had been cut and came floating down from the sky, a mad scramble by the street urchins would ensue, in their efforts to retrieve the prize.

The Frazer boys were well-acquainted with city life, and they would take Jamie with them on excursions, jumping on and off moving trams and buses, and going around the New Market and tasting the cheeses that the shopkeepers often offered as a free sample, but never buying anything. The vendors soon caught on to this wheeze and shooed the boys away whenever they approached. "You are very naughty babas! All the time you are eating, eating, and never buying. Go away from my shop."

It was the same when they explored toy shops, playing with the goods on show. They would often be kicked out of the shop by the irate store-keeper.

Like other parents of their day, mothers and fathers rarely accompanied children around on their excursions, but allowed them to wander about freely, and probably get into no end of mischief, and even danger. They would sometimes balance on the parapet of the terrace as a dare, or slide down the banisters of the long staircase that came down from the fourth floor.

An irritable elderly lady lived in a room built on the terrace, and would tell the boys off if they played there and made a noise. One day, they were playing football and Fredrick kicked the ball, which ricocheted off a wall and continued towards the lady's front door. At the same moment, she opened it and the ball bounced up and knocked the cigarette she was smoking out of her mouth. She didn't say anything, but just glared at the boys, picked up the football, and threw it over the balcony and onto the street below.

Another of the other permanent residents was an old colonel, who owned a female Dalmatian, and one day he asked the boys if they wouldn't mind taking her for a walk as he wasn't feeling very well. "But don't let any other dogs near her," he said, "because there might be a fight." He didn't tell the boys that the bitch was, in fact, on heat. As they walked the dog along Sudder Street in the direction of the *Maidan* beyond, the dog attracted a host of pi-dogs that followed in a line. One of them, a large husky mongrel, soon mounted her, and they got stuck together. The boys waited patiently until they separated again, and when they returned the dog to its owner, he asked, "Did she get into any fights?"

"No," the elder of the boys, Malcolm, said, "but a pi-dog came sniffing around, and they got stuck together."

A look of utter fury passed over the colonel's face, and it turned as red as a turkey-cock's. He snatched the leash from the boy, took the dog inside the room, and muttered, "Fucking little bastards!"

Jamie sometimes spent sleepovers with the Fraser brothers. They welcomed him as another brother, and since he had none of his own, he felt a certain camaraderie with them. They would play rough-and-tumble games — like pillow fights — and they all slept in three single beds placed together to make it into a large one. Although Malcolm was the eldest, it was the middle brother, Fredrick, who was the tallest. The youngest, Brian, was the same age as Jamie but bigger and stockier.

Just before Christmas, Lydia took the children to the New Market to shop for presents and the Christmas decorations. These were sold in the centre of the market in various stalls, and Lydia bought a small artificial Xmas tree, tinsel, and coloured glass balls with which to decorate it.

She received a telegram from Howard saying that he would be coming down with Frances for Christmas. They arrived a few days later.

"Mummee," Frances screamed, as she hugged Lydia. Then she embraced Jamie and kissed little Cissy. The hotel *durwan* brought in her tin trunk and bedroll, and Lydia noticed that Howard had no luggage with him. When she asked him about this, he replied:

"Mine's still in the taxi. I'll be going on to the Great Eastern, where I'll be staying for the next few days."

Inwardly, Lydia felt glad of this, as it would avoid the prospect of overnight sex, which she expected Howard would demand, having been on his own all this while. But instead she said, "That's very posh. I suppose you think it all right for the likes of me to stay in a cheap-jack place like this while you're off to stay in that expensive hotel."

"It's only for a few nights, Liddie. I'll be going back soon after Christmas. I thought it would save you the trouble of moving into a two-bedroom suite here to accommodate all of us."

"That's very considerate of you," she said in a voice heavy with sarcasm. "I'm only staying here to save your precious money."

"Yes, I realise this, Liddie," Howard said in a gentle tone, in an effort to console his wife. "Look, I can always change my plans."

"No, you go ahead, since you've already made the arrangements."

Howard did not stay long as the taxi was still waiting, so he said his goodbyes and went off with an, "I'll see you all tomorrow, then."

The family sat on the cane suite at one end of the room near the window, and Frances filled her mother in with all the news of her school year. Lydia thought she would wait for a more appropriate moment to broach the subject of her plans to remove Frances from Queen's Hill and admit her to Pinewood. For the time being she was content to exchange family news, although she had written to Frances at school quite regularly to keep her abreast of events.

That evening, Howard sat in his hotel bedroom smoking his pipe. He waited in anticipation. Soon it came, a light tapping on the door. He opened it, and Veronica stood on the threshold.

"Darling," she said as she hugged him. She gave him a long, enduring kiss. "Oh how I've missed you, and how glad I am that we can see each other again in private. I've been simply longing for you all these months."

"I've missed you too," Howard said. "It's been lonely for me in Panchpani without a woman, seeing that Lydia's moved to Maflong."

"Where is she now?"

"She's at The Evergreens Hotel. I've been to see her and made an excuse why I couldn't stay there. I really came here so that we could be together, dearest."

"Oh that's wonderful, darling. Look, let's get on with it. I'm simply dying for you and can't wait a minute longer. Then we can talk at our leisure." She placed her handbag on the chair, and undressed. Naked, she lay on the bed, with her legs spread wide apart.

Howard took off his clothes, and looked down at her. As usual, she was clean-shaven around the area of her vulva.

"I see you're ready for me, darling," she said, nodding at his erection. She flipped over on her stomach and adopted a kneeling position, her legs still spread wide apart. "Let's do it doggie style," she said. "I want to be taken like a bitch."

Howard got on the bed and knelt behind her. Then he entered with a deep thrust.

"Oh! Oh! Oh!" she cried as he pumped away. "Harder, darling. Harder."

He withdrew momentarily. Veronica reached between her legs and took hold of him. Then she guided him into her other tight little orifice. He grunted as he penetrated her, and she moaned in agony and ecstasy. "Oh darling. Deeper. Deeper. Oh! Oh! Oh my God!" she screamed as he thrust in and out, beads of perspiration collecting on his forehead. Then he cried out as he came.

They lay back on the pillows, completely exhausted.

"That was wonderful, darling," Veronica said as she placed a cigarette between her lips. "Want one?"

"Yes," Howard replied.

She took another cigarette from her case and placed it alongside the other held in her lips, and flicked her lighter and lit them together. She handed one over to Howard.

"So, I suppose you won't be having sex with Lydia this time around."

"I don't have it with her much anyway."

"Yes, she's a dull little creature. I can't imagine what she would be like in bed."

"Stiff and wooden."

"I suppose she only approves of the missionary position."

"Yes, that's the nub of it. Now that she's given me three children she considers her duties as a wife are over. She believes sex is for procreation not recreation."

"So, no sex for pleasure."

"Hardly at all," Howard said, and his lips drooped in gloom.

"And there's no one else you can turn to."

"No. I don't affiliate with the native women at all."

"My poor darling," Veronica said. "It's the same case with me. Alex is completely incapable now, and I don't have anyone else to turn to."

"Liar."

"Oh you rotten beast! Finish that cigarette and let's have another go. I don't want to waste a minute of our precious time together."

Just before Christmas Day, Howard took Lydia and the children to a children's fancy-dress party at Firpo's. Jamie went as a pirate, and Frances as Little Bo-Peep. Cissy dressed up as a fairy. Lydia hired the children's costumes at a local fancy-dress shop in the city. A Father Christmas attended the party, and all the children received gifts. Groups of children, singing Christmas songs, provided the entertainment, as well as clowns and a mimer dressed up as Charlie Chaplin. The tables were laid out with party food, and the children gorged themselves on cakes and other goodies. At the end of proceedings, someone with a long pole burst the customary kohi bag — huge kite-paper containers, in the shape of a fish, ship, or aeroplane suspended from the ceiling and filled with puffed rice and an assortment of small toys and sweets. When burst, the contents rained down on the floor, and a mad scramble by the children followed, to find the treats amongst the scattered rice.

On Christmas Day, the family attended the morning service at St. John's Church, which was located northwest of Government House. It had been modelled on St. Martins-in-the-Field in London and was one of the oldest churches in the city. Lydia wasn't much of a church-goer and her visits to church were confined to Easter and Christmas. They had their Christmas dinner at the Great Eastern, which Howard arranged, and to little Cissy's confusion all the servants serving at the table were dressed up as Father Christmases.

"How can there be so many?" Cissy piped up. "I thought there was only one."

"They're just his helpers," Lydia said, and then gave Frances a knowing wink as her daughter giggled.

After the Christmas festivities, Howard visited Lydia at The Evergreens. They sat in wicker chairs in the courtyard of the hotel, with their drinks.

"Are you really serious about having Jamie sent to England and admitted into school there?" Howard said.

"Yes, I am very serious," Lydia replied.

"Isn't he getting on at St. Vincent's?"

"Yes, in a fashion," Lydia said, "but the boys are a rough lot and his behaviour and manners are becoming worse. His accent is also deteriorating, and I would like him to speak more like an English boy."

Howard looked thoughtful. Then said, "Actually, I was speaking to Mohi the other day and I told him about your plans. He, Eleanor, and Zerina are going to England on holiday in April for a few months, and Mohi said he would be delighted to take Jamie with them and admit him into school there."

"Oh, they didn't mention this when I saw them."

"Perhaps they hadn't formulated their plans then. Mohi has to go anyway, because there are meetings in London between the British government and the Indian princes to discuss what will happen to them if India should be given its independence."

"That would be very helpful. It would save me having to take him and, of course, you never seem to have the time." Lydia's resentment was obvious.

"Yes, well, I can't very well leave things in limbo at Panchpani while I take a few months off to put Jamie into school. Did you get those school prospectuses? I would like to have a look at them to see if I can afford the fees."

"Yes, I'll show them to you," Lydia said. "I suppose you will say that they're all too expensive for you on the insufficient salary you're always complaining about."

"Well actually, Mohi has given me a very generous increase. He also offered to help out with the fare if need be. And he said he can make all the arrangements for Jamie's admission when they get to England. He suggested Wellingborough School in Northamptonshire, where Eleanor's brother went when he was a boy."

"That's one big problem solved then," Lydia said with relief in her voice. "I've been worrying and worrying about Jamie's schooling ever since Fern Hill closed down. Now it seems that at last he will have a decent education in England — something I have always wanted for him. It's been such a *tamasha* chopping and changing his schools."

"I'll tell Mohi, then, of your decision and we can get things moving. What have you decided to do about Frances?"

"I really want to get her away from Queen's Hill and the influence of her friends, like Maureen Kingsley. I'll admit her into Pinewood in Maflong as a day scholar, so I can keep an eye on her."

"Have you spoken to her yet?"

"No, not yet. She only has one more year at school, so it shouldn't make a great deal of difference."

"Well, I hope you're making the right decisions about the children's education — especially Jamie. He will feel very isolated in a strange school in a strange country, and I hope he won't be unhappy."

"It'll be the best for him," Lydia said. "And, who knows? With all this trouble going on in India we will probably very well land up in England ourselves in a few years' time."

"I expect you could be right."

"I am sure I am right," Lydia said. "It will be impossible for us to live in India under an Indian government. Things will change and they'll expect us to become like Indians."

Howard mocked, "Horror of horrors!"

"Yes, you may very well laugh. But mark my words. It will happen. Then you'll laugh on the other side of your face."

Howard ignored the remark. He filled his pipe with tobacco and said at length. "I'd like to take Jamie back with me to Panchpani for the rest of his school holidays."

"Oh, would you?" Lydia said. "In that case, I'll take Frances back with me to Maflong. I don't want to be on my own, and she'll be company for me and Cissy."

"Yes, you might as well do that. The admissions start in March, don't they?"

"Yes." Lydia nodded. "It'll give her a few months to get used to Maflong. I'm sure she'll like it there, and being a day-scholar will be a change for her."

"There'll be no need to have Jamie re-admitted to St. Vincent's then, if your plans work out. I can bring him back to Calcutta and you can meet him here for your last goodbyes before handing him over to Mohi and Eleanor. It will be a sad occasion."

"Yes, during the Easter Holidays would be best," Lydia said. "Then it won't interfere with Frances' schooling."

"Well, it looks as if everything has been settled now. I'm glad we've been able to have this chat about the children. I do miss not having you at Panchpani though, Liddie dear."

When Lydia told Frances and Jamie of her plans regarding their futures and the reasons for her decisions, she was met with howls of dismay. Frances was the first.

"I don't want to leave Queen's Hill, Mummee. I've only got a year more to go then I'll be finished school. And I'm not even friendly with Maureen Kingsley anymore."

Jamie said, "I don't want to go to bloody England. I've heard of their snobby, posh schools there, and I wouldn't fit in."

"How *dare* you use swearwords in front of me!" Lydia said, anger in her voice. "You see, this is the very reason I want to take you out of St. Vincent's and those badly-mannered ruffians you're mixing with."

"I'm sorry, Mum," Jamie said with a note of apology in his voice. "But I'm happy there, and I've made so many friends."

"Yes, like those dreadful Fraser boys who are leading you into such mischief. No, my mind is made up," she said firmly, hands on hips. "And you'll have to abide by my decisions, like them or not, so that's that."

However, Jamie was happier when she told him that Howard would be taking him back to Panchpani.

"Oh good," he said, "then I can see Blackie and Gingernut again." He was going to add "Jubra," but then remembered he was no longer there.

"Anyway," Lydia said to Frances, "you'll like Maflong. It's a lovely place, just like Scotland, and Pinewood is a very good school. Besides, I've been talking to your father, and it's likely that we will all settle in England, if India should get its independence."

The children didn't argue anymore. When their mother made up her mind about something, it was final.

CHAPTER 31

Being back in Panchpani made Jamie happy. It was good to see the smiling, familiar faces of the servants, and Gingernut and Blackie. The first thing he did was to get Kaila to saddle his pony up so he could take him for a ride. Of course, he sadly missed his friend Jubra, and also missed the company of Aaron, but he chummed up with *Humni* and *Thumni*, Dawa and Tulassa's children, so at least he had someone to play with. He didn't see much of his father, as Howard was always busy with the Estate affairs and toured around for most of the day.

However, the *Mela* was in full swing, so there was plenty of entertainment for Jamie, as he wandered around with *Humni* and *Thumni*. They attended the circus again and visited various side-shows, or the magicians with their clever tricks—including the famous Indian rope-trick. He could never work out how the rope would stiffen and rise high into the air from the basket below, and the little boy who climbed it would suddenly disappear from view as he reached the top, only to reappear a moment later at ground level. He guessed that some form of mass hypnotism was used to dupe the spectators into believing this was actually happening.

Then there were other incidents to keep the children amused. One day, a train came off the rails a short distance from Panchpani station. The front wheels of the steam engine hung right off the tracks, causing it to list. As the boys stood in the shadow of the engine, looking with fascination at the huge mass of iron and hissing steam, an official came bustling along waving his arms and telling them to move back as the engine could easily topple over and come crashing down on them.

Another amusing incident was when the *monkey-wallah* came around to Lal Kothi, carrying a monkey on his shoulder, and rattling his tom-toms. At the promise of payment of a few rupees, the man began the performance. The monkey suffered the indignity of being dressed in gaudy clothes and made to act out little plays in mime. Its master would sing and sway to the rhythms of his tom-toms, which he held in one hand and operated by twisting his wrist backwards and forwards.

To add a bit of variety to the act, Jamie suggested that the monkey ride a goat that was tethered nearby. The *monkey-wallah's* response was a firm "No," but when Jamie offered him two rupees more, he consented and the deal was clinched.

"Just walk the goat around the garden with the monkey on its back," Jamie said. They watched in anticipation as the monkey was placed gingerly on the goat's back. The goat, outraged by this liberty-taking, jumped about like a bucking bronco before bolting off with its petrified rider, clinging on for dear life.

Round and round the front lawn they went with the *monkey-wallah* in pursuit. Once the man managed to trap and hold the goat, the poor little monkey was pulled off with wisps of pale goat-hair still trailing from its tiny fists. Quite understandably, the *monkey-wallah* thought it expedient to cross them off his itinerary, for they never saw him again!

The days and weeks seemed to pass all too quickly for Jamie, and Easter fast approached. The time soon came for him to return to Calcutta to meet up with his mother, who was coming down from Maflong for the Easter break. His father couldn't take Jamie down to the city, as he was too busy with his work, so he arranged with Dawa, accompanied by his sons, *Humni* and *Thumni*, to take him. It would also give Dawa and the twins the chance of seeing Tulassa again, after such a long separation.

Howard saw them off at the station. He shook Jamie by the hand as he bid him farewell. "Chin up and all that, old chap," he said. Then Jamie suddenly gave his father a hug as tears sprung to his eyes. How long would it be before he saw him again? Or, for that matter, the servants, Gingernut, and Blackie. He stood on the threshold of a completely new life in a new school and a new country, and he was apprehensive to say the least. They reached Calcutta the following morning and went straight to The Evergreens by taxi. It was nice to see his mother again and his sisters. Frances chatted away to him gaily. She had settled into Pinewood School and seemed to be quite happy there, and had made new friends. Also, she enjoyed being a day-scholar and not having to abide by the rigours of boarding-school routine and the separation from her family.

A few days later, Eleanor and Zerina came to visit and take charge of Jamie. They would be leaving for England in the next few days.

"Don't worry about the boy," Eleanor said to Lydia. "We'll take good care of him. Mohi will see that he is outfitted for school and purchase everything in the Prospectus from one of the big London shops."

"How will we pay for it all?" Lydia said, worried.

"Oh, don't worry about the expense. Mohi will pay for it, and Howard can square up with him later. He will also pay the admission fees for the first term, until Howard can set up a system with the school. Just leave everything in our hands, dear."

"It is ever so good of you, doing all this for us," Lydia said with gratitude in her voice. "I don't know what we would have done without your help."

"It's a pleasure, dear. I only hope that Jamie will adjust to the school and not be unhappy as I was when dear Papa left me in England."

Jamie listened to their conversation with mixed feelings. He felt nervous and excited all at the same time. And, he was homesick before he'd even left.

"At least he will get a good education there, and mix with decent children—not like the riff-raff boys at Turnbull's and St. Vincent's." Lydia said.

"Yes, Wellingborough is a well-established school, and my brother George received a good education there. Previously, he had been at St. Paul's in Sing La. Unlike me, George adjusted to the school, although when he went into the town once, the street-urchins knocked his top-hat off with a stone." She gave a little giggle.

It was soon time to say their last goodbyes. Jamie gave his mother a hug and a kiss. "I'm going to miss you, Mum," he said, and tears filled his eyes.

"You be a good boy now," Lydia said, "and listen to Uncle Mohi and Auntie Eleanor." She wiped the lipstick off his cheek, where she had kissed him, with a handkerchief.

With goodbyes to Frances, Cissy, and of course Tulassa, Dawa, and the twins, they drove off in the Bentley to their residence at Alipore.

Jamie and Zerina stood at the stern of the P&O steamer, RMS "Strathnaver," watching the Gateway to India in Bombay fade away into the distance. They had travelled from Howrah Station in Calcutta on the Bombay Mail to Victoria Terminus, on this luxury express, which took them two days and two nights. Now, as the shores of India disappeared, Jamie felt a wave of sadness pass over him. He was leaving his familiar world to enter a new one—one that he was uncertain of. Everything he knew and loved was being left behind. He would miss India with its excitement; its colour; its sights; its sounds; its smells. He had heard that England was grey and gloomy—as he was feeling now.

He couldn't help but feel this was the end of an era.

"Don't look so sad, Jamie," Zerina said. "Papa and I will be going to Panchpani soon, and I'll look after Gingernut for you. I'll even take him for rides. And I'll write to you often—I promise."

"I'll write to you too," Jamie said.

He took Zerina's hand in his and they made their way back to their cabin.

EPILOGUE

In August of 1947 — ten years earlier than Mohi's prediction — India achieved its independence from Great Britain, with much pomp and ceremony. The country had been divided up between Hindu India and Muslim Pakistan — done all two quickly by Lord Mountbatten who was made Viceroy of India and given the job of partitioning the country. Those last years had been a tumultuous time, with the assassination of Mahatma Gandhi in 1948, and as Howard had correctly predicted, a blood-bath followed the leaving of the British, with hundreds of thousands of Hindus, Muslims, and Sikhs massacring each other. There were also three armed conflicts between Hindu India and neighbouring Muslim Pakistan. Following independence of both countries, an exodus began; the British were the first to leave, followed closely on their heels by the Domiciled Europeans, the Anglo-Indians, and the Jewish and Armenian communities, and finally many of the Indians themselves to seek better jobs in the UK. It seemed ironical that after struggling to rid themselves from British rule, Indians were content to live in England under British rule again!

The remnant of the Anglo-Indian community remaining on in India, felt their world was closing down around them, as the Indian government removed all vestiges of the British in India. Statues in the cities of old colonial rulers were removed and replaced by ones of Indian nationalist heroes. Then came the policy of banning most foreign imports—particularly from Great Britain. "Self- sufficiency" was the keyword the Indian government adopted and, as a consequence, the large departmental shops like Whiteaways, and Hall and Anderson had to close down as they depended on imported goods. Things had changed for the worse in Calcutta, and the once-vibrant city shut down around them, especially when a Communist government was installed. This resulted in the closing down of clubs, restaurants, and nightclubs, as they were considered bourgeois by the authorities. Even the cinemas now only screened Russian or Indian films, so that Western culture would not be encouraged. The familiar street names had been re-named after the long-winded names of Indian Nationalistic heroes, and even Communist ones—like Ho Chi Minh and Lenin Sarani. However, taxi drivers and the locals still followed the old names, and seldom recognised the new. Hitherto privately run companies, like the Calcutta Tramways Company and Calcutta Electric Supply Corporation, had been nationalised, which resulted in the deterioration of transport services, and frequent blackouts in the city when the power company was unable to supply all parts of the city with adequate electric power. All this was due to inefficiency and corruption. Bribery had always been a way of life in India and the British had struggled to eradicate it; but it persisted, and when they left, it became endemic. People like Abigail who remained behind in the city, felt isolated as most of her friends had left India for England, Canada, or Australia, so she felt lonely in her old age, trapped in her high-rise flat with only an *ayah* and a parrot for company.

Howard and family only remained on in India for three years after Independence. He would have been jobless, as a Socialistic Congress government under Pundit Nehru nationalised the Panchpani Estate and *Mela*. This affected all the Rajas and Nawabs of the Princely States of India, as although the British had assured them that their lands and property would be protected, this did not happen and huge states like Hyderabad and Mysore fell victim to a land-grabbing Indian government. Not only did the Indian aristocracy lose their lands and property, but their titles too, as they were always considered lackeys of the British, and did not fit into the pattern of a Socialistic India.

Mohi was spared most of the distress and hardship this caused, as he fell seriously ill with cirrhosis of the liver, brought on by his heavy drinking, and died in Mussoorie not long after Independence. Eleanor, grieving, remained on in India, because she had been expecting promised compensation from the Indian government for the acquisition of their Estate and the *Mela*, but this never materialised, and not an anna was ever paid. Eventually, she had to live in a small rented flat in the slummier part of the city, as all their money had been exhausted, as she had no other source of income. Fortunately, Zerina was able to leave India and settle in England when she reached adulthood, and although she hated the idea of leaving her mother behind, she felt she could help her more by sending her money from time to time.

Howard was unhappy in England, and never really settled down in this "alien" environment. He missed his life in India and pined for the colour, sights, sounds, and smells of the beloved country of his birth. Lydia did warn him that even if he returned, he would not find things the same, he still yearned for India and the privileged life he had enjoyed there. He managed to find himself a job, which was a mediocre one, far removed from the importance of his position in Panchpani. He did not live very long after his arrival in England—a mere three years—when a sudden heart attack resulted in a premature death. He had requested in his will that he did not even wish his ashes to be interred in England, so Lydia had to make arrangements to have these sent out to India and scattered in his beloved Sing La. This, his father Stanley arranged. He and Matilda too had had their troubles after Indian independence. Stanley had been unable to meet the crippling interest rates of the mortgage he had taken out on "Stone Valley," which resulted in foreclosure and loss of the tea estate. They lived out the rest of the few short years of their lives in impoverished circumstances in Sing La.

As far as Lydia was concerned, she was reasonably content in England. She hadn't made many friends, because she found the English rather aloof and unfriendly, so she was lonely in her old age. She did feel rather a misfit too, because anyone she did happen to meet would think she was Asian if she mentioned that she had been born in India. This she would vehemently deny, and when she explained she was an Anglo-Indian, they became baffled and confused. She had to give this explanation because there was no getting away from a swarthy skin and slightly oriental features. So she usually tried to avoid the question of her ethnicity whenever possible. However, she was glad she had come away from India, as it had become very much more "Indianised," and all vestiges of the British Raj were being carefully removed by the government of India. It seemed they wanted to erase that "chapter of shame" from their history. So, all in all, Lydia contemplated, things had not worked out too badly for herself. When she first came to England, she was able to get a teaching job without discrimination, so she had a small pension when she retired. She had never been back to India — not even for a holiday. She had no desire to. She didn't even watch documentaries about modern-day India on her television, though she never missed one about India in the old days, under the British Crown.

As for Jamie, he settled down to school in England eventually, although in his first few letters back home he was terribly homesick, and they were filled with unhappiness and woe. However, once the rest of the family settled in England, they were able to take him out of his expensive boarding school and admit him as a day boy to a grammar school in their locale. When he grew up, he made contact with Zerina again, and the happy outcome of this, was they fell in love and married. They now had two children of their own, and lived in Cornwall, so were not able to visit Lydia as often as they would have wished.

Frances had also married, a New Zealander, and her husband had taken her to live there. She had a large family of five children, and kept in touch with her mother regularly by letter. Little Cissy was yet unmarried, and lived and worked in Cambridge.

However, the Anglo-Indian community had been marginalised, and was rarely mentioned in any television documentaries about India. It seemed that the British, after having created this mixed-race community, were now quite happy to forget and abandon them to their fate. Almost all of them had moved away and found new homes in England and the former colonies. The dregs that had been left behind now lived in impoverished circumstances, and had to live in squalid conditions and become like Indians, who never wanted them in the first place.

So when the British left India, they took their *Shamiana* with them, and without its protection from the hot Indian sun, the forgotten Anglo-Indian community withered away as so many wild and unwanted flowers.

The End

GLOSSARY

ABBA—Father.

ACHKAN—Long coat with high collar.

AHM BAGH—Mango Garden.

ANGLO-INDIAN—Up to 1900 British born in India. Subsequently, of mixed British/Indian parentage.

AYAH—A native lady's-maid or nursemaid.

BABA—A child—usually a European one.

BABU—Usually a Bengali clerk.

BAKSHEESH—A small amount of money, generally a tip.

BAWARCHI—A male cook, usually Moslem.

BEARER—A manservant.

BEGUM—An Indian lady of high rank.

BENGALI—Relating to Bengal and a person of Bengal.

BIBI-GHUR—House of women—the residence of a British gentleman for housing his Indian mistresses.

BIDI—A smoke, made from a special leaf wrapped around tobacco.

BOX-WALLAH—Derogatory term for European businessman derived from Indian door-to-door salesmen.

BURRA—Large or big.

BURRA-PEG—A large measure of alcoholic drink.

CHA—Tea.

CHA-CHA—Uncle, generally the brother of your father.

CHAPALS—Open-toed sandals, usually made of leather.

CHAPATTI—Pancake made of wheat flour.

CHARPOY—A wooden-frame bed, with webbing of, generally, coir rope.

CHATTIS—Earthenware vessels – usually cups.

CHEE-CHEE—Derogatory term used to describe a sing-song accent or Anglo-Indian people of lower class.

CHEROOT—A cigar, cut at both ends.

CHITTIES—Small notes.

CHOKIDAR—A watchman or caretaker.

CHOTA—Small or little.

CHOTA HAZRI—Morning tea.

CHUTNEY-MARY—A person of low class and morals, typically a prostitute.

CHULA—A primitive stove made of clay.

CHUTUR—Anus.

COOLIE—A labourer or porter.

DAAB—Green cocoanut.

DAK—The Post or Mail.

DAK BUNGALOW—A rest house for travellers.

DAK-WALLAH—Postman.

DEGCHI—A utensil used for cooking.

DHAL—Lentils.

DHOBI—Washer man.

DHOTI—Long loose loincloth worn by caste Hindus.

DHURRI—A carpet of woven cotton.

DJINN—An intelligent being lower than the angels and having power over people (in Moslem mythology).

DURWAN—Gate-keeper.

DURZEE—Tailor.

EURASIAN—Mixture of European and Asian, sometimes used to describe the mixed-race community of India.

FAKIR—A Moslem or Hindu religious beggar who abstains from physical pleasure.

GARAM—Hot.

GARAM CHA—Hot tea.

GARI—A vehicle.

GEE—Yes.

GHARRY—A horse-drawn carriage.

GHAT—A series of steps or boarding place for boats beside a river.

GHORA—A horse.

GIDARPAHAR—The Hill of Vultures.

GOBUR—Dung.

GULAB JAMUN—A round, brown Indian sweetmeat.

GUMLA—Earthenware bowl or pot.

GURKHALI—Language of the Nepalese people.

GYMKHANA—Usually related to sports and athletics, horse-racing, tennis, etc.

HAH—An expression of agreement or assent.

HARAM—Forbidden.

HARTAL—A strike.

HINDUSTANI—Term used by the Europeans, generally the Urdu or Hindi language.

HUZOOR—A term of respect for European or high-class gentlemen.

JEHMELA—Anything problematic.

JOOTA—Leftover food that has been contaminated by another.

JALEBIS—Yellow pretzel-shaped Indian sweetmeat soaked in syrup.

KARAYA—Literally for rent or hire.

KARAYA ROAD—A notorious red light area of Calcutta.

KHADI—Handloom cotton cloth.

KHANNA—Food.

KHANSAMA—House steward.

KHASI—People of the Khasi hills in Assam.

KHAS-KHAS TATTIS—Screens of rough, sweet-smelling khas-khas grass.

KHITMAGAR—A house-steward or butler (sometimes referred to as '*khit*').

KHUD—Precipitous hillside or valley.

KUKRI—Broad knife used by Gurkhas, generally for hacking.

KURTHA-PYJAMA—White muslin shirt and white pyjamas worn by Muslim men.

LAL KOTHI—The Red House.

LATAI—Spindle used to hold the string for kite-flying.

LATHI—Thick stick made from bamboo.

LOWRA—Penis.

LUDOO—Round yellow Indian sweetmeat.

LUNGI—A sarong-like garment worn by Moslem men.

MADRASSI—People from the state of Madras.

MAAF KURO—Begging forgiveness.

MAHOUT—Elephant driver.

MAIDAN—A large open space.

MANJA—Kite string, coated with flour paste and powdered glass.

MELA—A fair.

MEMSAHIB—A title of respect for European ladies.

MISSYBABA—A young European female child.

MOFUSSIL—The Indian countryside.

MUSTH—Aggressive behaviour of bull elephants due to sexual excitement.

NAWAB—A Moslem Nobleman, the equivalent of the Hindu Raja.

NIMBU-PANI—Literally lime juice and water.

NULLAH—A small stream.

PAAN—The leaf of the betel-nut, usually chewed by the natives of India.

PANI-WALLAH—A manservant who usually deals with the carrying of water, lighting of fires, etc.

PARGANA—A region or district.

PERA—Circular-shaped Indian sweetmeat.

PI-DOG—A vagrant mongrel dog.

PUNKAH—A fan, generally a large fixed swinging fan, made of heavy cloth, suspended from the ceiling and pulled by a rope to agitate the air.

PUNKAH-WALLAH—A servant employed to pull the rope of the punkah.

ROSSOGOLLAS—Round, white Indian sweetmeat.

SADAH—White.

SAHIB—A title of respect for European gentlemen.

SAMAN—Luggage.

SARI—A native woman's dress comprising of a long length of cloth.

SATYAGRAHA—Non-violent protest movement.

SEPOY—A native soldier.

SHAMIANA—An awning or flat-tent roof, generally without sides.

SHIKAR—Hunting.

SHIKARI—A hunter.

SINGHARA—A samoosa—triangular-shaped pastry, filled with spiced mince or vegetable, named after the water chestnut for its similar shape.

SOLA TOPEE—Pith helmet.

SOWAR—Native horse soldier.

SYCE—A groom.

TAMASHA—Festivity.

THANA—Police Station.

TIFFIN—Luncheon.

TONGA—A small, light, two-wheeled horse drawn vehicle.

TOPEE—A hat.

URDU—The language of the Moslem people of India.

ZAMINDARI—A large portion of land, typically an estate.

Other Books by James Sinclair

Over Our Heads

Don't Water the Marigolds

Made in the USA
Charleston, SC
17 October 2016